I0631366

AGE OF THE
IMPERFECT
LEADER

Pawan Verma is an author, thought leader and professional speaker whose passionate intellectual curiosities have often led him to challenge conventional wisdom. His expertise in leadership stems from his wide experience in guiding start-ups, serving on boards and leading business initiatives in large organizations, such as the Reliance Group of Industries and the LIC of India. As the COO of an Indo-Japanese start-up, Star Union Dai-ichi Life Insurance, he led the designing and implementation of pioneering SOPs and customer-facing solutions, supported by an innovative technological platform.

Pawan has authored a crime thriller, *No Closure No Forgiveness*, and published a number of e-books and short stories. He has also written for some of India's leading dailies and periodicals.

Pawan has an MBA and a doctoral degree in management—honoris causa—from the Azteca University, Mexico. He is also a recipient of REX Karmaveer Award by iCONGO, the international Confederation of NGOs.

AGE OF THE IMPERFECT LEADER

LEADING FROM STRENGTH

PAWAN VERMA

RUPA

Published by
Rupa Publications India Pvt. Ltd 2019
7/16, Ansari Road, Daryaganj
New Delhi 110002

Sales centres:
Allahabad Bengaluru Chennai
Hyderabad Jaipur Kathmandu
Kolkata Mumbai

ISBN: 978-93-533-3644-8

First impression 2019

10 9 8 7 6 5 4 3 2 1

The moral right of the author has been asserted.

I dedicate this book to my parents,
who would have been delighted to see me achieve this milestone
but for their untimely departure from this world.

Contents

Introduction

Since its very inception, the destiny of human civilization has been shaped by its leadership. Whether it is the leadership of parents within a family, the captain of a game of football, the CEO of a company or the Prime Minister of a nation, the role of leadership is all-pervasive and, in more than one way, it impacts all of us and sculpts our individual and shared futures.

We may not immediately notice the impact of leadership in our lives, as we are too busy managing the challenges of our daily lives—going to work, feeding our children, managing the sick and the elderly... Whether it is a sleepless old man in a Dharavi slum wondering where his next meal is going to come from, or a boatful of helpless refugees on the high seas desperately scanning the horizon for a glimpse of land, or a single mother on her deathbed in a Chicago hospital worried about the fate of her child, they all have more pressing problems to think about than leadership.

Unfortunately, life doesn't give us a discount for not having a role to play in deciding the leadership we receive. It punishes or rewards everyone equally. Today, our stake in leadership, however, is much higher. At no point in history has mankind been confronted with challenges as daunting as those it faces today. In an increasingly complex and volatile environment, full of uncertainties and ambiguities, leaders of today are more prone to failures. Likewise, the fusion of infotech and biotech offers us choices, which, if not decided upon wisely and with some foresight, could be disastrous for the entire human race. Hence, understanding the phenomenon of leadership in its correct perspective is critically important now, more than ever before.

There's no doubt that leadership has been a widely studied and researched subject, but it has been studied mostly by researchers and academicians. In comparison, much less has been said about it by the actual practitioners of leadership. This book is essentially a product of my conversation with myself. As a practising executive throughout my career, I have been asking myself questions, answers to which haven't been easily forthcoming. Sometimes, my own experience on the job has given me the answers; at other times, it has been the observation of my leaders and fellow colleagues or the vast reservoir of knowledge provided by various leadership experts and authors that has explained the riddle. Overall, it is an attempt to provide a practitioner's perspective, which could be different from that of a researcher in many ways. While both perspectives are important, the difference lies in being on the high seas in real time, passionately battling life-threatening waves for survival, as against analysing the boatman's battle with the waves while seeing the video documentary in a detached manner.

In my study, while tracing briefly the history of leadership, I have also highlighted the prevailing contradiction between leadership practices and theories. Over the years, the practices of leadership have undergone a massive transformation, but leadership theories haven't been able to keep pace with the change. Even though new-age leaders are operating in a flat and digital world, leadership theories are still wrapped around the vertical structures of Victorian-age factories. As a result, leadership-development programmes continue to offer us outdated models. For example, while we are all operating today in a fast, flat and transparent environment, where our strengths and weaknesses are exposed, our leadership schools still prescribe *models of perfection* with a fixed set of mandated traits and virtues for success. Following these misconceived models, budding leaders are often modelling themselves into clones of iconic personalities, while established leaders are feeling inadequate and unsure of their own leadership capabilities. The result is the leadership crisis facing the world today and the consequent trust deficit in all organs of the state.

The problem with leadership studies has been that when we ask what leadership is, we are told what leadership ought to be. The question demands a plain, descriptive answer, but the answer one receives is a value-loaded normative response. My attempt here has not been to explore what leaders should be, nor have I attempted to study leadership in the framework of traits, values, ethics or morality. This book simply explores what contemporary leaders do to be effective and to deliver results. Moving away from benchmarking them on the parameters of traits and values, it uncovers the myth of the *perfect leader* and argues that leaders across ages have basically been *imperfect*. It further explores the way *imperfect leaders* of the contemporary age, being conscious of their imperfections, navigate their way in a complex and uncertain environment to deliver the results expected of them.

Prologue

Leadership in the Face of Death and Devastation

The ultimate measure of a man is not where he stands in moments of comfort, but where he stands at times of challenge and controversy.

–MARTIN LUTHER KING JR, AMERICAN CIVIL-RIGHTS ACTIVIST

5 August 2010

When fifty-four-year-old mining shift supervisor Luis Urzúa left for work in the morning, it looked like it would be just another day in his life. But come afternoon, all hell broke loose. Around 3 p.m., disaster struck and the famous San José copper and gold mine in Chile's Atacama Desert became the site of an unprecedented mining disaster in the history of mankind. About 700,000 metric tonnes of hard rock had suddenly caved in, blocking the passage to the tunnels underneath. At stake were the lives of thirty-three men working at a depth of 2,300 feet inside the earth and trapped under the weight of some of the hardest rocks, which blocked escape routes and even ventilation shafts. Given the odds at hand, like the hardness of the rocks, the blocking of the ventilation shafts and the uncertainty about the location of the miners, the feasibility of a successful rescue operation was less than 1 per cent.

Deep inside the mine, there was total confusion among the

people, panic-stricken, running helter-skelter, facing physical and psychological challenges for survival. There were wild clouds of dust all around and visibility was less than a metre. It was in such a moment of unprecedented crisis that Urzúa took control of the desperate situation. He told his people not to panic. He directed them to get into the refuge area—a small space with an area of approximately 530 square feet. As the dust settled, he took three of the men to explore the tunnel and chalk out the next course of action.

Soon, realization dawned upon Urzúa and the team that they were trapped under the earth and any possible rescue attempt was likely to take a long time. He explained to his team that they had to focus on safety and survival until they were rescued, and that they needed to be disciplined for it. He also appealed to them to keep their morale high and hope for the best. It took a few days before the team could get over the initial conflict and confusion, and restore some order under the calming influence of Urzúa.

The refuge area had food adequate for just ten persons for two days. Accordingly, the team enforced upon itself a strict rationing of food—a small portion of tuna or salmon every twenty-four hours. The water inside the mine was contaminated with oil from the machines, but they had no alternative but to drink it. Separate areas were demarcated for working, sleeping and waste disposal to reduce conflict and to bring about a sense of orderliness among the men. Tasks were clearly allocated to different members and a twelve-hour working shift was adopted by the team. Braving excessive heat and humidity inside the mine, the team simulated day and night with the help of miners' lamps to provide some semblance of normalcy. Above all, the team ensured that they always had their meals together to enhance the fellow-feeling and to strengthen team-bonding. They cheered up one another by narrating stories from their lives and eventually grew into an emotionally unified team, calling themselves Los 33, meaning 'The 33'.

While the miners struggled day and night to sustain their hope and faith, there was another example of heroic leadership on the ground led by André Sougarret, the chief of mine-rescue operations, with the full support of Sebastián Piñera, the newly elected president of Chile.

It was after seventeen days of Herculean efforts and drilling at alternative sites that the location of the trapped miners was pinpointed and the first contact made with them, on 22 August, when a borehole opened up on a ramp close to the miners' refuge area. During this long period, the incessant sound of drilling coming closer to them kept the miners' hopes up and sustained their faith. Once the probe reached them, with a surge of adrenaline, the group euphorically sang their national song, painted the drill head and stuck notes on it that conveyed their well-being. On pulling back the drilling instrument, the surface engineers were elated to find one of the notes saying, '*Estamos bien en el refugio, los 33* (We are well in the shelter, the 33).'

However, it was after yet another fifty-two days, on 13 October, that the rescue team—supported by the global expertise of NASA, the Chilean navy and others—was able to evacuate the trapped miners. During this period, Urzúa maintained order, and reinforced discipline and teamwork on the one hand, and instilled hope in the hearts of the team members and sustained their faith on the other. At the end of the rescue operation, like the captain of a ship, he was the last to come out of the sixty-nine-day ordeal. On their part, his team members, battling physical frailty and psychological disorders, refused to leave the rescue site until their leader was evacuated.

Later, recuperating in a hospital bed, Urzúa revealed that his primary focus during the crisis was to preserve the bonding among his team members and sustain their hope of survival. On being prodded further, he added that he was able to accomplish this through majority decision-making.

'You just have to speak the truth and believe in democracy… Everything was voted on. We were 33 men, so 16 plus one was a majority.'[1]

However, subsequent accounts from the other members of Los 33 clearly showed that like a true leader, Urzúa was just being modest, and giving credit to his team for his success. In an interview with *The Guardian*, Richard Villaroel, a member of Los 33, threw some more light on the plight of the miners in those dark days. He revealed that the situation inside the mine was not as simple as portrayed by Urzúa. There was hopelessness and frustration, a waiting for inevitable death, petty quarrels and the unspoken fear of cannibalism. As he put it, 'We were waiting for death. We were consuming ourselves— we were so skinny.'[2]

Villaroel also complimented Urzúa, who, according to him, tried to give them the emotional strength to face the situation and accept the reality of life.

'Every day [he] told us to have strength. If they find us they find us, if not, that's that. Because the probes [drilling towards the men] were so far away, we had no hope. Strength came by itself. I had never prayed before, but I learned to pray, to get close to God.'[3]

◆

---

[1] Rory Carroll in Copiapó and Jonathan Franklin at San José mine, 'Chile miners: Rescued foreman Luis Urzúa's first interview', *The Guardian*, 14 October 2010
[2] Ibid
[3] Ibid

Welcome to the VUCA World!

In many ways, the leadership story of Urzúa symbolizes the challenges of the VUCA world, an acronym formulated by the US Army War College to describe the volatility, uncertainty, complexity and ambiguity that characterize the post-Cold War world. When applied to modern business landscapes, they symbolize the challenges before new-age leaders. There is *volatility* in the environment, which keeps the operating landscape constantly unsettled. Both the nature and the dynamics of change have become different. Not only has the speed of change accelerated, the change catalysts, too, are often unrecognizable and unpredictable. The *uncertainty* about the shape of things to emerge in future adds to the unpredictability, often throwing up shock or surprise for the leadership. It adds to the confusion in understanding and interpreting the events and issues for future action. The *complexity* within the system, arising out of the multiplicity of closely interacting factors and forces, blurs the cause-and-effect relationship and brings about haziness, unintelligible to the human mind. The *ambiguity* in the operating environment adds to the cloudiness of judgements, often leading to the misreading of signals, erroneous perceptions of reality or even a cause-and-effect relationship.

No wonder that the world today is witnessing breakdowns of systems—social, political, economic and institutional—leading to uncertainties, susceptibilities and vulnerabilities, some of which are unprecedented and catch leaders unawares. What's worse, there is no time to prepare for change when circumstances demand instantaneous responses. On their part, leaders don't often find themselves equipped to manage the change, and, therefore, have to lean on their colleagues to deal with the situation. The stakes are high, because a failure to rise to the occasion and come up with appropriate responses could be suicidal for them.

However, even in the face of daunting challenges and their own inadequacies, leaders such as Urzúa have to generate hope and sustain the faith and commitment of their team members and deliver the results expected of them. As the Canadian astronaut Chris Hadfield put it, 'Ultimately, leadership is not about glorious crowning acts. It's about keeping your team focused on a goal and motivated to do their best to achieve it, especially when the stakes are high and the consequences really matter. It is about laying the groundwork for others' success, and then standing back and letting them shine.'

PART I

Grasping the Existential Challenges

When a leopard threatens a band of chimpanzees, the leopard rarely succeeds in picking off a stray. Chimps know how to respond to this kind of threat. But when a man with an automatic rifle comes near, the routine responses fail. Chimps risk extinction in a world of poachers unless they figure out how to disarm the new threat. Similarly, when businesses cannot learn quickly to adapt to new challenges, they are likely to face their own form of extinction.[1]

∞

---

[1]Ronald Heifetz and Donald L. Laurie, 'The Work of Leadership', *Harvard Business Review*, December 2001

1

Turbulence in the Environment

If you continue doing business today with the methods of
yesterday, you are bound to go out of business tomorrow.

−UNKNOWN

During the Industrial Revolution of the late eighteenth and early nineteenth centuries, there was just one new force that brought about massive transformation in thinking, working and managing styles. In comparison, the world today is constantly impacted by a host of change catalysts— be it globalization, liberalization, privatization, technological breakthroughs or innovations. Naturally, not only is the speed of change much higher than during the Industrial Revolution, but even the impact of change is more disruptive. Feeding upon one another, these changes get amplified, magnifying the scale and magnitude of disruptions in the environment.

Leadership around the world has been an easy casualty of these onslaughts, resulting in some of the most unimaginable upheavals in the recent past. Businesses are struggling, institutions are facing a credibility crisis, political leaders are beleaguered by falling approval ratings and humanity is facing famine, internal strife, civil unrest, war, terrorism, ecological catastrophes and other serious problems. In recent times, five of the ten major economies in the world—the United States

(US), the United Kingdom (UK), Brazil, South Korea and Italy—have seen upheavals in their leadership space, impacting global politics and economies in significant ways. In March 2017, Park Geun-hye, then president of South Korea, was dismissed from office after the constitutional court upheld by an 8-0 verdict the parliamentary vote to impeach her. A year earlier, in August 2016, President Dilma Rousseff of Brazil was impeached and removed from office after being found guilty of breaking Brazil's budget laws.

The facts that these two presidents happened to be women and that President Geun-hye happened to be the first female president of South Korea and the first popularly elected president in East Asia get added significance from the leadership perspective. In a world where women are perceived to provide a different, more honest kind of leadership, the impeachment and removal of both female presidents on counts of corruption and misdemeanour sent shock waves among students of leadership.

Italy, the third-largest economy of the eurozone, continues to struggle between Eurosceptic populists and pro-European Union establishment politicians, driving its economy to become more and more anaemic as time passes. Brexit and the 2016 US presidential election results indicated that political leaders were not able to decipher the social undercurrents. The Panama papers have shown that even sports and media celebrities have betrayed the system and thus lost their leadership appeal.

What we are witnessing today is a serious trust deficit, which is no longer confined to class versus mass—it is, rather, a systemic issue. On the basis of its latest research, the 2017 Edelman Trust Barometer observes, 'Trust in all four institutions—business, government, NGOs and media—to do what is right declined broadly in 2017, a phenomenon not recorded since Edelman began tracking trust. Two-thirds of countries now fall into "distruster" territory with trust levels below 50 per cent.'[2]

The implosion of trust in all four pillars of human society is well captured in the following graph from Edelman's annual global study:

Trust in Institutions Declines
Per cent trust in the four institutions of government, business, media and NGOs, 2016 vs 2017

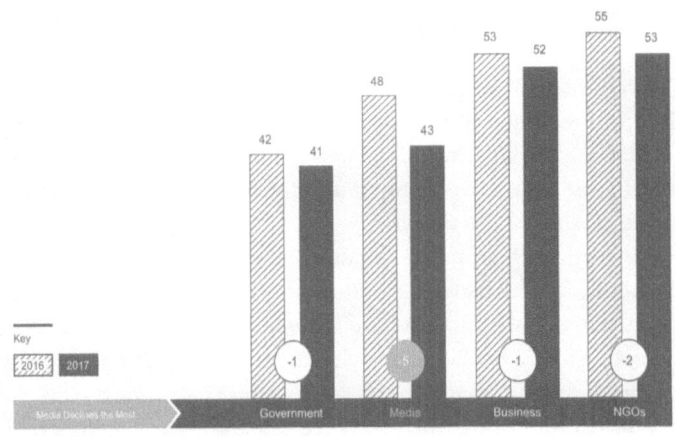

Source: The Edelman Trust Barometer 2017 Report—Executive Summary

According to the report, the vast majority of people do not trust their leaders' ability to solve problems. On the business side, the CEOs' credibility index lost twelve points, falling to a poor 37 per cent globally. It is just 18 per cent in Japan. Even though it could be a matter of some satisfaction that the 2018

---

[2]The Edelman Trust Barometer 2017 Report—Executive Summary

Labor Day Survey[3] conducted by the Conference Board has recorded improvement in the overall job satisfaction among employees in the US, the fact remains that even now only 51 per cent of the employees happen to be satisfied with their work and a whopping 49 per cent are still outside the ambit of job satisfaction. In fact, the 2017 survey by the board was the first since 2005 that recorded the US employee satisfaction percentage crossing the 50 per cent mark.

Perform, or Be Purged: The Changing Face of Leadership

The loss of faith in institutions and their leadership reflects an alarming feeling among the masses that the system is broken or that it doesn't work for them. This, in turn, fuels mass anxiety and fear, leading to some of the upheavals that we are seeing in the world today.

Even though human civilization has evolved considerably, and globalization and better communication have brought societies and nations closer and we have a much better understanding of leadership today, one wonders why leaders are proving inadequate to lead the way. Organizations are coming face-to-face with the painful realization that people processes and their outcomes are not in consonance with the demands of the time. The leadership crisis around the world is getting more and more severe and the common refrain is: *Where have all the leaders gone?*

This deepening leadership crisis remains largely unrecognized and grossly misunderstood. To operate in the neo-normal, leaders have to shake off their inertia and take note of the changes in their operating environment, some of which demand new leadership skills that have been ignored so far.

---

[3]The Conference Board, 'Labor Day Survey: 51% of U.S. Employees Overall Satisfied with Their Job', Cision PR Newswire, 29 August 2018

What are the challenges emanating from the operational landscapes today that are demanding a leadership transformation? Let's take a look.

In these volatile and uncertain times, when organizations are becoming increasingly networked and transparent, leadership is being determined more by the value one adds to the organization than where one is placed in the hierarchy. As a natural corollary, leadership does not flow from the power of the position of the leaders—it flows from the power of the ideas they propound and the solutions they offer. The interesting thing is that in this brave new world, organizational hierarchies are getting redefined and leaders hold their influence as long as they add value to the community they represent. Take, for example, social media, which provides a forum without any hierarchies and has no formal levels of authority. But, even here, there is a hierarchy of influencers who shape opinions within the network, based on the number and nature of their followers. A religious leader such as the Dalai Lama or a Nobel Peace laureate and social reformer such as Kailash Satyarthi could be ordinary members of a social networking site, but it is the influence they exercise on the community that determines their position and authority in the network hierarchy. It follows, therefore, that leadership in the modern context is not bestowed upon anybody—it is earned by the value people add to the community. Also, leaders continue to be leaders only till they contribute to their cause, not beyond.

This situation is not unique to social organizations—the trend is catching up with other forms of organizations as well, whether they are academic, commercial or political. In today's complex and globally networked environment, where the resolution of complex issues requires the pooling of diverse expertise and relevant market intelligence, leadership is more spread across an organization than concentrated at the top. The sword of Damocles—that is, the fear of constant disruptions—looming over business organizations also demands that thinking is not left to the leader at the top—everyone in the organization has to contribute to the strategy and complement and supplement the leadership.

What Now? A Complex and Unpredictable Business Landscape

First, the leaders of today have to deliver in a more complex business environment. A multiplicity of interconnected heterogeneous factors have the potential to impact the outcome of an event. The unpredictability of outcomes leads to a high degree of uncertainty, as it becomes difficult to predict the future and take a reasonable bet on the consequences of a move. On the one hand, the degree of complexity overwhelms an individual's cognitive limits, and on the other, the past outcome of a situation no longer serves as a guide to the future.

A case in point is the global economic crisis of 2008, which was a result of a host of interconnected activities in the financial market, coming together to lead to a disaster in the global financial ecosystem beyond anybody's anticipation. While everyone could make sense of issues like the relaxation of banking regulations, the liberalization of credit standards, the innovation of derivative instruments taking risk off the lenders' balance sheets, low-interest-rate monetary policies or market-value accounting norms, nobody could foresee the impact of the fall in housing prices on the entire system.

The flow of labour and capital beyond national boundaries, the global nature of trade and commerce and the emergence of transnational corporations have added to the complexities of the business landscape today. An organization remains susceptible to myriad influences that can hit it from any corner of the world any time. If a subsidiary of a global corporation is found guilty of a regulatory violation in its country, the parent company in another country also gets impacted. Likewise, the interconnectedness and interdependence of different markets across the globe leads to a situation where developments in one market impact the performance of enterprises in another, with companies having practically no control over the outcome.

This unpredictability of outcomes has a profound impact on the role of business leaders today, as they have to manage the uncertainties in critical business operations like market forecasting, product development and customer-behaviour patterns.

IT Makes the World Open and Transparent

The role of information and communication technology (ICT) is among the most critical factors impacting business landscapes today and influencing behaviour patterns of business leaders. These impacts are visible in two distinct areas. First, from its initial role of being a business support system and later as an enabler of business, information technology (IT) today has evolved into a potent driver of business. In this role, it has moved far ahead of law and regulations. Factors such as social media, mobility, analytics and cloud computing technologies have expanded business landscapes beyond national boundaries, whereas law and regulations are still struggling with the same. Mobility and cloud computing are enabling business leaders to venture into areas and segments that were earlier thought to be inaccessible and unprofitable. At the same time, advancements in technologies such as artificial intelligence (AI), machine learning and bioengineering are opening up new possibilities.

Secondly, unlike in the past, when the state or the enterprise was the source of information and citizens or customers its passive consumers, today IT has created a universe where ordinary citizens and customers have become producers of information that could be critical to the fate of the government or the enterprise. It could be an asset for the organization in brand-building, and internal and external communication. But, conversely, it could also pose a threat to the establishment, as all its dealings become transparent and open to the world outside. Any wrongdoing could become an issue of global concern, as information dissemination and customer interactions transcend geographical barriers within moments, taking into its loop various interest groups across the world. The resultant storm on social media, for example, could bring an empire to its knees.

The Arab Spring of 2010 is an example of the masses shaking up mighty governments in north Africa and the Middle East against oppression and injustice. The #MeToo movement provides yet another example of how social media has given voice to the weak and the oppressed and shaken powerful establishments.

What does the impact of ICT mean for the leaders of today? Clearly, ICT has placed them in a glasshouse where all their actions are exposed to the outside world 24x7. Their planning and performance, successes and failures get evaluated and commented upon by interested stakeholders around the world. Leaders of today do not have a hideout or a moment of respite, being under the scanner all the time. They have to carve out a place for their enterprise in the virtual space and ensure that it is handled with speed and integrity, because any lack of timely and proper response may lead the organization and its leader being hammered on social media.

The Start of the #MeToo Movement

On 15 October 2017, American actress Alyssa Milano tweeted, 'If you've been sexually harassed or assaulted write "me too" as a reply to this tweet.'[4] Soon, word spread like wildfire, mushrooming into the #MeToo movement. According to Wikipedia, by the end of the day, the hashtag had been used more than 200,000 times and tweeted more than 500,000 times. Over 4.7 million people used it in 12 million posts on Facebook within the first twenty-four hours. The result was the fall of Harvey Weistein, the co-chairman of the Weinstein Company. When the #MeToo storm reached India, it took into its fold powerful personalities, including an important minister in the Government of India.

Leadership of Pathos in the Era of Post-Truth

The power of emotions is tested in the post-truth era. The *Oxford Dictionary* defines post-truth as an adjective 'relating to or denoting circumstances in which objective facts are less influential in shaping public opinion than appeals to emotion and personal belief'. The post-truth scenario, systematically built up and utilized during Brexit and the 2016 US presidential election, has become a force to reckon with. The increasing reach of the Internet, social media and 24x7 television push leaders, particularly political leaders, to embark on the romance of leadership, where leaders and their followers feed off each other to create their own truths and perceptions.

Clearly, leadership cannot be taken out of the context in which it operates. Therefore, leaders, particularly business

---

[4]https://twitter.com/alyssa_milano/status/919659438700670976?lang=en

leaders, have to take into cognisance the post-truth environment in which they are working and nuance their approach to an issue suitably. It is not only them who have to be politically correct, but also the organizations they represent. They must be seen following and supporting values and beliefs cherished by contemporary societies.

The story of the killing of Cecil, a lion in Zimbabwe's Hwange National Park by the American hunter Walter Palmer, is symptomatic of the post-truth world in which we live. It is a burning example of how public perceptions on issues matter more than the cold facts of common sense and rationality. It also provides a glimpse of how, in the modern world, a local cause can become global overnight and impact people, jobs and societies.

The lion was killed on 1 July 2015, but the news hit the media a few weeks later, on 26 July. On 28 July, Palmer was identified as the hunter and the news went viral in both mainstream and social media. As a local newspaper put it, the international response to the event was 'the largest reaction in the history of wildlife conservation'. In fact, the University of Oxford's Wildlife Conservation Research Unit (WildCRU), which had been tracking the lion since 2009, engaged a multimedia monitoring company, Meltwater, to examine the reasons behind why the story went viral on the Internet and how the 'Cecil moment' was transformed into a 'Cecil movement'.

Meltwater counted more than 12,000 articles in the mainstream media mentioning 'Cecil' on 29 July, while social media mentions peaked at 90,000 on the same day. The WildCRU website tracked 4.4 million visitors on the day and finally crashed due to server overload. Between 1 July 2015 and 30 September 2015, there were over 100,000 mainstream media mentions while social media accounted for nearly 700,000 posts.

Cecil the Lion

On 26 July 2015, it came to light that Cecil, the much-loved lion of Zimbabwe's Hwange National Park, had been killed on 1 July 2015 by bow and arrow, before being beheaded and skinned by a US tourist. It caused a massive furore among conservation groups as, apparently, the thirteen-year-old lion was known to tourists and much loved. Cecil enjoyed human contact, roamed free in the park and never frightened anyone. His black mane was the centre-point of tourists' attraction. He was collared, as he happened to be part of a study by WildCRU.

On 28 July 2015, the world came to know that the killer was Walter James Palmer, a dentist and a professional hunter from Minnesota, who had organized a £35,000 hunting trip to the Hwange National Park to kill the lion. The lion was first baited out of the park at night and wounded by an arrow. The next day, he was traced, killed, beheaded and skinned.

What followed was global outrage. As this news broke, within a day, Palmer was forced to shut his dental clinic and go into hiding. His clinic as well as his Google+ profile were vandalized by furious animal rights activists with hate mails and posters. Even as Palmer regretted the killing, clarifying that he did the hunt under the impression that it was legal, social media was flooded with images of him posing with other animals that he was supposed to have hunted earlier. His Florida mansion was vandalized, with 'Lion Killer' painted on the garage.

The former Bond star, Sir Roger Moore, called for Palmer to face criminal charges while Sharon Osbourne, an English media personality, called him a 'killer' and 'Satan' in her tweet. People for the Ethical Treatment of Animals, or PETA,

> demanded the immediate execution of the dentist—no trial, no defence. Horrified people organized demonstrations outside Palmer's clinic and threatened to kill the killer of Cecil.
>
> While a criminal case was registered against all the professional hunters involved in the hunt, the Zimbabwe government was preparing to ask the US government for the extradition of Palmer to face prosecution in Zimbabwe.

Reacting to the story and its wild media coverage, leadership speaker and journalist Steve Keating wrote in his blog LeadToday in August 2015,

> The death of Cecil the Lion was indeed a big deal. Mere miles from the dentist's office is the Hennepin County Morgue. As the protest for Cecil was taking place, the body of a little boy was at the morgue. This child was also innocent, he didn't bother anyone, he was beloved and he was also murdered while doing what children do. But there was no outrage, there was no protest. … Did I mention the fact that the child was a human being and the lion was an animal? Has the whole world gone crazy?[5]

Keating goes on to point to the grim reality of a perception-driven world, where what catches people's imagination takes precedence over what they should be concerned about. He argues that an outrage over the killing of a lion is quite fine, but he wonders why there is no outrage when an innocent boy is murdered while playing on the streets.

The story of Cecil is an example of how popular perceptions about seemingly remote issues impact the operating

---

[5]https://stevekeating.me/2015/08/02/cecil-the-lion/

environment in which leaders are expected to deliver. The speed and volume of response is so high that it hardly provides time for analysing, examining and determining the truth. This cacophony of perceptions reaches a crescendo that often stifles a dissenting voice, howsoever sensible or logical.

Public Perceptions Influence Law and Governance

In democratic societies, governance is as much about public perception as about rules and regulations. Laws are often a reaction to what seems politically correct rather than what is factually correct. In view of the pervasive role of the media in our public lives, the existence of various advocacy groups and the speed at which information flows and opinions get formed, governments and regulators are careful about doing something that can lead to public outcry. Whether it is the killing of a 'black' citizen by the 'white' police in the US or the case of police raids on hotels in Mumbai to check prostitution, issues can rapidly acquire different overtones, never intended by the administrative or regulatory authorities.

The story of Maggi noodles in India is a case in point. The speed at which different states went about banning the product, leading to a ban by the Food Safety and Standards Authority of India (FSSAI), the national regulator, within a period of just a fortnight, without even giving an opportunity to its manufacturer, Nestlé India, to argue its case, displays an agonizing tendency on the part of state governments and regulators to present a picture that they are concerned about the health of citizens. However, the studied silence with which the Bombay High Court's order lifting the ban was received only goes to show that governments were more concerned about their own image rather than about public good.

The Maggi Noodles Crisis

Nestlé India, a subsidiary of Nestlé S.A. (Switzerland), is a Large Cap company incorporated in 1959, which operates in India's food processing sector and has an annual sales turnover of approximately ₹100 billion. Its flagship product, Maggi Noodles, enjoyed a market share of over 60 per cent in the instant noodles segment in the country. Over the thirty-year period since its launch, 'two-minute Maggi' grew as one of the most popular fast food items in the country and developed into a $500-million category. It contributed around 23 per cent of the company's total sales and 25 per cent of its operating profits.

But after a random test of a batch of Maggi Noodles in Uttar Pradesh, it was found to contain lead and monosodium glutamate (MSG) beyond permissible limits. The product was declared 'unsafe and hazardous' and Nestlé India was accused of compromising with the food safety of Indian citizens. On 21 May 2015, the company was ordered to recall its products from the market in the state.

Nestlé India disputed the results and maintained that the product was safe for consumption. However, the issue soon snowballed into a nationwide controversy, with different states sending product samples to laboratories for testing and subsequently banning the product. On 5 June 2015, the FSSAI banned the product in India on the grounds that it contained excessive lead and that there was mislabelling related to the MSG content.

What followed was a near disaster for Nestlé. The company's stock prices got a massive hammering. The crisis led to the biggest product recall in the more-than-100-year history of the brand. As per estimates, more than 27,000 tonnes of noodle packages worth ₹3.2 billion were transported to an unnatural destination—to be used in cement factories as fuel—all at a huge cost to the company. In another move, the Government of India filed a class action suit against the company before the consumer disputes redressal forum, NCDRC, claiming damages to the tune of ₹6.4 billion. Further, according to global valuation consultancy Brand Finance, Nestlé suffered a brand loss of ₹12.7 billion. What is worse, for the second quarter ended 30 June 2015, the company reported a net loss of ₹644 million, its first quarterly loss in seventeen years. This followed the reporting of a net profit of ₹3.2 billion in the previous quarter ended 31 March 2015.

In a major shake-up at Nestlé India, the company's India MD, Etienne Bennet, was repatriated and Suresh Narayanan, Chairman and CEO of Nestlé, Philippines, was called to handle the crisis.

On 13 August, the Bombay High Court quashed the order of FSSAI and the Maharashtra Food & Drug Administration, banning Maggi Noodles in the country, and pronounced that the company could manufacture and sell its products if three independent laboratories in India certified its suitability based on fresh tests. The Minister for Food Processing, Government of India, expressed happiness at the judgement of the court.

This is the reality of modern business landscapes, which leaders can afford to ignore at their own peril. Businesses today not only have to promote public good, but also communicate it to society as well. Further, in situations where their intent or action comes under scrutiny, they have to be quick to respond to rectify the situation and communicate that to the public.

It's a Small World: The Changing Profile of the Modern Consumer

The fast pace of urbanization in emerging economies is transforming today's customer profile rapidly. India, for example, is a young country with more than 50 per cent of its population below the age of twenty-five and over 65 per cent under the age of thirty-five.[6] The process of urbanization, accelerated by certain transformational government projects like the creation of a hundred smart cities, Digital India and Skill India, is placing more purchasing power in the hands of millennials and Gen Z, while the creation of digital platforms and access to global markets is raising their aspiration levels in terms of the nature of products and standards of customer engagement. Similar trends can be observed in the Chinese, African and Latin American markets as well.

Globalization, on the one hand, has enabled multinational corporations to open shop in developing economies, where customers earlier had no access or exposure to products and services from developed markets. Thus, not only are products and services in the developing markets getting a churn, but the production and delivery systems and the customer-engagement processes are also being redefined and reinvented. This obviously puts a great demand on the new leadership. Those in developing markets need to recognize the change fast, reorient their product and market strategies and understand the new rules of attracting and retaining customers. On the other hand, leaders from developed markets are required to understand the dynamics of the developing markets and their cultural and behavioural nuances, which could be drastically different from their own. Any failure to come to terms with

---

[6]https://en.wikipedia.org/wiki/Demographics_of_India

these realities is only going to place them on the sidelines.

However, many of today's leaders are unable to understand and appreciate the changing profiles of their customers and their emerging needs and motivations. They think they know best what their customer wants, and accordingly design their products and services. In that sense, their mindset still reflects that of Henry Ford, the pioneer in the automobile industry who, out of his preference for black cars, once said, 'Any customer can have a car painted any colour he wants so long as it is black.'[7]

Leaders like him tend to depend upon their own knowledge and understanding while anticipating and responding to customer needs. They will not tire of saying, 'Look at Steve Jobs, he didn't ask the customer. It's no use; people don't know what they want.'

However, it must be realized that not every leader happens to be a visionary like Steve Jobs and not every Steve Jobs can succeed every time. In today's competitive environment, leaders have to remain in the learning phase. They have not only to keep making sense of their customers' emotional, cultural, psychological and intellectual preferences, they also have to anticipate their latent and unarticulated needs and aspirations, and deliver better than the competition.

The New-Age Workforce

The Internet has not only changed the workplace, it has transformed the workforce like never before too. First, the skills and expertise available within the workforce, coupled with the free flow of labour across different markets, have now enabled employees to choose their employers. Not only do they have access to an organization's management culture

---

[7]https://en.wikiquote.org/wiki/Talk:Henry_Ford

and compensation plans on social media, there are websites that provide a window into the management philosophies and practices within different organizations as shared by employees, often in anonymity.

Secondly, unlike in the past, people today do not work for wages alone. They need to be excited and motivated about the job they are performing. They look for collaboration rather than command.

Third, unlike in the past, when the employer had an exclusive right to employees' time during their shift, today's employees want to have control over their time and remain connected to the outside world through social media. Going beyond, they prefer to use their own devices for connecting to the outside world and hence an enterprise has to devise ways and means to ensure data security. The story of the young lady who resigned from her job at a sophisticated bank branch saying that she felt that she was working in a coal mine depicts the mindset of Gen Z. The alarmed bank learnt only on subsequent enquiries that she felt suffocated as she was not allowed to connect to her social media account during work hours.

Fourth, it is not about the work environment alone. The workforce today is more oriented towards delivering results than spending mandated hours during a shift. At the same time, it is more assertive about its own personal time and individuality. To the modern generation, serving an employer does not necessarily mean subjugating one's personality to the dictates of the job. If a worker is feeling happy about something, they may smile genuinely, but, if feeling otherwise, they may no longer fake a smile to please the customer.

It is interesting to note that the workforce is slowly waking up to the tyranny of forced smiles on the job, arising from the culture of 'service with a smile'. A number of studies have shown that the mandate to smile at every customer to give them a feel of 'superior service' drains employees in the same way as physical or mental labour might. Constantly wearing a mask, or 'emotional acting', could lead to anxiety, distress and emotional exhaustion. As journalist Anna Almendrala writes in *HuffPost*,

> Customer service with a smile is the American way, but faking it all day can take an emotional and physical toll once workers head home, according to a small but compelling new study published in the journal *Personnel Psychology*.[8] The findings should give employers pause about just how much they can fairly expect in terms of 'emotional labour'—the requirement to display certain emotions or feelings toward customers, clients and others at work.[9]

What does all this mean for the enterprise today? Clearly, organizations today have to compete not only for their customers, but for attracting talent as well. Both hiring and retaining the right talent has become competitive, as employees not only make a choice while accepting to work for an organization, they keep reviewing their choices as well, depending on circumstances. This has a great bearing on today's leadership, as it has to create and maintain the right environment within the organization to both attract and retain talent.

◆

The new economy today is demanding new leadership styles based on current realities. The old style has become outdated

---

[8]David T. Wagner, Christopher M. Barnes and Brent A. Scott, 'Driving it Home: How Workplace Emotional Labor Harms Employee Home Life', *Personnel Psychology*, 9 May 2013
[9]Anna Almendrala, 'Customer Service with a Smile Comes at a Big Price', Huffingtonpost.in, 7 July 2014

and ineffective in a business environment characterized by speed, openness and complexity. The weakening of class structures and the democratization of wealth and education have bridged social and intellectual gaps between today's leaders and followers to a large extent. As organizations are getting flatter and the information revolution is seamlessly equipping people with knowledge and information, people are expecting better standards of performance and behaviour from their leaders. In such an environment, it is no longer possible for leaders to lead through command and control. The old shepherd is failing not because he is unwilling to lead but because the sheep have become smarter.

2

The Leadership Conundrum

Life isn't about waiting for the storm to pass. It's about learning how to dance in the rain.

—VIVIAN GREENE, VISIONARY, ARTIST,
AUTHOR AND ENTREPRENEUR

In essence, the basic premise of leadership is universal in nature. All organizations—social, political and commercial—need leaders to provide a vision, set up goals, and inspire and motivate people. Leadership also has a symbiotic and mutualistic relationship with organizations. While it tries to optimize value creation for organizations, the organizations, in turn, impact leadership models, styles and philosophies with their changing structures, values, systems and challenges. Further, insomuch as all the four essential components of human civilization—human beings, societies, organizations and leadership—keep impacting one another, there is a need for them to be in sync and remain relevant to their times.

In the past few decades, global economies have seen increasing competitiveness in innovation around business models, strategies, products, services and operating models. However, the need of the hour is a radical innovation around leadership, which has become outdated. As leadership provides the essential competitive edge to business and society, organizations have to innovate their leadership models and adapt to the new normal in managing themselves.

The leadership crisis that the world is witnessing today basically emanates from two sources. First, the failure of the twenty-first-century leaders to realize that their operating landscape has undergone a massive transformation, which requires them to reorient their leadership styles and behaviour patterns. Secondly, over the ages, leadership literatures have presented a misplaced profile of successful leaders and thereby created wrong models for the grooming of future leaders. These models impart some kind of Shakespearean 'fatal flaws' to the leaders, leading to the failure and collapse of their leadership. Groomed by the misconceived models, they go on to perpetuate behaviour patterns that are not in sync with the demands of the time. Ultimately, confused and confounded, they act like Alice in Wonderland, unable to feel the pulse of the solution they need to come out of the crisis.

Working Out the Leadership Puzzle

To understand the misconceptions around the subject, we need to go back to the history of leadership, which, in its refined manifestations, is essentially a product of human civilization. Human beings are creative, ambitious and dynamic. Ever since they learnt to live in groups, they have endeavoured to form and develop appropriate organizations to fulfil their needs, realize their goals and overcome the challenges confronting them. In a way, these organizations also reflect the cultural moorings and traditions, beliefs and value systems cherished by societies. However, as these beliefs, values and traditions evolve over time, these organizations innovate themselves in terms of their structures or governance systems, so as to maximize their benefits to society and remain relevant. Leadership is one such innovation that provides meaning and relevance to an organization.

Even though the scientific study of leadership has its origins in recent times, mankind has known the leadership phenomenon since time immemorial. At the initial stage of civilization, human beings learnt to live in groups, formed tribes and developed a common identity and purpose driven by their common need for food and survival. At this stage, as in the case of animals, physical force became the sole determinant of power within the group and the source of leadership as well. A person who was physically stronger was in a better position to lead his nomadic tribe to victory in its frequent fights with other nomadic tribes, all competing for limited resources—food and shelter. It is probably at this stage that command and control became the most potent and, possibly, the only tool of leadership for influencing human behaviour.

It was only with the human-chimpanzee split that Homo sapiens started to explore new kinds of leadership. As mankind learnt farming and agriculture, it led to another key milestone in the development of human organizations and their leadership. The development of agriculture induced people to stop being nomadic and start settling down across contiguous pieces of land. The relative stability further led to the development of craft and artisanship, followed by the development of art and literature. At this stage, along with physical power, other supplementary and complementary sources of leadership started to emerge, such as intelligence, skill and esteem.

This phenomenon of esteem as a source of power is beautifully illustrated in the 1960s' American prison movie *Cool Hand Luke*. A maverick, Luke keeps challenging prison authorities and the pecking order among prisoners. He is thrashed and battered repeatedly by prison authorities and Dragline, the bully leader of the prisoners. Yet he earns the respect of the prisoners, because every time he is beaten to the ground, he gets up to challenge them. In the boxing scene in the prison, he is battered by a brawny and burly Dragline, so much so that he can barely stand. But every time he is floored he gets up, to the point where the bully ultimately gives up and leaves. Shown to a group of chimpanzees, they would unequivocally declare Dragline to be the hero. But humans see it differently—Luke generates a sense of esteem, standing up to a powerful adversary. He earns prestige and becomes the leader of the prisoners.

It is not without reason that the hero of *The Iliad* is Achilles, the greatest warrior in contemporary Greece, and not Agamemnon, for whom Achilles worked.

The Evolution of Kingship

The emergence of kingship as an institution added a new dimension to leadership. It made position and hierarchy the dominant source of power and leadership. While in tribal societies leadership would get replaced more frequently depending upon which member of the tribe had greater physical prowess, the institution of kingship acquired an element of divinity over time. Thus, even a child or a weakling anointed as a king acquired power and was in a position to lead his people. In India, the institution of *'chatur-varna-vyavastha'*—the four varna system (varna refers to an occupation-based class of people)—further consolidated the system of positional power with consequent impact on leadership. The emergence of professional armies maintained by kings for the defence of their territories further saw the development of other facets of leadership, such as planning, strategizing, reward and recognition.

Impact of the Industrial Revolution

The Industrial Revolution, ushering in the age of mass production of goods, provided a milestone in the development of leadership. For the first time, work was studied and analysed as an economic activity. With a host of innovations taking place around machinery, technology, power sources and organizational structures, focus shifted from artisanship to engineering as the driving force of production. The emergence of the services sector and, more recently, the onset of the information revolution have added new dimensions to leadership.

In an age where information is an alternative source of power, the portrait of a leader has undergone substantial transformation. Likewise, leading in the post-truth era has its own demands, making the leadership methods of yesterday irrelevant. Going forward, the ongoing technology revolution, with the advent of AI, machine-learning or 3D printing, is going to make the future of work volatile and uncertain, demanding a new generation of workers to handle it and a new breed of leaders to optimize value creation for the organizations they lead.

Leadership 1.0

A scientific study of leadership was started in Britain, Germany and the US during the Industrial Revolution as part of the overall effort to maximize production and profits with the best utilization of time and resources. This drive led to the study of organizational systems and structures in a critical manner. It also brought about a greater focus on the study of leadership—the qualities and attributes that could optimize gains from organizational activities and maximize production. In-depth studies of factors such as human behaviour, motivation, reward and recognition, work environment and operational processes shifted the focus to a host of leadership attributes, such as vision, communication, intuition, knowledge, expertise, and intelligence and emotional quotients (IQ and EQ). Experts studied these phenomena from various angles, trying to explore the characteristics that made or defined a leader. They wondered if people were born with certain leadership traits or could acquire them with training and observation. The proponents of the behaviour theory focused on what leaders actually did, rather than what leaders were. They studied leadership behaviours in terms of task and people orientation. Yet other theorists studied it from the angles of leadership styles and philosophies.

Leadership as a concept has been studied in terms of traits, behaviour or working styles. Different theories have also been propounded. However, in view of the complexity and diversity comprising the idea of leadership, it has been difficult for experts to come up with a comprehensive definition of the term—perspectives have been changing with the prevailing sensibilities of the times.

In his book *Leadership for the Twenty-First Century*, Joseph C. Rost, professor of leadership and administration at the University of San Diego, includes an insightful analysis of most of the writings on leadership between 1930 and 1990. He collected and analysed 221 definitions of leadership across decades. What emerges from Rost's study is that the twentieth-century leadership studies were dominated by what he calls the 'industrial paradigm'. He further maintains that the idea of leadership is predominantly influenced by the thinking and sensibilities of the times. In the first three decades of the twentieth century, the notion of leadership was focused more on the leader's ability to exercise control and ensure obedience, respect, loyalty and cooperation from followers. In the 1940s, the focus shifted from control to persuasion, and the representative definition of leadership could be stated as, 'Leadership is the result of an ability to persuade or direct men, apart from the prestige or power that comes from office or external circumstances.'[10]

---

[10]Joanne B. Ciulla, *The Ethics of Leadership*, Cengage Learning, 2002, p.306

Going further, in the 1960s and the 1970s, leadership meant influencing followers, while during the 1990s, leaders and followers mutually influenced each other. However, what is relevant here is that the evolving definitions of leadership differed when it came to the relationship between the leaders and their followers. Who decides the organizational vision and mission? Do followers have a role in deciding the goals and how they are to be pursued? What should the relationship between leaders and followers be?

The Role of Leadership

While the definition of leadership has varied with the contemporary sensibilities of a society, there can be a consensus on what leadership objectives are. The 'leadership circle' provides a broad perspective on the role leaders perform in an organization and the values they need to promote to achieve their defined objectives.

The Leadership Circle

The outermost circle defines the four core functions of leadership—providing direction for change, inspiring and engaging the team, building organizational capabilities and nurturing an organizational culture. Each of these functions leads to a set of outcomes marked against them in the next inner circle. While providing direction for change would result in defining the relevant vision, mission and strategies of the organization, the function of inspiring and engaging followers would require the leader to motivate their team and drive change in the right direction. In the same way, the function of building organizational capabilities would result in the formation of teams, organizational structures and relationships to help realize the vision and the mission. Finally, when leaders take up building an appropriate culture for their organizations, it results in diversity and inclusion within the enterprise and promotes a culture of innovation.

The innermost circle describes the four critical values—commitment, trust, integrity and habits—leaders must possess and demonstrate in their conduct and behaviour while promoting the same within their teams.

Who Is a Leader?

Usually, when we talk of leaders, we think of presidents, prime ministers, military generals, and CEOs and chairmen of corporate bodies—people who are at the top of an organized structure, having the onerous responsibility of setting goals and priorities for their teams, monitoring their performance and administering reward and recognition. But this offers a limited view of leadership. In real life, we find leadership all around—in our homes, at our workplaces, in social life and practically everywhere else. When our children are young, we act as their role models and provide them leadership. At work, we lead teams to plan and execute projects. A philosopher propounds a philosophy and influences millions of people, thereby becoming a thought leader. A poet inspires an entire generation of poets, which follows the norms and sensibilities championed by him or her, thereby ushering in a distinct age or school of literature. So does a politician or a social reformer, who challenges the status quo and brings about change in society.

Leaders need not be at the apex of their organizations. They could also be corporate executives at the middle level, taking their teams to the envisioned destination or goal. The leader could also be an artist or the conductor of an orchestra, who doesn't communicate directly but sets performance standards, which generations follow as the benchmark.

Leadership is also not limited by values and morality, organized groups or unorganized followers. An authoritarian dictator such as Adolf Hitler was a leader, but so was Mother Teresa or Martin Luther King, who were at the other end of the spectrum. Henry Ford, commanding a huge organization, was a leader to reckon with, but so was the great poet William Wordsworth, who inspired the Romantic age of English literature.

In his book *Leading Minds: An Anatomy of Leadership,* Howard Gardner describes the 'Churchill-Einstein Continuum' and explains the two ends of the leadership continuum. Whereas Winston Churchill, being the prime minister of the UK, exerted his influence in a direct manner, conveying his vision and mission to the world, the great scientist Albert Einstein exercised his influence indirectly through the power of his ideas, propounded in his theories and treatises. The former had a well-orchestrated organization with authority and power, while the latter worked on his own.

The leadership conundrum further confounds, as there are

no definite traits that can identify a leader. We have examples of successful leaders failing miserably when circumstances change. Likewise, leaders who look inept and ineffective in certain circumstances go on to display overwhelming leadership when the time is opportune. Thus, leadership is a multidimensional factor, which goes beyond the personality of the leader.

Myth of the Perfect Leader

Have you ever been surprised by a market move but pretended to have seen it coming? Or do you tend to feign familiarity with a new technology when your chief technology officer (CTO) tries to explain it to you? Do you give the impression of a man always in command of the situation?

If the answer to these questions is a plain 'yes', there is nothing wrong about it, except that you are subscribing to the myth of the *perfect leader*, created by traditional leadership literature. The historical focus on leadership traits and styles has led to the idea of a perfect leader, the flawless person at the top of the organizational pyramid who can craft a grand vision of the future, sell his dreams to others, develop strategies to translate the vision into action and, finally, make it happen on the ground.

No wonder that this leadership stereotype perpetuates the belief that to be a leader one has to have a complete personality with an intellectual depth to decipher the complexities of the operating landscape, an unbounded imagination to create a magnificent vision of the future, the operational excellence to translate the vision into reality and, above all, the charisma to ensure that everyone in the team lives and breathes the vision crafted by the leader. Leaders, therefore, are expected to have superlative IQ and EQ as well as traits such as charisma, integrity, empathy, effectiveness, decision-making, humour, humility, listening skills…and the list can go on. They also have to be flexible enough to keep alternating between different leadership styles, depending upon the people, task and situation. In a nutshell, leaders are supposed to be perfect, the shepherds who guide their flocks to the destination. Not surprisingly, in his book *Developing the Leader Within You*, John C. Maxwell puts his idea of good leaders as those 'who know the way, go the way, and show the way'.

The macho image of leaders as persons who are infallible and born to lead is all-pervasive and not limited to leadership literature alone. Look at William Shakespeare's *Richard II*: 'We were not born to sue, but to command.' ('Sue' here denotes the older French-English expression conveying 'follow after'.)

Even business communications, advertising in particular, have tried to create the *romance of leadership* by perpetuating the myth of an accomplished and infallible leader, capable of leading his team to its goal single-handedly—the pilot who doesn't need a co-pilot. While leaders are persons of flesh and blood, with formidable strengths and natural weaknesses, this stereotype of an infallible and omnipotent individual often leads to flawed behaviour patterns among leaders as well as their followers. On the one hand, the followers start having misplaced expectations from their leaders; on the other, the leaders end up creating around themselves an artificial aura of perfection with assumed strengths. Decisive and authoritative, they set the agenda, direct their teams towards the goal, command performance, control the direction and finally bestow performance-based reward and punishment on the team.

Command and Control

In the process of promoting a macho image, leaders often take recourse to the earliest leadership tool known to mankind:

command and control. This is a top-down style of leadership, which is authoritative in nature and therefore leaves little scope for questioning and participative management. This culture is still prevalent in most organizations, reflected in their management structures and functions, like organizational diagrams, goal-setting from the top, micromanaging performance, budget controls, employee evaluation, and reward and punishment based on fixed performance targets. There is no dearth of literature pointing out the inadequacies of this system, but the cultural legacy and historical dominance of this management tool is hard to escape. Leaders who are the product of the command-and-control culture feel at home perpetuating the same expectation in the next generation of leaders too.

Commenting upon the popularity of command and control, Herminia Ibarra makes a forceful point in her article titled 'Why Command-and-Control Leadership Is Here to Stay', '...We talk about the death of command and control leadership, and praise the rise of a new, more collaborative, breed of leader. But when push comes to shove, being in control sells. Collaborative is vegan; directive is meat and potatoes.'[11]

End of the Perfect Leader

Stories of successful leaders around the world tell us that like other mortals, they, too, happen to be vulnerable to various factors—personal weaknesses, incompetence, unfavourable circumstances or change in the operating landscape. The classical leaders of yesterday looked invincible and infallible simply because of the stability, continuity and opacity characteristic of the old economy. The slow pace

---

[11]Herminia Ibarra, 'Why Command-and-Control Leadership Is Here to Stay', *Harvard Business Review*, 20 September 2012

provided enough response time to the leaders and the lack of transparency provided a cover for their weaknesses. But no longer, no more!

In the knowledge-intensive economies of today, characterized by globalization, hyper-specialization, high transparency and increasing accountability, the command-and-control style is fast losing its relevance. Once they are asked to lead in the new economy with the changing landscapes, they fail miserably. As Tacitus put it, 'No-one would have doubted his ability to rule had he never been emperor.'[12]

An Unreal Idea of Leadership

Part of the leadership problem today emanates from misplaced leadership models, which are hardly able to provide any useful guidance towards leadership-development. Essentially, they have their fundamentals wrong. As mentioned earlier, when we ask them what a leader is, they tend to tell us what a leader ought to be. Consider the following as an example: 'Do you have what it takes to become a great leader—the kind that not only attracts people but actually makes things happen as well?' asks Lolly Daskal, leadership expert, president and CEO of Lead from Within, a global consultancy that specializes in leadership and entrepreneurial development.

In a blog post dated 12 June 2015 and titled 'The 10 (and a Half) Commandments of Leadership',[13] Daskal goes on to prescribe the 10.5 commandments for successful and effective leadership.

---

[12]From *Histories*, the Roman historical chronicle by Tacitus, written CE 100–110
[13]Lolly Daskal, 'The 10 (and a Half) Commandments of Leadership', Inc.com, 12 June 2015

> **The 10 (and a Half) Commandments of Leadership:**
>
> 1. You shall be more concerned with your character than your reputation.
> 2. You shall be committed in all that you do.
> 3. You shall listen more than you speak.
> 4. You shall bring the best of who you are into everything you do.
> 5. You shall stand brave even in the face of fear.
> 6. You shall live by your convictions.
> 7. You shall focus with consistent excellence.
> 8. You shall be clear in your vision.
> 9. You shall seek knowledge and wisdom.
> 10. You shall honour others and know their importance.
>
> And finally, here's 10.5:
>
> > You shall make everything count.

Even a cursory look will tell you that all these attributes are indisputable mission statements, signifying the ideal state of the human mind and a model pattern of human behaviour. The emphasis on 'making everything count' aims to portray a leader as a paragon of virtues, which is far from what happens on the ground.

In fact, Daskal is not alone here. Leadership scholars across ages and geographies have contributed to this ideal-state perception of leadership. In *Leading Minds*, Gardner suggests that great leaders exhibit their leadership in two ways—through the stories they tell and through the kind of lives they lead. Likewise, in their book *Leadership by Example: The Ten Key Principles of All Great Leaders*, authors Dr Sanjiv Chopra and David Fisher convert the word 'leadership' to an acronym, associating each of the ten letters in the word with one essential quality. Thus, to qualify as a leader, one must possess the ten qualities of *listening, empathy, attitude, dreaming, effectiveness, resilience, sense of purpose, humility, integrity* and, finally, the willingness to *pack others' parachutes.* The virtuosity woven around leadership by other authors are equally exhaustive, talking of universal human virtues: listen, empathize, share credit, be consistent, remain committed, have a clear vision and guard your character. They tell us that integrating these virtues in our character is the sole route to becoming a successful leader.

The confusion around leadership gets further confounded due to another factor. No doubt, apart from knowing what leadership is, we also need to know what *good leadership* is. But here, the word 'good' has two connotations—morally good and effective. Instead of focusing on effectiveness, leadership experts have been combining both the moral and effectiveness aspects in their definition of good leadership. While it could be an ideal situation, this, again, creates a misplaced leadership model that doesn't match with the realities on the ground.

Putting a Lid on Morality Tales

Is morality relevant to leadership? Scholars will tend to answer in a vehement affirmative. However, the reality can't be seen in terms of black or white—there are shades of grey as well.

While morality and ethics add up to leadership effectiveness, before going further, we must first make a distinction between private morality and public morality. The first refers to an individual's conduct in his personal life, which does not come within the purview of societal or governmental concern. The latter, popularly termed 'ethics', on the other hand, relates to the acts of individuals within the social and legal norms framed by society. To put it simply, private morality relates to what executives do in their bedrooms while public morality concerns what executives do in their boardrooms.

Moral and ethical behaviour does enhance the appeal of leaders, as it brings honesty, authenticity, genuineness and dependability to their discourse. Public morality, in any case, is the bedrock of leadership, which leaves no scope for transgression, and every leader must conform to it.

However, what leadership scholars have been lax in pointing out is that transgressing the boundaries of private morality has not always been a barrier for effective leadership. Some of our most towering leaders, who have transformed generations, have been flawed in one way or the other, some very seriously. Life sketches of some of the most admired leaders, such as Mahatma Gandhi, Martin Luther King, John Lennon, Michael Jackson, John F. Kennedy and Steve Jobs, tell similar stories.

The morality argument has been taken further to distinguish between good and evil. John W. Gardner discusses the issue at length in his book *On Leadership*. In the chapter titled 'The Moral Dimension of Leadership', he distinguishes between good and bad leaders, and insists that leaders must be caring, compassionate and benevolent, and that they must work for the common good of the masses. This morality-driven perspective takes us to the oft-quoted 'Hitler dilemma' and raises the question of whether Hitler should have been considered a leader.

The good-versus-evil approach must be avoided in understanding leadership, simply because our perception of good and evil is based on a lot of variable factors. What is good to one may be evil to another. Hitler was a leader with a mass appeal in contemporary Germany, but people saw his actions as evil in the greater part of Europe and the US. Even in present-day Germany, he is not looked upon as a hero.

Then again, sometimes certain extraneous factors also prevail in endorsing what is right and wrong. Even when a leader is morally deviant, if he is seen to be helpful to the community, people may come up with a trade-off such as, 'Of course, he is a son of a bitch but he's our son of a bitch.'

Going further, if Hitler cannot be considered a leader on the grounds of public morality—not doing good for society at large—applying the same criteria, Indians could dispute Churchill's being a good leader on the grounds that his handling of the Bengal famine during 1943–44 was callous and inhuman. The Bengal famine, systematically engineered by the British for their own commercial profits, was one of the worst man-made calamities in human history, as it saw three million people die of hunger. The Churchill government, pursuing its harsh economic agenda for India, mercilessly focused on tax revenue without any positive intervention or any show of benevolence to ease the problem. Churchill is on record for his insensitive comments, such as, 'I hate Indians. They are a beastly people with a beastly religion. The famine was their own fault for breeding like rabbits.'

Likewise, Harry S. Truman, a former president of the US, could also be denied leadership credit for his bombing of Hiroshima and Nagasaki, which destroyed the two cities and resulted in the mass killing of innocent civilians and maimed their next generations.

A moral distinction between good and bad, therefore, could further confound our understanding of leadership, and hence is best avoided. Across ages, successful leaders are considered to be those who bring about a change in society, for better or for worse. Judged by this amoral standard, Hitler has as much claim to leadership as those at the other end of the morality spectrum, such as Mother Teresa, Gandhi, Churchill and Martin Luther King. We must also remember that history has always been written from the perspective of the winners, who decide what is moral and what is evil. Hence, we must avoid complicating the concept of leadership with our own biases and prejudices.

No True Measure of Leadership

The ideal-state approach to leadership oversimplifies the issue and deprives us of any meaningful guidance on the subject. Researches into human behaviour show that it is shaped not only by inherent traits but also by the circumstances people are placed in. Human beings are complex and multidimensional, and possess all kinds of traits, sometimes even opposing ones, in varying proportions. These traits become dominant or weak depending upon the people one is dealing with or the circumstances one is placed in. Thus, the same person can behave one way within the family and differently at the workplace. He or she may exhibit a different persona in a place of worship and on a picnic with friends. Likewise, human behaviour is determined by the role one is expected to play in a group. Thus, one's behaviour as a follower could be different from one's behaviour as a leader. Even in a leadership role, a person's behaviour is likely to be different when placed at the top of the leadership ladder.

◆

The misconceived leadership models, focusing on essential leadership traits, styles and values, have created a lot of confusion. First, they have driven organizations to search in the wrong direction while looking for leaders from outside or nurturing them in-house. Secondly, the larger-than-life image of leaders is terrifying to budding executives, who are learning to scale up the leadership ladder. They start developing a sense of deficiency and incompleteness, leading to a lack of confidence in their own leadership potential. Even in the minds of established leaders, the misconceived models create persistent doubts as they try to benchmark themselves against the standards enumerated by experts. Thirdly, and what is worse, in trying to conform to the laid-down benchmarks, leaders try to cover up their weaknesses by keeping up a false façade. They attempt being everything to everybody and, in the process, deviate from the agenda they had originally decided to follow.

It's high time, therefore, that we bust the myth of the perfect leader and bury it. Forever!

3

Celebrating the Imperfect Leader

*There is no need to be perfect to inspire others. Let people
get inspired by how you deal with your imperfections.*

−ROBERT TEW, BRITISH SPORTSMAN, AND
CHAIRMAN, NEWCASTLE KNIGHTS LTD

The twenty-first century offers an interesting canvas for
leaders. The political, economic and business environments
across the globe are becoming increasingly complex and
challenging. The social, political and business milieu is turning
out to be more transparent and open to questioning. As a natural
corollary, leadership in all its manifestations is taking on a new
avatar, which can be defined as 'Leadership 2.0'. In a world
where old hierarchies based on class and social order are giving
way to a new pecking order based on intellectual, emotional
and entrepreneurial attributes, leaders are compelled to turn
away from the factory-based Victorian model of leadership and
adopt a new style of leadership. This is now taking root slowly
but steadily across geographies around the world, thanks to
globalization and liberalization.

So what is new about this new-age leadership? What are
the defining characteristics that separate these leaders from
the earlier brand?

Leadership 2.0: Emergence of the Imperfect Leaders

Leadership 2.0 represents a new generation of leaders who accept their vulnerabilities and shake off the psychological pressure of looking perfect. The imperfect leaders of today believe that they are essentially human, with their own strengths and weaknesses. Therefore, while they are aware of their formidable strengths, they are equally comfortable with their natural weaknesses. In fact, it is being realized that in today's world, acceptance of one's imperfections is the stepping stone to good leadership.

This confidence of new-age leaders emanates from their perception that leadership is largely a group activity, as against individual heroism. The earlier approach focused exclusively on the individual as the leader and, therefore, mandated a set of traits, skills and styles for success. Thus, leadership expert Daniel Goleman would expect a leader to alternate between six distinct leadership styles—coercive, authoritative, affiliative, democratic, pacesetting and coaching—'each in right measure and at just the right time'. As against this, the imperfect leaders of today consider leadership as a group activity, where individuals in a diversified leadership team lend their strengths to it and compensate for the weaknesses of their teammates. This approach relieves leaders of the perceived burden of having a complete repertoire of skills and traits for their success. Instead, they prefer to build a well-rounded leadership team of individuals with the required skill sets for organizational success.

It is not that new-age leaders are different from their predecessors, who projected an aura of perfection and infallibility around themselves. The bare truth is that with the progress of civilization, even though Homo sapiens have changed their behavioural patterns, their basic nature, strengths and frailties have remained the same. There has been no fundamental change in their fears and apprehensions, aspirations and motivations. It is therefore not out of place to observe that even across ages, leaders have been imperfect, as they, too, have had their strengths and weaknesses. The entire history of leadership can hardly project a personality without fallibility or imperfection. We have numerous examples of epoch-making leaders who have transformed generations of people and moved human organizations to newer horizons in spite of their own frailties. However, except for some rare examples of transformational leaders, such as Gandhi, who openly declared his weaknesses and converted them into his strengths, leaders in the past usually covered up their weaknesses and projected an aura of perfection and invincibility. The standalone, opaque and stable economies of their times, supported by a hierarchical society with an unquestionable respect for higher-ups, enabled them to create a smokescreen of perfection—a luxury modern leaders can ill-afford.

The driving forces behind this new approach to leadership are quite strong and pervasive. The onset of the knowledge economy, along with rapid globalization, is ushering in organizational changes that are making modern corporations less hierarchical. As information today is readily available across geographies, it facilitates long-distance teamwork by pooling in expertise from different parts of the world to deliver the required solutions. Further, with the emergence of multinational corporations, businesses have to cater to a variety of markets and customer needs, conform to their varying cultural sensibilities and comply with local laws and regulations. In a globally networked environment, marked by constant disruptions— economic, political and technological—and increasing ambiguities and complexities, organizational responses have to be swift and appropriate. With competitors breathing down their neck, coupled with analysts' and shareholders' activism, companies are already on a tightrope walk. The stakes are higher, as misplaced or delayed organizational responses could be disastrous for the company, with wider implications.

In such a scenario, it is not possible for any one leader to have all the knowledge and competence required to address the issues facing the organization. The urgency with which issues need to be addressed and the required collaboration by distant and multi-location players having specialized skills also rule out the possibility of any one leader at the top dictating all the solutions. Further, in this age of increasing openness and transparency, if a leader attempts to hide a weakness and project a non-existent strength, the bluff is likely to be called soon.

In fact, in the extremely uncertain, volatile and disruptive environment in which organizations are operating today, any attempt by leaders to aspire for perfection would be counterproductive and may lead to organizational distress. Contemporary leaders, responding to the demands of their environment, are therefore quick to embrace their imperfections.

I Am That: Embracing Imperfections

Imperfections in a leader may be of different kinds. Some may be deficient in certain desirable soft leadership attributes such as communication, humility and consistency; others could be lacking in professional or technical skills related to their business. For example, there could be leaders who are not good at communication or do not understand the nitty-gritty of IT or may not have an in-depth understanding of the financial statements of their organizations. A clear understanding of their own strengths and weaknesses, therefore, becomes the bedrock of their leadership strategy.

At a personal level, the awareness and acceptance of their vulnerability enables leaders to ward off criticism targeted at their weaknesses. In fact, it helps them set the right expectations from them and enables them to focus on their strengths. Also, shorn of the burden of looking perfect, they don't waste their time and energy in creating a façade of perfection. Once they are their natural selves, they do not have to pretend to be on top of everything concerning their organization. In the process, they save their organization from any possible damage arising out of immature and uninformed decisions they could make in an attempt to look perfect.

However, the most important benefit from this shift in approach is that it gives leaders the much-needed emotional and intellectual space to look for the missing expertise outside of themselves—within their own organization or outside it. Thus, by bringing in missing expertise from outside, they make the leadership team more competent and ready to face challenges. Instead of the age-old practice of command and control, they tend to collaborate and co-create for achieving their common vision. As organizational complexities increase and business landscapes get globalized, they feel the need to take decision-making closer to the scene of action. To achieve this, they groom leadership within the organization and delegate authority and decentralize decision-making to improve organizational agility.

It must, however, be appreciated that being imperfect does not mean being incompetent. Imperfect leaders are the ones who convert their weaknesses into an opportunity to add to the organization's collective strength and make it ready to face the myriad challenges before it. It is, in effect, a strategic shift of focus from the leader's own personality to the needs of the organization and the demands of the environment.

Celebrating the Imperfect Leader

In the light of these postulates, let's look at some leadership stories to understand how great leaders have sidestepped their weaknesses and gone on to accomplish their mission and vision. These leaders belong to different ages, generations and professions. Their challenges were different and the environments in which they worked were also different. They had only two things in common, though—all of them were flawed in one way or the other, but they rose to the pinnacle of effective leadership. All by working on their strengths!

Mahatma Gandhi: His Experiments with Chastity

Gandhi, one of the greatest leaders the world has seen, is a fascinating example of an imperfect leader. The 'half-naked' and 'seditious fakir', as Churchill once described him, was the person who galvanized India to fight against the mighty British Empire and led India to freedom from colonial rule.

Was he an epitome of perfection in public perception? By no means was he even close to it. In his autobiography, *My Experiments with Truth*, he admits his personal failings—giving in to unethical pleasures, mistrusting and maltreating his wife, not being an ideal son and so on. With respect to his relationship with his wife, he writes,

> Her duty was easily converted into my right to extract faithfulness from her, and if it had to be extracted, I should be watchfully tenacious of the right. I had absolutely no reason to suspect my wife's fidelity, but jealousy doesn't wait for reasons. I must be forever on the lookout regarding her movements, and therefore she could not go anywhere without my permission.[14]

In fact, judged by the yardstick of personal ethics and public

[14]M.K. Gandhi, *An Autobiography: The Story of My Experiments with Truth*, Chapter 4, 'Playing the Husband', translated by Mahadev Desai, Beacon Press

morality, Gandhi comes out as an abject disappointment. His personal conduct and sexual life were always mired in controversy and invited widespread public disapproval. It was in 1906, when both he and his wife were thirty-eight, that he took a vow of brahmacharya, enforcing celibacy upon himself, and persuaded his wife to do the same. While this was a purely private vow, without caring for his wife's privacy he made it public so as to create an aura of sainthood around himself. But what became more questionable in the public eye was that while he advised newlyweds to stay celibate for the sake of their souls, he himself slept naked next to young, nubile and naked women to test his self-control.

The fact remains that while Gandhi could successfully embrace poverty, chastity always eluded him. In his own ashram, while even husband and wife were forbidden to sleep together, for himself he had a different set of rules to conduct his 'experiments' and test his spiritual resilience. As he grew older, he increased the level of his challenges. Thus, when Dr Sushila Nayar, who was part of his 'experiments' for a long time, turned thirty-three in 1947, she was replaced by a much younger eighteen-year-old Manu, Gandhi's grand-niece, to sleep with him and test the seventy-seven-year-old man's spiritual fortitude. While people criticized him and started to desert his ashram, Sardar Vallabhbhai Patel wrote to him saying that what he was doing was 'adharma' (immoral). To this, Gandhi retorted, 'For me Manu sleeping with me is a matter of dharma (moral duty). If I don't let Manu sleep with me, though I regard it as essential that she should, wouldn't that be a sign of weakness in me?'[15]

It was quite evident that like many great leaders, Gandhi

---

[15]'An odd kind of piety: The truth about Gandhi's sex life', *The Independent*, 2 January 2012

made his own rules as he went along. He lived by them and often elevated them as a demand of the cosmic order. In the 1970s, Dr Nayar revealed that the 'brahmacharya' experiment was only in response to criticism for his behaviour. As she put it, 'Later on, when people started asking questions about his physical contact with women—with Manu, with Abha, with me—the idea of brahmacharya experiments was developed… In the early days, there was no question of calling this a brahmacharya experiment.'[16]

Going beyond his personal life, even in his political life, Gandhi didn't live by some of the cherished values of the times. A self-opinionated person, he was highly undemocratic in his approach to issues of national interest. Some of the milestones in his political life bear testimony to his dictatorial attitude. During the Congress Tripuri Session in 1939, when Subhash Chandra Bose was elected the president of the Indian National Congress (INC), defeating Gandhi's candidate Dr Pattabhi Sitaramayya by a clear margin of 1,580 to 1,377 votes, Gandhi took it as a personal blow and almost declared war against Bose.

He said, '…I am glad of his (Subhash's) victory…and since I was instrumental in inducing Dr Pattabhi not to withdraw his name after Maulana Azad Sahib had done so, the defeat is more mine than his…'[17]

At this point of time, Bose was posing the greatest challenge to Gandhi's ideology and stature. As the Congress Working Committee (CWC) was still being controlled by Gandhi's followers, through a well-orchestrated scheme of

---

[16]'An odd kind of piety: The truth about Gandhi's sex life', *The Independent*, 2 January 2012

[17]'Subhash Chandra Bose and Congress Tripuri Session 1939', GKToday. in, 9 August 2018

non-cooperation against the president, Gandhi ensured that while Bose could reign, he could not rule. Under his influence, twelve members, including Patel, resigned from the CWC. Frustrated, Bose resigned and went on to take an altogether different course of action to work for India's freedom.

Gandhi's undemocratic nature was again evident when it came to deciding who the prime minister of Independent India should be. After the Second World War, the British were actively considering granting freedom to India, and, by 1946, it was clear that India's Independence was just a matter of time. Following the 1946 elections, in which the INC won the maximum number of seats, an interim government was to be formed, headed by the INC president. At this point, the position of the INC president had become all the more crucial, as the person occupying the position would be the prime minister of Independent India. The then Congress president, Maulana Abul Kalam Azad, was interested in contesting for the president's position once again, but Gandhi made his opposition clear. A dejected Azad had to fall in line. It was well known that Gandhi had a soft corner for Jawaharlal Nehru. However, when nominations for the post of president were made, of the fifteen regional Congress committees, twelve voted for Patel. None of them had voted for Nehru. Then Gandhi asked Acharya J.B. Kripalani to organize a few nominations for Nehru by members of the CWC, knowing fully well that only the regional committees were authorized to nominate.

He asked Patel to withdraw his name and thus Nehru became the first prime minister of India, against all democratic norms.

Did the moral aberrations in his personal life or the undemocratic behaviour in his public life deter Gandhi from rising to the pinnacle of transformational leadership? No. While all Gandhi's weaknesses were in the public domain, what was it in him that made the people of India love him as a leader and catapult him to the heights of glory, so much so that even today he is revered as the Father of the Nation? Quite clearly, his leadership was built on his strengths and not on his weaknesses. His strength emanated from his undying commitment to truth and non-violence, which he used as powerful weapons in his fight against the British.

Gandhi's strengths overshadowed his weaknesses. His commitment to truth was so absolute that he disclosed all his weaknesses in his autobiography, written and published between 1927 and 1931. The highly conservative Indian society could have shunned him for the revelations made in his book. But his weaknesses were overshadowed by two of his indisputable virtues: the commitment to truth and the courage of conviction that truth had to be told, howsoever inconvenient it was.

Equally unflinching was Gandhi's commitment to non-violence, which was repeatedly tested during the thirty-year struggle for India's Independence. His pledge to the ideal of non-violence was so strong that he suspended the nationwide Non-Cooperation Movement, launched by him against British imperial rule in India, because of an isolated incident of violence during the Civil Disobedience Movement based on non-violence, or satyagraha. The incident took place on 4 February 1922 at Chauri Chaura in present-day Uttar Pradesh. A peaceful crowd of protesters was fired at by the police, resulting in the death of a few agitators, which led to the burning of a police station by the angry mob, killing the policemen inside. Even though the agitation was at its peak across the country, Gandhi did not hesitate to call it off, much against the advice of his lieutenants.

Likewise, Gandhi refused to intervene and save the lives of three of India's celebrated revolutionary freedom fighters—

Bhagat Singh, Rajguru and Sukhdev. On 8 April 1929, Bhagat Singh, along with his friend Batukeshwar Dutt, had thrown two low-intensity bombs and leaflets in the corridors of the Central Legislative Assembly, seeking to draw the attention of the British government to their misrule in India. The revolutionaries thereafter shouted slogans and waited to be arrested. They didn't intend to kill anyone, and, indeed, the bombs hadn't.

However, Gandhi was not convinced, as he didn't approve of their violent means of freedom struggle. In spite of massive public sentiment in favour of the three revolutionaries, Gandhi agreed, as part of the Gandhi-Irwin Pact of March 1931, that Bhagat Singh, Rajguru and Sukhdev be hanged.

Gandhi's success is a classic example of leadership inspired by the strength of character and personal convictions, and a unique ability to convert weaknesses into strengths. He was a person who never denied his weaknesses; rather, he was one who had the courage to disclose them to the masses. This strategy took the sting out of any criticism against him. Further, with single-minded focus, he utilized his strengths and converted them into a potent weapon in his fight against the British Empire. Before Gandhi came on the scene, India's struggle against the British was more or less an elitist movement, led by a few Western-educated leaders. It was Gandhi, dressed as the poorest of the poor Indian, who transformed it into a mass movement, cutting across geography, caste, creed and religion. His appeal for peaceful non-cooperation against the British struck a chord with the Indian masses, which showed unflinching resilience throughout the freedom struggle, even in the face of extreme violence at the hands of their oppressors, at times leading to mass death and destruction.

While Gandhi belonged to a different age, US President Donald J. Trump is the face of the imperfect leader in today's world. He is the most telling rebuttal of the trait-based understanding of leadership.

Right through his presidential campaign, he displayed a number of deeply problematic character flaws, any of which could have been good enough to throw him out of the race. His idiosyncrasies were not limited to his personal character but extended to his declared stance on public policies as well.

On the personal front, during the election campaign, not less than twenty-four women came forward accusing Trump of inappropriate sexual behaviour on multiple occasions spanning a thirty-year period.[18] He was accused of being a misogynist, a womanizer, and even talking lasciviously about his own daughter, Ivanka. Memes of his wife, Melania Trump,[19] a former model, were splashed across social media, as she was mocked about bringing transparency to the White House. While some of these were hotly discussed in the public domain, on his part, Trump, too, added to the negative vibe around his personality. Quite a few of these accusations, such as walking into the green room of beauty-pageant participants and patting naked models, were admitted by him and dismissed as 'locker-room talk'.

In his useful biography *Trump Revealed: The Definitive Biography of the 45th President, Washington Post* journalists Michael Kranish and Marc Fisher talk about 'Trump's morals failings'. It mentions his cheating on his wife, admitting to trying to

---

[18]Amber Jamieson, Simon Jeffery and Nicole Puglise, 'A timeline of Donald Trump's alleged sexual misconduct: who, when and what', *The Guardian*, 27 October 2016
[19]https://me.me/i/melania-trump-will-bring-transparency-to-the-white-house-8shit-4235206

'seduce a married woman', and bragging about how he could 'grab women by the crotch...'[20]

Going beyond his lack of moral compass, Trump's stance on matters of public policy displayed a horrible disdain for political correctness. He was perceived as indulging in tax evasion, appealing to racism, destroying social cohesion, and polarizing American society on issues of immigration and border security, among others.[21] Even worse, he was accused of taking the help of the country's arch-enemy Russia to win the election.[22]

Further, in the three presidential debates with Hillary Clinton, he came across as brash and brazen, and an indiscreet and intemperate person. To top it all, in the age of live television, he criticized, ridiculed and insulted the media in no uncertain terms. Even now that he is the president of the US, every time he tweets on matters of state, he puts out an array of negative traits that old-school leadership scholars would be quick to denounce as Shakespearean 'fatal flaws'.

Following eight years of an 'honourable leadership' provided by Barack Obama, ably supported by his graceful wife Michelle, the prospect of Trump's leadership appeared to be outrageous and outlandish, verging on near-disaster for the US. Not only is the US the richest nation in the world today, it has a high stake in the global order as well. The White House has been the seat of the most powerful head of state in the world since 1945, and the US president has at his fingertips the power to unleash nuclear disaster, which could

---

[20]Walter G. Moss, 'Unlike Obama, Trump Has No Moral Compass', History News Network, George Washington University, 6 October 2018
[21]https://en.wikipedia.org/wiki/Donald_Trump_2016_presidential_campaign
[22]Max Boot, 'Let's not lose sight of the real scandal: Trump was elected with Russia's help', *The Washington Post*

annihilate the Earth. The entire world had watched Trump's unorthodox presidential campaign with anxiety, concern and curiosity. And yet, the US elected Trump as its leader. How?

Evidently, Trump's weaknesses did not come in the way of his being anointed the leader of the most powerful nation in the world. It is, rather, his strength—the power of his dream for the American people and which appealed to the American electorate, who voted in his favour—that got him the presidency. His call to 'make America great again' resonated with the majority of American voters, who were getting impatient with the rising cost of living and healthcare, the falling employment rate and the decreasing influence of the US in the affairs of the world. Fed up with conventional and manipulative politicians, the people of America saw in Trump a successful businessman who talked straight and could lead them to a better life and living, and bring back the fading glory of the US.

It is not that Americans have been unmindful of the moral aberrations of their leaders. The recent example of Harvey Weinstein, the former Hollywood mogul, is a case in point. He was sacked as co-chairman of The Weinstein Company following charges of sexual abuse and harassment levelled at him by a host of Hollywood actresses during the #MeToo movement. In similar circumstances, recently, Josh Randle, the then president of Miss America Organization, had to resign following his remark about the physical appearance of 2013 winner Mallory Hagan, even though the comments were made in a private e-mail conversation and even before he had joined the organization.

Even in the past, the leading Democratic Party aspirant, Gary Hart, had to bow out of the presidential race in 1987 once his affair with Donna Rice was broken by *The New York Times* and *The Miami Herald*.

The moral and behavioural transgressions of Trump could be considered far worse than those of the others cited above. In fact, Trump could be a perfect example of what a leader should not be in a conventional sense. However, even in the face of all the fatal flaws in his character, the liberal democracy of the US elected him as its leader, ignoring the tough challenge from a suave, eloquent and experienced Hillary Clinton, who was on the cusp of making history by becoming the first female president of the US. This example should wake us up to the need for a relook at the morality tales that we have been fed for ages and to face the fact that a leader's character is never the be all and end all of his leadership. While positive character traits are important for leadership success, they are not its sole determinants. Leadership, being a multidimensional phenomenon, has multiple factors that determine its success. Moreover, as human beings are complex, displaying both positive and negative traits, a one-way approach to understanding leadership leaves much about it unsaid. It has to be studied in all its dimensions.

M.S. Dhoni: An Imperfect Captain Cool

The previous two examples were from politics. Let us see one example from the world of sports. Mahendra Singh Dhoni, considered the most successful captain of the Indian cricket team, appropriately nicknamed Captain Cool, is a living example of an imperfect leader. Popularly known as Mahi among his friends, he is as admired for his cricketing skills and achievements as for his cool and charismatic leadership. During his nine-year captaincy from 2007 to 2016, he led the Indian team to unprecedented heights and unparalleled glory. He led India to victory in different formats of the game, winning the World Twenty20 Cup, the World Cup, the Champions Trophy, the Asia Cup, the Commonwealth Bank series, the

Compaq Cup series and the Celkon Mobile Cup, to name a few. In the Indian Premier League (IPL), he led his team, Chennai Super Kings, to the trophy in both 2010 and 2011. Under his leadership, India won eleven bilateral ODI series and the country's winning percentages in ODIs and Twenty20 were 59.57 per cent and 59.28 per cent, respectively. In a rare recognition of his charismatic career, a biopic titled *M.S. Dhoni: The Untold Story* was also made in 2016, which was quite a box office success.

But more than his cricketing genius, it is his leadership that has mesmerized sports lovers. On his giving up the captaincy in 2016, *The Indian Express* wrote:

> With him, it was clear that someone was in control out there. His fielders felt it, his bowlers felt it, the opposition batsmen felt it and the fans too cottoned on to it. And the spooky calmness behind the stumps would surely have had a detrimental effect on the batsmen. It definitely had a beneficial effect on his team-mates, and also changed the way, we, the viewers, watched the Indians play.[23]

The aforesaid portrayal of Dhoni's achievements and leadership profile might give one the impression that he possessed all the leadership qualities in abundance. Unfortunately, that is not true. One of Dhoni's serious drawbacks is his communication skills, which most of us would recognize as an essential leadership trait. An intensely private person, his off-the-field communication was extremely poor. To the rest of the world he has always appeared inscrutable and unpredictable. He resigned from Test captaincy in the middle of a Test series abroad without any obvious provocation. He further shocked

---

[23]Sriram Veera, 'MS Dhoni, former India ODI, T20I captain', *The Indian Express*, 5 January 2017

the cricketing fraternity by his sudden and unanticipated resignation as India's ODI captain. To add to this, he has also been mired in controversies involving professional ethics and financial integrity.

And yet, if the cricketing world looked at the leadership of Dhoni with awe and an entire generation of youngsters drew inspiration from him, it was simply because Dhoni focused on his strengths, which completely overshadowed his weaknesses. Starting out as a small-town boy with humble beginnings, he earned the position and respect he enjoys today. Then, his performance as a cricketer—both as a batsman and a wicketkeeper—has been superlative. As the leader of the Indian team, he has always delivered, often taking risks and leading from the front. Faced with an impending defeat in the 2011 World Cup, his decision to promote himself in the batting order—even after a mediocre run with the bat—over Yuvraj Singh, the Man of the Tournament, is the stuff legends are made of. The winning runs coming off his celebrated helicopter shot underscored the self-belief that is characteristic of Dhoni the leader.

The other great strength of Dhoni always on display is that he appears to be a team person. Not given to narcissism, which leaders usually fall prey to, Dhoni passed on whatever trophies he won to his teammates so they could savour the moment and be in the limelight while he himself moved to position himself behind the others.

Yet another noticeable strength of Dhoni was that he increased the 'cool quotient' of the game to an unparalleled level. With him in command, the team seemed to be less nervy, the bowlers didn't throw up their arms in frustration or look angry when there was a misfield or if a yorker ended up as a full toss and was hit for a six. It is as if his pervading calmness, darting eyes and the occasional wave of hand to set the fielding cast a hypnotic spell on the team, which did his bidding.

If Dhoni was able to transform the Indian team as a world beater, winning the World No. 1 ranking in spite of his glaring weaknesses, it was all because he focused on his strengths and built upon them. He was conscious of the fact that it is always easier to swim with the current, i.e. work on strengths, than swim against it. It was true of Dhoni, and it is true of all leaders.

Albert Einstein: The Energetic Leadership of an Eccentric Genius

If we study the lives of leaders and geniuses with the expectation that they are fundamentally different from common men and women, we are in for a huge disappointment. Albert Einstein, the celebrated genius, has attained an iconic status as a scientist and a humanist. Acknowledged as Person of the Century by *Time* magazine and voted as the greatest physicist of all time by *Physics World*, Einstein mesmerized the world with his scientific theories and provided intellectual leadership to generations of human beings. His contributions to science were indeed path-breaking and revolutionary. His works were instrumental in recognizing cosmology as a branch of science, dealing with enormous ideas such as the origin of the universe, and studying exotic cosmic phenomena such as the Big Bang, black holes and gravitational waves.

No wonder that he was considered a mystic genius by his own generation and perceived to be drastically different from the rest of humanity in some fundamental manner. It was this larger-than-life persona of the iconic genius that led the pathologist Thomas Harvey, who conducted his autopsy, to preserve his brain for scientific experimentation later.

However, while Einstein's glorious scientific legacies stand on one side, his idiosyncrasies and weaknesses stare us blatantly in the face on the other, marking him as just like the rest of us. He was a deeply flawed individual, who was often viewed as a philanderer, an absentee father, a plagiarist and even a fraud. The Princeton Press's *The Collected Papers of Albert Einstein* tells the story of the man and his first wife, Mileva Maric, who was once his lover and intellectual companion. Einstein, who was 'crazy with desire' initially, later wrote in July 1914 to the mother of his two sons in a cold and calculated manner, laying down the conditions for continuing their marriage: 'A. You will see to it (1) that my clothes and linen are kept in order, (2) that I am served three regular meals a day in my room. B. You will renounce all personal relations with me, except when these are required to keep up social appearances.' And: 'You will expect no affection from me... You must leave my bedroom or study at once without protest when I ask you to.'

As far as his moral fibre went, the great scientist was no different from a common man. He is reported to have cheated on his first wife and had an affair with his cousin, Elsa Einstein, whom he married later but cheated on as well. He didn't have a normal relationship with his children, whom he often ignored during their childhood.

Many also wonder if Maric, Einstein's first wife, who too was a Physics student, had made substantial contributions to Einstein's theories but was denied any credit for it. The US TV documentary *Einstein's Wife*, which came out in 2003, only added substance to this theory. In fact, the accusations go beyond the denial of credit to Maric and on to whether Einstein stole the work of other physicists. In an article published in the digital magazine *Aeon*, on 22 July 2014, Matthew Francis, a science writer and speaker specializing in Physics, Astronomy and the Culture of Science, makes an assessment:

> He was also justifiably modest about his mathematical ability. He relied on others, including his first wife Mileva

and his good friend, the physicist Michele Besso, to help him work out thorny problems. Today they would receive co-author credits on Einstein's papers, but that wasn't the practice at the time.[24]

John Stachel, director of the Center for Einstein Studies at Boston University and editor of *The Collected Papers*, sums it up well: 'Too much of an idol was made of Einstein... He's not an idol—he's a human, and that's much more interesting.'[25]

Why is it, then, that in spite of his eccentricities and weaknesses, Einstein is viewed as a genius with a larger-than-life persona? The answer is not far to seek. It is all due to Einstein's strengths and his circumstances that made him a celebrity, way above some of his equally talented contemporaries, such as Niels Bohr, Marie Curie, Werner Heisenberg and Erwin Schrödinger. Einstein was able to convey powerful messages with extreme simplicity. The equation derived from his theory of special relativity, expressed in the simple-looking formula $E = mc^2$, caught the imagination of people, even though they may not have been able to understand it.

Further, Einstein had a much louder amplifier than most of his contemporaries. He became the poster boy of American liberalism once he migrated from Nazi Germany to the US. It was also a time when the mass media—radio and newspapers—arrived on the scene and carried his anti-racism and humanism messages to the public. Einstein's wit and unique coif were also factors that portrayed him as a rare kind of genius.

The recognition of Einstein as a superhuman cognitive celebrity and the poster boy of genius, in spite of being a flawed human being, tells us the strengths story. When the

---

[24]Mathew Francis, 'Cognitive Celebrity', *Aeon*, 22 July 2014
[25]Tarun Mittal, 'Albert Einstein: the great scientist who was a flawed human being', YourStory.com, 14 March 2017

message of the leader is powerful and his vision of the future compelling, and he is able to communicate that to his audience, his weaknesses take a back seat in the minds of his followers. It was no different for Einstein.

Steve Jobs: An Arrogant Maverick Who Changed the World

In recent times, if there has been one person who has transformed the way we live and think, it is Steve Jobs. You don't need to be an Apple fan to appreciate that he was the genius who created a unique connect, an emotional attachment, between man and his machine. Innovations such as the iPhone, the iPad, the iPod, the MacBook, the iMac and the iTunes Store tell a saga of entrepreneurial excellence. Nearly a billion iPhones have been sold around the world, with each new version being lapped up by fans who do not mind waiting in queues overnight to buy one. The insurmountable global appeal of his products is testimony to the creative genius of the man who is now ranked with all-time greats such as Henry Ford and Walt Disney.

However, even after his death, the question keeps surfacing, 'Does Steve Jobs deserve to be admired? Could he be a role model for leaders?' In the documentary *Steve Jobs: The Man in the Machine*, released in September 2015, celebrated filmmaker Alex Gibney paints Jobs as 'ruthless, deceitful and cruel'. Writing for *The New York Times*, Andrew Ross Sorkin says, 'Mr Gibney goes through a laundry list of Jobs's sins: backdated stock options, factory conditions in China and secret agreements with Silicon Valley rivals to prevent employee-poaching.'[26]

Gibney is not alone in an adverse assessment of Jobs's leadership. Even Jobs's foremost admirers have admitted that

---

[26]Andrew Ross Sorkin, 'Decoding Steve Jobs, in Life and on Film', *The New York Times*, 7 September 2015

he was a complicated leader—a brilliant innovator with a keen eye on each and every aspect of his product, but, at the same time, an insufferable maniac who could drive his colleagues to tears. In a *Harvard Business Review* article titled 'Was Steve Jobs a Role Model for Leaders?', authors Darren Overfield and Rob Kaiser conclude, 'According to our data, Jobs should be regarded as a statistical outlier and a managerial anomaly rather than as a model of leadership worth imitating.'[27]

A maverick he was, no doubt, but that did not prevent Jobs from becoming an outstanding leader who transformed an entire generation and set uncompromising benchmarks for competitors. A few decades on, history will forget his idiosyncrasies but remember him for his contribution to the development of human society.

Does It Pay to Be a Jerk?

On the other end of the morality and virtuosity spectrum is the question: Does it pay to be a jerk? Fed on the Manichaean principles of morality as well as our religious convictions, we have always been made to think that leaders have to be honest, virtuous, kind and merciful. They must have complete harmony of thought, speech and action as envisaged in the Indian philosophy of *manasa-vaacha-karmana*—harmony of thought, speech and action—akin to Rotary International's Four Way Test, which, too, implores that our thoughts, words and actions be truthful and fair, promote goodwill and be beneficial to all.

However, this has not put an end to the good guy-bad guy debate. While the Bible says 'Blessed are the meek, for they shall inherit the earth', and Dale Carnegie advises us to 'begin with

---

[27]Darren Overfield and Rob Kaiser, 'Was Steve Jobs a Role Model for Leaders?', *Harvard Business Review*, 1 October 2012

praise and honest appreciation', there is always the apprehension that 'nice guys finish last'. Some recent books, such as *The Power of Nice* by Linda Kaplan Thaler and Robin Koval and *The Upside of Your Dark Side* by Todd Kashdan and Robert Biswas-Diener, have taken this debate further. In an article written on the 500th anniversary of the writing of Machiavelli's *The Prince*, the authors John T. Scott and Robert Zaretsky summarize the crux of Machiavelli's teachings:

> Yet Machiavelli teaches that in a world where so many are not good, you must learn to be able to not be good. The virtues taught in our secular and religious schools are incompatible with the virtues one must practice to safeguard those same institutions. The power of the lion and the cleverness of the fox: These are the qualities a leader must harness to preserve the republic.[28]

Leaving aside the academic debate, what do we see on the operational landscape? Kissing up and kicking down may not be a great human virtue, but in the corporate world, many have successfully adopted this route to reach the top of the leadership ladder. On the global scene, the Western Bloc sees shades of Machiavelli in the leadership style of Russian President Vladimir Putin, with the Western media calling him 'Czar Putin'. To the world he appears to be a ruthless autocrat and his forcible annexation of Crimea has shown that he hardly cares for world opinion where Russian interests are involved.

Says Ilya Matveev, a researcher and lecturer based in St Petersburg, Russia,

---

[28]John T. Scott and Robert Zaretsky, 'Why Machiavelli Still Matters', *The New York Times*, 9 December 2013

Putin's style of governance has always assumed, on the one hand, the elimination of independent players and, on the other, the encouragement of competition between dependent players. Here, Putin acts as a referee between them, making his role irreplaceable.[29]

In spite of the fact that a lot of negativity surrounds Putin's leadership style, he has been rated as the sixth most admired person in the world in an annual global survey conducted by pollster YouGov. Putin's global popularity is neither sudden nor accidental—he has been riding the popularity wave for quite a few years now.

While the role of virtuosity in leadership has always been accepted and acclaimed, some amount of empirical data exists on the other side of the spectrum, which suggests that certain not-so-desirable qualities could also contribute to leadership success. Attributes such as a deliberate display of power, narcissism, self-promotion or the act of manoeuvring one's success through lies and fabrications have also been seen to contribute to leadership success.

In a brilliant article in *The Atlantic*, 'Why It Pays to Be a Jerk', Jerry Useem argues that 'a touch of jerkiness could be helpful'.[30] He analyses research findings of Wharton professor Adam Grant's book, *Give and Take: Why Helping Others Drives Our Success.* He also discusses the research conducted by Professor Donald Hambrick of Penn State on narcissist CEOs. Interestingly, in the respective studies, both the narcissist CEOs and Grant's 'givers' formed a U-shaped distribution, clustering near both extremes of the success spectrum.

Useem quotes Hambrick as suggesting that 'there is such

[29]Ilya Matveev, 'The big game: Ulyukaev, Sechin and Russia's neopatrimonial privatisation', Opendemocracy.net, 21 November 2016
[30]Jerry Useem, 'Why It Pays to Be a Jerk', *The Atlantic*, June 2015

a thing as a useful narcissist'. Unlike average CEOs, narcissist CEOs, being gamblers, are more prone to making high-profile acquisitions, some of which will obviously work out. 'To the extent that innovation and risk-taking are in short supply in the corporate world, narcissists are the ones who are going to step up to the plate,' Useem quotes Hambrick in *The Atlantic* article.

However, the interesting part is that the contribution of the not-so-desirable traits has been ignored by leadership experts, confirming that people only see what they are motivated to see and believe.

4

Leading from Strength

Great leaders are not defined by the absence of weakness,
but rather by the presence of clear strengths.

–JOHN PETER ZENGER,
AMERICAN PRINTER AND JOURNALIST

Tasha Roy was disturbed and distracted. Twice she had nearly hit the car ahead of her in the peak-hour traffic, meandering its way through the outer circle of Connaught Place in New Delhi. Driving to work, she felt sick and nervous and wished that she didn't have to go to office that day. She took a deep breath and her focus returned. But the sinking feeling returned soon enough. It was the day staff promotions were going to be announced. She was almost sure she was going to be left behind. The head of her department had often cautioned her to improve her performance and the behind-the-back mocks and taunts of her colleagues had eroded her sense of self-worth. Shattered, she didn't know how she was going to face her colleagues or tell her family members that she had not been rated good enough to be elevated.

It had not been so in the past. When Tasha had been transferred from Lucknow, Uttar Pradesh, to the Delhi division of the insurance office, her Lucknow manager had spoken highly of her, saying that she had made a difference to the team performance. Encouraged by the recommendations, she had been placed in the Claims department, which was facing the onerous challenge of speeding up settlements of long-pending death claims, which was causing customer dissatisfaction.

As the list of employees to be promoted was placed for approval before Gaurav, the divisional head, out of curiosity he looked for Tasha's name. Not finding it there, he called the HR head to discuss her Annual Confidential Report. The HR head informed him that the report spoke of an average performance. She further added that with such a low rating, Tasha was not going to make the mark, given that there were plenty of people with 'Excellent', 'Well-Above Average' and 'Above Average' ratings. When Gaurav took it up with the Claims head, she corroborated Tasha's lower rating, revealing that Tasha had not been up to the mark in her understanding of the rules and regulations governing claims and had been inconsistent in putting up claims notes.

Gaurav was irked that Tasha's erstwhile manager had taken him for a ride and pushed an average employee into his division by talking highly of her—not an unusual practice in the public sector. But he decided to talk to Tasha and understand for himself what the problem was.

As Tasha walked into his office, he found that she had a distinct personality. Tall and graceful, she exuded charm and confidence.

'How are you, Tasha?'

'Fine, Sir! Thank you.'

'You've been with us for over a year now. How has your experience been?'

'Well, Sir, thank you for enquiring. Frankly speaking, I haven't enjoyed my work...,' she said with a note of sadness in her voice. 'In fact, I haven't contributed my best...'

'What explains that? You wanted to come to Delhi and your boss said you were an excellent performer.'

'I really don't know. Somehow, I'm not able to relate to the work.' She looked sideways as her eyes started to well up.

Gaurav offered her a glass of water and tissues, and waited for her to compose herself.

'What did you do in your previous assignment?'

'I was in the Marketing department and was liaising with vendors, designers, the press and others.'

'Any bright moments there that you remember?'

'Oh, yes,' her face lit up, her voice regaining composure. With a glint in her eyes, she narrated, 'You know, the year before last, when the chairman had come down to the division to inaugurate the local area network, our divisional head had organized a press conference...'

'I remember—the press coverage was excellent.'

'Right, Sir! But our press conference was nearly wiped out before we could salvage it.'

'Oh, I see! Something went wrong?'

'Yeah! Just a couple of days before our event, there was a sudden law-and-order problem and the police declared a curfew in the entire town. Our press conference was going to be a flop. As it had been widely announced, both the marketing head and the divisional head were apprehensive of a loss of face.'

'I see. So how did you retrieve the situation?'

'Well, Sir, I remember the grim faces during our meeting. And then I decided to do my humble bit. I asked our marketing head if I could persuade some journalists to come over so that even if we had a few, it could be a face-saver. With his permission, I took my bike from one press office to another, persuading journalists to come over and cover the event.'

'But the curfew...?'

'You know, the police usually do not perceive a lone woman riding a bike as a threat. They rather sympathize with her... sometimes patronize her with advice to stay at home,' she said with a smile, 'and the press guys manage with their press card.'

'Interesting!'

'So we had a full house during the press conference. The chairman was extremely satisfied with the coverage. I, too, was happy having done my bit in saving the day.'

'Well, I now have some idea about your areas of interest! Let's see how we can find a suitable job profile for you.'

'I'd be grateful, Sir. Thank you.'

The following week, the Claims head assigned Tasha a new role. She was entrusted with the responsibility of procuring claim-related documents in difficult and long-pending cases, particularly from various hospitals and police stations. This was a persistent problem delaying many claim settlements for years, because poor widows were not in a position to procure hospital reports, police FIRs and other documentation as required, and the agents were not much help either.

Tasha took upon herself the task of accomplishing the job. With her charm and persuasion skills, she was able to get the reports in a much shorter time. She moved around with a camera and wherever she encountered bureaucratic hurdles in obtaining the reports, she would talk her way to getting a photo of the relevant documents. Very soon, the position of claims settlements brightened, the number of complaints reduced and the agents were able to knock on customers' doors for fresh business again.

Needless to say, Tasha was promoted in the next round. Not only did she get her confidence back, her self-image was also restored. At the same time, she won the respect of her colleagues, who now often sought her help and cajoled her to prioritize their cases. But, most importantly, she made a difference in the lives of a number of families who were anxiously waiting for the settlement of their claims.

◆

The Tasha Roy story provides a lesson for individuals as well as for organizations. It tells us that when people are encouraged to perform drawing upon their strengths, their performance shows an upward progression, with a range of positive outcomes. It leads to enhanced self-esteem and improved job satisfaction among employees, which, in turn, goes on to boost higher employee engagement and greater commitment to the organizational vision and mission.

Focusing on strengths is the biggest differentiator for people and organizations to make the journey to their dreamland more satisfying, engaging, fulfilling and enduring. Therefore, while individuals must build on their strengths, organizations must ensure that their talent management and people processes are aligned to the strengths of their employees.

At Ease with Your Imperfections

One of the basic rules of the universe is that nothing is perfect. Perfection simply doesn't exist... Without imperfection neither you nor I would exist.

–STEPHEN HAWKING, PHYSICIST AND COSMOLOGIST

A reality check would, however, reveal that our standard approach to life has been different. All of us have grown up with the conventional wisdom that we should try to become well-rounded persons by overcoming our weaknesses. The universal expectation from leaders has been that they should convert their weaknesses into strengths and become epitomes of strength. They should be great visionaries, gifted communicators, perfect team leaders, superb strategists, excellent executioners...the list is endless. However, nothing could be farther from the truth as the approach is basically fallacious. As Tom Rath, the author of

Strengths Based Leadership, says, 'If you spend your life trying to be good at everything, you will never be great at anything.' In your leadership journey too, if you keep going after fixing your weaknesses and chasing elusive skills and traits to make you perfect, you are most likely to end up in mediocrity. And sure enough, the path to leadership is never paved with mediocrity—it demands excellence.

A study of some of the greatest leaders, such as Gandhi, Churchill, Kennedy and Abraham Lincoln, reveals that while all of them had some of the leadership qualities in great measure, none of them had all the leadership attributes at an exceptionally high level. All of them were essentially different persons with their own strengths, who effectively used their dominant leadership qualities to realize their visions and missions.

The secret of one's leadership success lies in identifying one's core strengths and cultivating them into one's strong suit. Look at the case of Madonna, for example. She became a world-class singer even though she didn't have the best voice in the world. But rather than trying to fix her voice quality and be seen on stage as a solo performer, she focused on her talent, which lay in her mesmerizing stage performance. And a star was born! Likewise, when Apple launched its first iPhone, it wasn't the best phone in the market on many counts, including connectivity and battery performance. But Apple placed it differently by igniting desire among people and creating an altogether new user experience, so much so that it was able to create an emotional bond between man and his machine.

It follows from the aforesaid examples that the way we address our strengths and weaknesses is critical to the success of our leadership. Human beings are essentially imperfect, and we should all learn to be at ease with our imperfections while focusing on developing our individual strengths.

Spotlight Your Strengths!

Why is it desirable to focus on our strengths rather than on our weaknesses? It is for the simple reason that focusing on our strengths gives us quicker and better results than any effort to overcome our weaknesses. Sowing on fertile land always yields a better crop than sowing on infertile land. When you swim with the current, you always move faster in comparison to when you swim against it. The reasons are based in our psychology. Our effort to fight weaknesses invariably meets with resistance from within, building up an urge to avoid the tasks at hand. Failures in the process drain our energy and fill us with despair. Repeated failures build up a sense of frustration and desperation within us, leading to loss of self-confidence and, ultimately, a negative impact on our psychology. The time and effort utilized in fixing weaknesses ultimately end up being less rewarding, as they could yield better results if the focus was shifted to our areas of strength.

On the contrary, when we operate in our zone of strength, we feel more motivated and energized as we are rewarded by quicker and more positive results. The resultant successes keep filling us with new energy and opening up new vistas of exploring our full potential. Over a period of time, our strengths get multiplied by repeated successes and we experience a rising level of confidence.

Everyone has inherent strengths and the potential to develop them into their forte. The mantra for leadership success is that one should have the courage to be imperfect and the determination to make one's strengths so formidable that one's weaknesses become irrelevant. Every time a David is confronted by a Goliath, he must focus on his mental prowess to win the battle rather than try to improve his physical power.

The Matthew Effect

Awareness of one's strengths and the resultant increase in self-confidence are critically relevant to success in life. In 1968, social researcher Robert K. Merton carried out a sociological research on scientific careers and came up with a revealing finding that productivity and awards accumulated disproportionately for scientists who had tasted success early in their careers. This group of people had a much steeper career growth trajectory, leading to increasing inequalities in achievements and rewards.

The concept was named the Matthew Effect or the Matthew Principle, taking a cue from a parable in the Bible: 'For to everyone who has will more be given, and he will have abundance; but from him who has not, even what he has will be taken away.'[31]

Even though Merton's research was about scientific careers, sociological researchers have been studying the cumulative effect of the Matthew Principle applied to other careers in general. In this sphere, a study conducted by Timothy A. Judge and Charlice Hurst of the University of Florida,[32] utilizing a dynamic design from participants in the National Longitudinal Surveys of Youth (NLSY79), is quite significant.

In this study, spanning twenty-five years, Judge and Hurst studied the self-evaluation of 7,660 men and women. When first studied in 1979, these participants were in the age group of fourteen to twenty-two years, and were followed for the next twenty-five years. The self-evaluation measures included questions related to their educational levels, job status, career

---

[31]The Holy Bible, *Matthew 25:29, RSV*
[32]Timothy A. Judge and Charlice Hurst, 'How the Rich (and Happy) Get Richer (and Happier): Relationship of Core Self-Evaluations to Trajectories in Attaining Work Success', *Journal of Applied Psychology*, 2008, Vol. 93, No. 4, pp.849–863

success, health, etc. The exercise was repeated in 2004.

What Judge and Hurst discovered was quite insightful. Their study revealed that participants with higher confidence in their abilities at the beginning of the study, in 1979, had higher levels of income and steeper career-success trajectories at the end of the study in 2004. What was more surprising was that the group that had started with a much higher level of self-confidence at an early age saw its income grow at an entirely different rate as compared to the low-confidence group. The average annual income of the high-confidence group in 1979 was higher by a meagre $3,496 as compared to the low-confidence group. This small difference in income level kept increasing every year and eventually widened to a difference of $12,821 in the average annual income of the two groups.

Astonishingly, researchers were also able to find a link between participants' self-confidence and their physical health. People with a higher level of self-confidence were found to be experiencing fewer health problems at the end of the study period, in comparison to those who had started with lower self-confidence. The low-confidence group had experienced nearly three times more health problems, interfering with their jobs over the twenty-five-year period, as compared to their counterparts.

In essence, Judge and Hurst suggested that individuals with higher self-confidence at a younger age have a more ascendant career progression, remuneration, occupational status and job satisfaction. In their own words,

> Results indicated that higher core self-evaluations were associated with both higher initial levels of work success and steeper work-success trajectories. Education and health problems that interfere with work mediated a portion of the hypothesized relationships, suggesting that individuals with high core self-evaluations have

more ascendant jobs and careers, in part because they are more apt to pursue further education and maintain better health.[33]

What explains this phenomenon? The possible explanation is that the self-awareness of one's strengths and the consequent increase in self-confidence has far-reaching and long-term implications for an individual. At an early stage in life, when people utilize their strengths to accomplish a task and get recognized for it, they feel motivated and energized to continue working in the same direction, utilizing their strengths again and again. In the process, their strengths get honed further to ensure greater success and higher rewards. Incremental success and rewards build up in due course and make a huge difference over a period of time, in comparison to those who start their journey trying to focus on their weaknesses, thereby starting with lower self-confidence and consequently, lower success.

Leading by Imitation?

The core of authenticity is the courage to be imperfect, vulnerable and to set boundaries.

–BRENE BROWN, AUTHOR, DARE TO LEAD

Have you heard the story of the CEO who gave a new mantra to his leadership team every time he returned from a leadership conference? He was a well-meaning and passionate individual who was always sold on the theme presented during

---

[33]Timothy A. Judge and Charlice Hurst, 'How the Rich (and Happy) Get Richer (and Happier): Relationship of Core Self-Evaluations to Trajectories in Attaining Work Success', *Journal of Applied Psychology*, 2008, Vol. 93, No. 4, pp.849–863

the conference. Hence, his message to his team would vary from change management to people-focus to value creation for shareholders, and so on. Such CEOs are like the surgeon who will perform a cardiac surgery on a patient needing a renal transplant. Leaders like these try to lead their teams by imitating the vision and mission of someone else, and, in the process, invite failures for themselves as well as for their organizations. Just like the leaders who are fascinated by an idea, there are individuals who are mesmerized by an iconic personality and make them their personal role model. They start imitating his or her leadership style, forgetting their own inherent personality types, core strengths and competencies, which could be entirely different. Unfortunately, by the time they realize the futility of this, it is too late.

During the period that Jack Welch was the chairman and CEO of General Electric, his leadership style was imitated by his admirers across the industry. However, while Welch remains an iconic leader, none of his copycats were able to make the grade on the leadership scale.

For sure, imitation could be the best recipe for leadership failure. In the first place, you can be sure that people around you will trust you more easily when you are being your authentic self in comparison to imitating someone and being a carbon copy, howsoever good, of any other person, howsoever great. Also, you will be more effective while working with your own inherent strengths instead of feigning to have the elusive strengths of another individual.

In Bollywood, some of the most celebrated singers, such as K.L. Saigal, Mohammad Rafi and Mukesh, had outstanding successes with long career spans. After their death, there were many who ventured to fill the void by singing in their hero's style. Although they could create a semblance of the voice and style of their respective icons, none of them could come close to their ideals in popularity or career success, even after getting ample opportunities. Because once one has seen the original, who wants to see the imitation, howsoever good? In fact, Mukesh had started his singing career by imitating Saigal. However, it was only after he developed his own unique style that he became a phenomenon, capturing millions of hearts.

Know Thyself. Be Thyself. Invest in Thyself

People would rather follow a leader who is always real than one who is always right.

—CRAIG GROESCHEL, AUTHOR,
FOUNDER AND SENIOR PASTOR, LIFE.CHURCH

Over the years, philosophers have been telling us to 'know thyself'. We could add 'be thyself' to it, as nowhere else is it more applicable than in the case of leaders on whose shoulders lie the responsibility of a number of people and their organizations.

This must be appreciated from the perspective that leadership is highly contextual—it cannot be taken out of the context in which the leader is required to operate. As a leader, you are required to chalk out your own path and develop your own strategies, depending on your operating landscape, the nature of the problem, the kind of support available and the nature of obstacles or opposition likely to be placed on the way. Your response to these challenges has to be determined by your personality type and your strengths and weaknesses. Hence, you have got to develop your own leadership style based on your inherent strengths and the demand of the operating environment.

We have countless volumes written about epoch-making leaders such as Gandhi, Churchill, Lincoln, Golda Meir and Martin Luther King Jr, but the one uniform lesson that emerges from the study of their profiles and challenges is that all of them had their own unique challenges and the experience of one cannot be replicated with another's. Both Gandhi and Churchill lived in the same age, but their leadership styles had more differences than similarities. In fact, it is their differences, arising out of their personalities and the demands of their operating landscapes, that defined their leadership styles and ensured their success.

In recent times, we have had the examples of two tech wizards, Bill Gates, the founder of Microsoft, and Steve Jobs, the founder of Apple Inc. Both of them happened to be outstanding leaders from the technology sector who founded and nurtured their respective enterprises into Fortune 500 companies. But much more than that, their transformational leaderships reshaped the way we looked at the world.

In their leadership styles, Gates and Jobs are a study in contrasts and offer a good example of strength-based leadership. Both had similar missions, were in the same industry and of the same age, and in the same geographical region. But they approached their missions in entirely different ways, based on their individual uniqueness and strengths. Gates is a participative leader, given to group-thinking. His mission was to explore the boundaries of what a common man could do with an ordinary computer. His passion for his mission was so infectious that it could ignite the imagination of his team members to deliver results beyond expectation. Jobs, on the other hand, was idiosyncratic and autocratic, but his passionate creativity had no parallel in the contemporary world.

The results are before all of us to see. Gates was able to create a computing platform that is not only nearly ubiquitous, but can also be operated by just about anybody without any technical skill or expertise. Jobs, on the other hand, created a unique user experience for his customers.

These technology wizards could accomplish their transformational missions only because they used their unique strengths to realize their dreams. We can only imagine the disaster if either of them had tried to imitate the leadership style of the other.

In essence, no two leaders are similar in their traits and personalities, nor are the circumstances in which they operate identical. In fact, it is the unique circumstances and the distinctive styles adopted by them that define their leadership. Hence, there can never be a common list of traits for leadership success, nor can there be a common prescription for achieving leadership greatness.

It goes without saying, therefore, that in their leadership journeys, budding leaders need to identify their personal strengths and invest in them to hone their skills. As they grow, they should be able to marshal their skills with expertise and dexterity. As American psychologist and leadership researcher Donald O. Clifton puts it:

> A leader needs to know his strengths as a carpenter knows his tools, or as a physician knows the instruments at her disposal. What great leaders have in common is that each truly knows his or her strengths—and can call on the right strength at the right time. This explains why there is no definitive list of characteristics that describes all leaders.[34]

How to Identify Our Strengths

How do we identify our areas of strength? As social scientists say, every individual is gifted with capabilities in three basic areas:

[34]Tom Rath, *Strengths Based Leadership: Great Leaders, Teams, and Why People Follow*, Gallup Press, 2008, p.13

Play Skills: It consists of sporting skills that we start learning right from our childhood. Strengths in this faculty include traits such as competitiveness, gamesmanship, imagination, creativity and dexterity, along with physical, cognitive and emotional strengths. This also inculcates in us social skills such as fellowship, teamwork and communication, including both verbal and non-verbal communication such as speech, gestures, facial expressions and body language.

Personal Traits: Strength of character is built over a period of time since childhood. While it bears the stamp of one's family and environmental influence, an individual's mental and psychological disposition, too, contributes to it immensely. These strengths include virtues such as honesty, integrity, curiosity, perspective, judgement, bravery, perseverance, empathy, humility, social intelligence and self-regulation.

Professional Competence: This comprises of competencies such as leadership, management, coordination, planning, problem-solving, conceptualization and strategizing. They are learnt and honed over a period of time.

Normally, every individual has all these strengths in different proportions, but with a dominant share in any one area. Some people have some of these skills in abundance, which, when identified and applied to the task, leads to their success.

But how do you find your passion and identify your strengths? To begin with, identify your talents by asking yourself a few questions related to your performance and performance-related experience.

How good you are at performing a task?

Do you find the experience of task-performance energizing or does it sap your energy?

How often do you use that strength and in what way?

You can consider a particular attribute or competency to be your talent if you are good at it; you feel energized while using it and are able to use it often and in newer ways. The next step should be a professional self-assessment using some standard analytical tool, which will not only confirm your subjective evaluation but also give you a detailed analysis of your personality type and talent areas. An objective assessment made by such a tool would also be helpful in discovering the latent potential within you, which may otherwise remain unnoticed. Overall, such a tool would help you discover yourself and indicate your future potential. Having identified your talent zones, you should start focusing on them. To begin with, you must notice things such as what you like doing, what kind of work makes you happy, who you like working with or at what time or place you enjoy working. There are people whose productivity goes up when they team up with someone of their choice, while someone else could be more comfortable working solo. Likewise, some people enjoy working during their preferred hours of the day or night.

To develop your talents, you must hone them by using them more often at right moments, in the right proportions and in newer ways, so that they develop into skills. Ultimately, they should become your forte and be identified as your signature traits.

Converting Your Talent into Your Strength

Honing your talent and skills is not enough. In your leadership journey, you need to achieve a level of expertise and excellence so as to be able to lead others. This requires converting your talents and skills into your strengths. This will require undergoing dedicated training for sharpening your relevant skills at regular intervals. Further, as they say, practice makes perfect. Hence, regular and concerted practice of your skills will help you gain expertise in the area and, in the process, enable you to evolve as a continuously improving version of yourself. In the article 'The Making of an Expert',[35] authors K. Anders Ericsson, Michael J. Prietula and Edward T. Cokely discuss a landmark study by Dr Benjamin Bloom, a professor of education at the University of Chicago, published in his book *Developing Talent in Young People.* As part of the study, Bloom took a deep retrospective dive into the childhoods of 120 distinguished achievers who had won some kind of international award or competition in fields such as music, arts, mathematics, neurology, medicine, chess and sports. Surprisingly, except in sports, where height and physical build mattered, in other areas there were no early indicators of the virtuosos' success. In fact, the study didn't support any correlation between IQ and expert performance.

If not IQ, then what determines expertise and excellence? The authors of the article go on to suggest that the one thing common to all experts is that they practise their skills extensively to achieve excellence in their area of work. According to them, 'Later research building on Bloom's pioneering study revealed that the amount and quality of practice were key factors in the level of expertise people achieved. Consistently and overwhelmingly, the evidence showed that experts are always made, not born.'[36]

This is equally true of leadership skill as well; it is regular and guided practice that can make it a natural extension of yourself. A guided practice not only draws you out of your comfort zone, it also broadens your range of skills.

Case studies in leadership schools are good examples of

---

[35]K. Anders Ericsson, Michael J. Prietula and Edward T. Cokely, 'The Making of an Expert', *Harvard Business Review*, July-August 2007, pp.1–2
[36]Ibid

such guided practices, as they provide situations where one can undertake repeated practice in dealing with real-life situations and benchmark one's response against the actual consequences.

For accelerated leadership-development, it is equally important to seek the help and support of a coach or a mentor, because they can offer objective and constructive feedback. It is not without reason that even accomplished tennis players such as Roger Federer and Rafael Nadal use the services of a coach even after attaining the highest rankings in the tennis world. Even in the executive world, celebrated CEOs are known to look up to their coaches for advice. Celebrity coaches such as Bill Campbell and Ram Charan are persons whose services have been availed by senior executives at Apple, Google, eBay, Twitter, Next Door, GE, Verizon, Tata Group and a host of others.

However, as you progress on the leadership curve, you must practise the art of self-coaching as well, where you observe those experts who accomplish a job with excellence and learn from their experiences. At the same time, you must also learn from your own experiences of displaying expertise in any given field or on any specific occasion, and practise the same repeatedly in different situations.

In essence, it is practice that makes a person perfect. Let's remember that Mozart was not a born expert—he became one due to sheer grit and sustained practice since early childhood. Also, even a charismatic leader and great orator like Churchill was not originally a natural orator. He had a raspy voice, which was often marked by a stammer and a lisp. But he became one of the finest orators the world has ever known through sheer practice. It is common knowledge that even after becoming the Prime Minister of Great Britain, he used to practise his speeches in front of a mirror before delivering it in parliament.

Leadership, too, is a skill that needs to be improved with constant practice.

Imperfect Leaders Build Perfect Teams

Perfection is the willingness to be imperfect.

−LAO TZU, CHINESE PHILOSOPHER

Our work today essentially involves teamwork, demanding a varied set of skills to accomplish a task. In a corporate setup, it would require a host of skills involving product designing, marketing, sales, accounting, investment, operations, risk management, etc. Likewise, a game of cricket requires different kinds of expertise, ranging from batting to bowling to wicketkeeping. Even batsmen have varied skill sets; some could be opening batsmen while others could specialize in middle-order batting and yet others could act as finishers. Bowling, too, has its diverse specialization, like fast-bowling, spin-bowling, etc.

Winning a match is always teamwork, where everyone contributes with their unique expertise. You can't win a cricket World Cup by putting eleven Virat Kohlis in a team, even though he may be the best batsman in the world today. For a team to win a match, it requires a balance of different kinds of expertise, depending upon the need of the hour and the nature of competition.

Leadership, too, operates on a similar principle. Even though imperfect leaders do not strive to be well-rounded persons, they do ensure that their teams are well rounded, with team-members possessing varied kinds of skills required for carrying on the corporate mission. They surround themselves with people with the right skills and experience to maximize their team strength.

For this reason, they avoid filling up their leadership team with their own clones, who could be like-minded or identical in experience and expertise. Rather, they bring in people who can fill in the talent and skill gaps in the team. They strive to see that the leadership team consists of professionals with varied skill sets that can maximize team effectiveness and unlock the growth potential of the company.

This calls for a drastic rethinking of leadership strategies followed by companies. As per the current practice followed by most corporations, promotions in the executive teams are primarily based on one's performance in the current role. This naturally ends up with the best marketing professional becoming the marketing head or the best IT executive getting elevated to Chief Information Officer (CIO). Such performance-based elevations don't take into account the extended or alternative job functions in the higher role—for example, conceptualizing, strategizing or people management. Also, our current practices do not ensure whether the newcomers in the leadership team are going to complement and supplement the existing skills and strengths of the team beyond their functional roles and competencies. Are they relationship builders who can offer valuable intangibles such as caring and smiles that can bind the team together in conflict situations? Or are they influencers who can communicate the vision of the company across the institution? Leadership is essentially teamwork, and the composition of the executive team can be the real differentiator in whether the company is going to be a market leader or not.

Strength-Based People Strategy

It takes far less energy to move from first-rate performance to excellence than it does to move from incompetence to mediocrity.

–PETER DRUCKER, MANAGEMENT CONSULTANT AND AUTHOR

If focusing on strengths makes a leader more effective, it makes the followers more productive as well. Hence, while dealing with employees, there is a need to change the conventional deficit-based approach, which looks at the weaknesses in people with a view to rectifying them. Leaders would do well to have a gentle shift in mindset and apply the strength-based approach to their followers as well, and count on their strengths rather than discounting their weaknesses.

This is critical for organizational success, as there is a business case for this. When we orient our people strategy with a focus on their strengths instead of their weaknesses, we get measurable business returns in terms of increased productivity and revenue, with reduced costs. Further, going beyond these solid outcomes, it also leads to improved corporate performance indicators in terms of employee engagement, customer satisfaction, and employee satisfaction and morale.

An extensive performance management survey done by the Corporate Leadership Council in 2002, involving thousands of employees across different organizations, revealed that when organizations focus on employees' strengths, their performance improves by 36.4 per cent. As against this, when the focus is on people's weaknesses, the performance drops by 26.8 per cent.

Clearly, when the focus is on employees' strengths, it encourages performance-enhancing behaviour patterns—positive self-image, positive self-talk, greater engagement with work, higher job satisfaction and, consequently, improvement in productivity and customer engagement, along with a reduction in cost. On the other hand, focus on employees' weaknesses is the most negative factor, adversely impacting employee performance.

These results are well supported by another survey conducted in 2015 by Michelle McQuaid, an honorary fellow at Melbourne University's Graduate School of Education. The *2015 Strengths at Work Survey*, published in conjunction with the VIA Institute on Character, covered more than 1,000 employees from a cross-section of American companies. Among other things, it revealed that 78 per cent of employees who had their strengths taken into account during their performance review felt recognized, appreciated and encouraged, with a feeling that their work was making a difference to the organization. Further, over 61 per cent of them felt they looked forward to going to their workplaces at the start of the day.

The strength-based focus can be meaningful only if it is embedded in the core of the organizational philosophy and ingrained into its action plan, covering the four critical areas of recruitment and promotion, performance management, talent management and organizational design. Organizations need to embed the following five strength principles in these core areas for improving employee engagement and organizational success.

Focus on Strengths, Not Weaknesses: Leaders must ensure that across their organizational chain of functions, a clear focus on strength becomes the guiding principle, which is not limited to employees alone. Leaders must decipher and determine the areas in which their organization's strengths lie and then strategically design their vision and mission in a way that utilizes its strengths to compete in the marketplace and fulfil its objectives. Apple, for example, has its core strength in innovation. Likewise, Walmart specializes in large-scale distribution at low cost, while Amazon excels at its centricity to customers. All these companies are successfully deploying their core strengths to serve their existing markets and create new ones.

Align Job Definitions with Strengths: Job definitions are usually structured to look for talent in a particular age group with the relevant skills and experience. The strength required for a high degree of performance in the organizational context is hardly highlighted. HR managers, therefore, would do well to restructure job definitions in a way that not only highlight the skills and expertise required for the job but also consider the organizational context, like company culture, priorities and role expectations. A mutual fit between role and employee strength goes a long way in enhancing employee engagement, retention and productivity. Mere experience and skill-based recruitment, on the contrary, could dent organizational purpose. For example, if a company has a culture of decision-making through consensus, the relevant job definition must emphasize this strength, and recruiters must look for this in potential candidates for the role. In the absence of such clarity, if they recruit an alpha male for the role, he may negatively impact productivity and team morale with uncalled-for aggressiveness.

Emphasis on Strengths in Recruitment and Promotions: Organizations generally recruit people based on their qualifications, experience and performance in the previous job. This is also mostly true when elevating an employee to a higher role. This often results in wrong selections, leading to a mismatch between expectations from the role and delivery by the employee. Organizations end up being losers in the process in terms of higher recruitment costs, loss of time and opportunity, and the resultant deficiency in performance. Recruiters, therefore, must begin by identifying the strengths needed for high delivery in a role, keeping in mind the organizational context in which the person is required to operate. They should also define their talent-management strategies so as to attract people who possess the required talents. What is important is that the people selected must display their potential for the growth of their talent as well. The process must also consider the competencies already available in the existing team and what is required to be brought in by the person being recruited. Further, managers must also be trained and sensitized to identifying latent potential in employees as well as support them through strength-focused discussions, guidance and assessment.

Manage Change through Strengths: Change is a constant phenomenon in the volatile markets today. To survive and succeed, organizations must keep anticipating and embracing change throughout their functioning cycles. However, change is often resisted by people because it is disruptive and demands behavioural changes and adjustments. Organizations can manage change more efficiently by looking out for employees who display the relevant strengths for leading the change. Recognition of their inherent strength is good motivation for them, which, in turn, will help them hone their strengths and sharpen their skills further. At the same time, once operating within their zone of strengths, employees are more confident and prone to learning and adapting to the new behaviour patterns required for success in the unfolding environment. The success of this set of employees can further motivate others, who have the potential strengths within them, to venture out and join the change-management team. The snowballing effect of the strength-based approach can indeed infuse new dynamism into the organization.

Collaborate to Create a Shared Language of Strength: Organizations need to ensure that people know their own strengths as well as the strengths of their team members. They should further encourage teams to leverage their collective strengths for organizational success. A way to encourage this strength partnership is to ask team members to identify which part of a task they can do well instead of the role being assigned by the manager. A voluntary acceptance of tasks is always more fulfilling and engaging for employees and is bound to lead to higher performance levels.

Managing Your Weaknesses

A focus on strengths does not mean a denial of weaknesses. We all need to manage our weaknesses in a way that they do not come in the way of our success. Let us see an example from the corporate world on how to manage weaknesses. When Paresh Kathuria, the young and dynamic publicity head of a pharma brand, moved to another company, everyone felt that he had left a void that the company would find hard to fill. The apprehensions were genuine, because Kathuria was an expert at copywriting and networking. Typical of the pharma sector, the company would organize frequent meetings with various stakeholders, and Kathuria would ensure that his reporting of the meetings got widely published in newspapers, highlighting the company's market presence effectively.

His successor, Sumant Nagar, a greying man in his fifties, was no match for him in his drafting and reporting skills. That was the biggest concern for the top management, which was apprehensive of the likely hit the image of the company would take. However, within a few months of Nagar's taking over, the management was all smiles, contrary to expectation, and its image projection had also qualitatively rocketed. The secret of Nagar's success was that he was a relationship man par excellence and had cultivated excellent relationships at all levels in media houses. He had also adopted a different strategy for media coverage. He would go to the newspaper offices late in the evening, when senior editors had already called it a day, and with the support of the junior staff, would get a photo of the event inserted with an aptly descriptive caption. Each photo was worth a thousand words of text reporting. With this skilful approach, Nagar was able to turn the tables in his favour.

◆

It is no one's point that weaknesses do not matter—they do. But their management matters more. First, you should be aware of your weaknesses and accept them to be yours. Secondly, if it happens to be a fatal weakness, threatening your job or career, you would do well to look into this area and improve it to an extent where it no longer poses a threat. Thirdly, if weaknesses are not threatening, it would be more rewarding for you to manage them through a workaround. This may involve working closely with your team members, where jobs are scoped in such a way that someone having strengths in the area of your weaknesses takes over that part of the job while you compensate by lending your strength in another area. For example, if you are required to make presentations but are not comfortable with it, can you swap roles with someone in your team and just prepare the presentations, leaving it to that someone else to present it to the audience?

Like Sumant Nagar, you may discover an alternative skill or strength to get the desired outcome.

PART II

Leadership Attributes for Success

When geese fly in a V-formation, they display some unique leadership characteristics. They retain a clear vision of their destination and are able to keep track of their path even in the haziness of the vast, cloudy skies. They share a common goal, with everyone flying in the same direction. The orchestrated teamwork ensures that as each bird in the flock flaps its wings, it creates an aerodynamic effect, reducing the air resistance for the birds that follow, which adds to their flying agility. If any of them strays out of formation, it is soon included back in the flock, as flying solo is extremely tiring. While flying, they also honk to identify and encourage those leading in the front to keep up their speed. Interestingly, when they perceive danger, the entire flock reacts as a team to save itself from the threat.

However, the most interesting thing about these birds is the way they distribute leadership within the team. Flying in the V-formation, the lead bird has to work the hardest. But the beauty of their teamwork is that all the birds perform the lead role by rotation. Thus, every leader becomes a follower and every follower gets a chance to lead. This not only ensures the survival of the birds but also allows them to sustain the flight duration and fly longer distances.

Imperfect leaders of today cultivate some of these attributes, such as clear vision, collaboration, agility, inclusion and distributed leadership, to achieve their shared vision and mission in an environment that is increasingly complex and fuzzy. The chapters ahead discuss some of the key skills and attributes modern leaders need to have or inculcate within their team to ensure success in the turbulent environment of today.

ॐ

5

The Dream Merchants

*The very essence of leadership is that you have to have
a vision. It's got to be a vision you articulate clearly and
forcefully on every occasion.*

–THEODORE HESBURGH, FORMER PRESIDENT OF
THE UNIVERSITY OF NOTRE DAME

The ability to develop a vision is the essence of leadership,
and this has been the most common attribute among
leaders across ages. Ford visualized a car that families could
afford with ease. Kennedy envisioned putting men on the
Moon. Karl Marx dreamt of a society where labour would
command capital. Nobel laureate Aung San Suu Kyi dreamt
of a democratic and egalitarian Myanmar. Jobs wanted to
develop a powerful computer with his hallmark creativity
and innovativeness. Mukesh Ambani envisioned an affordable
communication network to usher in a communication
revolution in India.

It is in their ability to set the direction for their organization
and craft a vision for the future that makes successful leaders
stand out from the crowd. They are essentially storytellers,
dream merchants who paint a beautiful picture of the future and
promise to lead everyone there. It is the power of the messages
they convey through the stories they tell and the dreams they

sell that inspires their followers and creates a bond with them. As followers buy into the leader's dream, they make common cause with their leader. Soon, the followers themselves become advocates of the change envisioned by the leader. In the process, both leaders and followers strengthen one another.

In a sense, a leader determines the vision and the vision defines the leader. As John Quincy Adams, the former US president, put it, 'If your actions inspire others to dream more, learn more, do more and become more, you are a leader.'

Sense-Making: Creating the Vision

The process of creating a vision necessarily involves what is called 'sense-making', a term used in the field of information and computing science earlier, and later applied to organizational studies by organizational psychologist Karl Weick. Sense-making essentially is a collaborative process, where people within an organization try to create a shared understanding and awareness to fulfil an organizational purpose, leaning upon common and unique experiences, insights and perspectives of the members. In essence, sense-making provides leaders insight into the existing state of affairs and the possible direction of change. Vision, on the other hand, is the direction the leader would like the organization to take and the envisioned state of the organization in future.

Creating a vision is usually a dynamic and collaborative process. As we very well know, organizations are a complex and connected network of individuals, having varied expertise and experiences, perceptions and beliefs. In the process of making sense of the future, organizations are always faced with situations laden with uncertainty and ambiguity. As leaders try to understand the context relevant to their businesses, and make sense of the ambiguities and uncertainties, they start asking questions and seeking answers from people both within the organization and without.

What is going to be the political, economic and social outlooks within the medium and in the long term? What is expected to be the impact on the industry? What kind of technological advancements are likely to happen, and what will their impact be on business models, products and profitability? And, finally, how can the organization remain afloat and competitive?

These are questions that prompt leaders to seek answers from stakeholders with the required intelligence and expertise. They further analyse the varied responses and try to synthesize the same cohesively. They develop a vision of the future, paint a picture of the times to come and build a framework of solutions that could lead the organization to the next level.

The process of sense-making has two essential components—inquiry and advocacy. Inquiry is an attempt to take the honest opinion of team members about the existing state of affairs and the possible directions of change. Advocacy is the proposition made by leaders with respect to the direction of change for the organization and the possible solutions and outcomes. Leaders are expected to strike a balance while conducting inquiry and advocacy. At the stage of inquiry, they should listen to their followers with the intent of understanding—and not refusing—their ideas. It is only then that employees will get the confidence of giving their frank and honest opinion. Likewise, for advocacy, leaders must avoid being aggressive so that followers don't feel brow-beaten and refrain from giving their honest feedback. Leaders must appreciate that change and innovations are costly processes and losing the balance during inquiry and advocacy itself could derail the process and jeopardize the desired outcome.

Creating a Supporting Framework

Going forward, there is also a need to create a supporting framework, without which a vision, crafted by the leader, would hang like a castle in the air without any foundation. Leaders must ensure that the necessary organizational processes are put in place to convert the vision into reality. To this end, they need to create teams and structures and ensure that the new structures are able to break down the existing silos that keep people ticking old checkboxes rather than making any meaningful movement forward. The results of the anticipated change can be realized quickly only if the clutters around the processes that slow down the system are removed.

It is also required that leaders align teams and place change advocates at suitable points in the organization. Any change induced in the organization or an innovation done by a company has some natural opponents. It remains fragile until it takes deep roots and its benefits are visible to the people around. Therefore, any change or innovation has to be hatched and supported with sensitivity and care, and protected from adverse influence and circumstances until it stands by itself and becomes a force to reckon with.

Communication: Aligning People to the Vision

Good business leaders create a vision, articulate the vision, passionately own the vision, and relentlessly drive it to completion.

–JACK WELCH, AUTHOR AND
FORMER CHAIRMAN AND CEO, GENERAL ELECTRIC

The increasing complexities and interdependence of modern organizations go down to the level of employees, as their performance is impacted by hierarchies and structures, technologies and systems. In such a situation, if an organization embarks on a transformational agenda, it is essential that all its components fall into alignment and move smoothly like a juggernaut in the intended direction.

The role of leaders in aligning people to the organization's collective vision is crucial. It is not enough for leaders to be passionate dreamers and visionaries—they have to act, sometimes even like the Chief Meaning Officer for the organization as well, as Jack Welch of General Electric puts it. Once the leader floats the idea of change, he has to explain to his people what the change is about, where it is going to take them and, above all, how it is going to benefit them and the organization on the whole. As we know, change is often disruptive. Hence, unless the rationale behind the change is communicated well to the people it will impact, it is going to be resisted.

While communicating their vision to the people, leaders have to transmit to them some of their passion and enthusiasm. Only when followers are inspired do they start owning the leader's vision, and the further they move on the path of its realization, the more they win followers to the cause, thereby making the group stronger. In the process, their personal purpose in life gets aligned with the larger organizational purpose—the realization of the organization's dream becomes their personal mission. It no longer remains a task to be performed—it becomes a source of personal fulfilment, satisfying their innate human need of a sense of achievement and recognition, which ultimately enhances their self-esteem.

Developing Authentic Communication

To initiate the process of aligning others with their vision, leaders have to show an exemplary degree of conviction and perseverance. They have to live their vision, exemplify it—as is said in Sanskrit, '*Manasa, Vacha, Karmana*'—in thought, speech and action. The sincerity of purpose exemplified by leaders helps them persuade and win over people sitting on the fence of the ideological divide, as well as blunt opposition from across the fence. Any deviation from the stated vision results in erosion of trust even among the leader's followers.

In an age of global connectivity and transparency, former US President Barack Obama provides a classic example of aligning people through authentic communication. When he started his US presidential campaign in 2008 with the slogan 'Change we can believe in', he talked of it all the time. He talked about it so often and so sincerely that the word 'change' got associated with him. He spoke about it with so much earnestness and conviction that it won him a billion hearts. People looked at him with hope and expectation of a real transformation and revolution. Riding the wave, Obama kept reaffirming his sincerity and commitment to change with his pet phrase 'Let's get back to work'. A master communicator, he always used the word 'we' instead of 'I', thereby giving a feeling to people at large that they, too, had contributed to his mission. This in itself was enough to win him millions of followers.

Communicating through Non-Verbal Symbolism

Communication is often mistaken to mean oratory. Although oratory is a critical part of communication, leaders utilize a number of non-verbal methods to communicate to the outside world and win over followers and supporters. Mahatma Gandhi provides a classic example of communication through non-verbal symbols, such as attire and action.

Even in an age of slow communication channels, he was able to effectively convey his vision of truth and non-violence to the Indian masses. At the same time, he was able to portray to the world outside the miseries suffered by Indians under British rule and the atrocities being committed by colonial imperialists. During the Second Round Table Conference in 1931, when a scantily clad Gandhi stood beside the well-clad British emperor George V, the difference in their clothing very tellingly conveyed to the world the exploitation and mistreatment Indians were facing. Internally, within India, his dress helped him identify with the poor and the downtrodden across the country and helped him galvanize the entire country in opposing British rule.

Gandhi's historic Dandi March in March 1930—the twenty-four-day, 240-mile-long journey on foot—along with thousands of followers, is a classic example of communication through alternative mediums. Known as the 'Salt Satyagraha', this epic march to the seashore to break the salt law that prohibited Indians from making salt from sea water not only launched a civil disobedience movement in the entire country against the British, but also made the world sit up and take notice of the plight of Indians. It was a masterstroke in communication.

Is Vision Required to be Grandiose?

The vision created by a leader need not be grandiose and ground-breaking, like those by epoch-making leaders, such as Jeff Bezos, Mohammed Yunus and Elon Musk. It need not be magical and mysterious either. If we think that creating a vision is the preserve of *gifted* people only, nothing could be farther from the truth. We know that the main attribute of leadership is to produce change and, hence, a vision is mostly about setting the direction for change, preparing a roadmap for it and aligning people to walk on the path. Visioning, therefore, is an inductive process, whereby the leader analyses a broad spectrum of data, finds linkages and correlations, patterns and relationships, and tries to build a scenario for the future and defines a strategy for achieving it. More than magic, it calls for strategic thinking, the ability to analyse the situation and conceptualizing how to make everything better than the present.

A vision, therefore, could be as mundane as the concept of a new product line that fulfils emerging customer needs, or a process re-engineering that drastically cuts down on cost and time, besides enhancing customer satisfaction. It could be a small change to inspire one's team and create a strong buy-in from others.

According to Eric Hoffer, American philosopher and author, 'The leader has to be practical and a realist, yet must talk the language of the visionary and the idealist.' As a matter of fact, most leadership visions are never exotic but mundane and commonplace. But the magic lies in designing a unique offering that integrates features sporadically available in the market and therefore captures the imagination of people. For example, when entrepreneur Mukesh Ambani talked about enabling Indians to talk to each other at the cost of an ordinary postcard, he wasn't creating something new. People were already talking over the telephone, communicating through postal mails, and Airtel was already offering mobile telephony. All the same, his Reliance Infocomm created a communication revolution by combining the unique features of all three—enabling people to make calls over its technologically advanced network at the cost of a postcard—and much more. Likewise, a unique innovation like Uber simply integrated products and services already available in the market to create a unique platform for public and private transportation.

Alcoholics Anonymous: A Vision Born of Helplessness

Creating a vision is not always an orchestrated organizational action with systematic inquiry and advocacy. Quite often, a great vision has a modest beginning. It could just be a thought born of a crisis situation or one's personal circumstances. It is after one has tasted initial success and gained some support from others that the thought becomes a vision and its proponents start dreaming of bringing the benefits to the masses. In the process, dreams get converted into movements and ordinary individuals propelling it become icons and larger-than-life personalities.

Take the example of the great social movement Alcoholics Anonymous (AA). Its co-founder Bill Wilson's early life hardly gave any indication of the invaluable contribution he would make to humanity. Born on 26 November 1895, he became a compulsive alcoholic by the time he was thirty-nine. His alcoholism had taken a toll on his education, career, family life and, finally, his health, making it a life-threatening condition. He had to be repeatedly hospitalized in New York for treatment, each time returning in a worse condition.

It is not that Wilson didn't want to stop drinking, but he just couldn't keep away from it. He was so overpowered by the disease that all his efforts to get rid of it were proving to be futile. It was a chance encounter with God, in a state of hallucination induced by a drug administered to him in Towns Hospital, that changed his life forever. It was this transforming spiritual experience in 1934 that gave him the reassurance that he would be saved. It also gave him the courage to say no to alcohol for the rest of his life.

During those days, alcoholism was considered a moral failing rather than a mental obsession. It was Dr William D. Silkworth, the psychiatrist under whose treatment he was in Towns Hospital, who told him that alcoholism was a physical and mental condition that triggered a desire to drink alcohol when the affected person saw someone else drinking it.

Once out of Towns Hospital, a sober Wilson, buoyed by his spiritual experience and newfound knowledge, set out to help other alcoholics. He frequented the streets and bars of Brooklyn trying to keep people sober, but no one was listening, drinking being preferred over sobriety.

A completely sober Wilson had not touched alcohol for six months now. Along with some of his friends, he tried to take over a small company in Akron, Ohio, hoping that it would improve his financial condition. But as the deal collapsed, a disappointed and depressed Wilson was once again tempted to seek solace in a bar.

But his next steps created history. Instead of walking into a bar, he went out to a telephone booth to talk to someone in a similar situation. He got in touch with a local church, which put him in touch with Dr Bob Smith, a surgeon, who incidentally was also an alcoholic and a member of an evangelical group. Dr Smith agreed to give fifteen minutes to the man who claimed to have a cure for alcoholism; when they met, they came out of the room five hours later.

Dr Smith took his last alcoholic drink on 10 June 1935. But, more importantly, it was the day AA was founded by two sober men. Together they tried to wean others off alcoholism. They were happy to get proof of their notion that alcoholics could support one another in their effort to abstain. Slowly but steadily, the numbers started to multiply and soon there were small groups of sober alcoholics trying to help each other.

After a few months, Wilson returned to Brooklyn Heights and continued his work. The baby steps that he took gradually developed into long strides, and the movement started gathering momentum, with regular meetings of the alcoholics trying to support one another.

In the early days, alcoholics used to meet as part of the Oxford Group, a Christian organization founded by a Christian missionary, Dr Frank Buchman. However, soon, Wilson felt the need to have an exclusive organization of alcoholics only.

This growing realization led, in 1937, to the official launch of AA, an organization promoting 'a fellowship of men and women, who share their experience, strength and hope with each other that they may solve their common problem and help others recover from alcoholism'.

Wilson wrote a book titled *Alcoholics Anonymous* in 1939, which has helped millions of men and women recover from alcoholism. Together, Wilson and Dr Smith developed the twelve-step programme, which is the cornerstone of AA's spiritual recovery and development plan. Later, in 1946, they developed the Twelve Traditions, a guide to remaining stable and sober.

AA is the result of an ordinary individual's dream, born out of his personal circumstances, which transformed him into one of the greatest visionaries and reformers of the modern age. Through his own misery, Wilson empathized with the sufferings of others and in his own redemption, he visualized the emancipation of a million others trapped in similar circumstances. Today AA is an international movement spread across diverse geographies and among people of varied cultures, values and beliefs. As of 2016, AA had close to two million members, while it has transformed the lives of millions of other alcoholics over the years. All this, because Wilson had a dream and believed in it!

In a telling and evocative biography of Wilson, *My Name Is Bill*, author Susan Cheever vividly portrays Wilson's passion to share his experience with others so as to show them a way out of their misery. Talking about his influence across generations, she writes:

> In the thirty-three years since Bill Wilson's death, his influence has grown much more than anyone—even he—could have guessed. Although his name is not

famous, his ideas are among the most influential in the twentieth century. His writing has changed the way we think about addiction and, in turn, the way we think about human nature... Alcoholics Anonymous has spawned a dozen parallel programs, all of which depend on the book *Alcoholics Anonymous* and most of which also use the book *Twelve Steps and Twelve Traditions*.

Twelve-step programs for gamblers, debtors, people with eating disorders, drug addicts, and sexual compulsives have changed the lives of millions more people and their families... As a result of these burgeoning programs, each adding members every year, Bill Wilson's ideas have entered the common consciousness and changed how we define being human in a way certainly as powerful as the ideas of Sigmund Freud or Thomas Jefferson...[37]

Vision to End Global Poverty

> *There are two kinds of businesses in the world. One is a business that makes money, and the other solves the problems of the world.*

> −MUHAMMAD YUNUS, NOBEL LAUREATE
> AND FOUNDER OF GRAMEEN BANK

Visioning has myriad dimensions. Sometimes it is done with organizational objectives focusing on performance and profitability; at other times it is done purely for altruism. Yet, there are organizations that see a rewarding opportunity in combining organizational objectives with a larger social purpose.

---

[37]Susan Cheever, *My Name Is Bill: Bill Wilson—His Life and the Creation of Alcoholics Anonymous*, Washington Square Press, 2005

They make purpose the beating heart of their organization and use it to power the performance of their teams.

In 1976, a young professor of economics visited some of the poorest households in the village of Jobra near his university in Chittagong, Bangladesh. He was struck by the plight of the village women, who used to make bamboo furniture for a living. Anticipating default, the banks were not ready to extend any loans to them without collaterals. The poor women were compelled to take loans from greedy moneylenders at exorbitantly high rates of interest to buy bamboo, and practically pay all their profits towards the repayment of the principal and the interest thereon. At this rate, these families were destined to remain in poverty and indebtedness all their lives.

The young professor was Muhammad Yunus, the social entrepreneur who had seen the poor women's enterprise and believed that even small loans to them could make a huge difference in their lives. He also strongly believed that to sustain their business, the poor women would like to repay the small loans given to them. This is where he conceptualized the scheme of microcredit and put it in operation. To begin with, he advanced a loan of $27 to forty-two women in the village from his own resources. The loan was repaid well in time and the women in the group made an average profit of BDT.[5] ($.02), good enough to reinforce the young entrepreneur's belief in the proposition. His resolve was strengthened by the fact that there were millions of poor women in Bangladesh who could set up profitable businesses for themselves if they got small loans without collaterals.

Yunus continued to help the poor by arranging loans for them from government banks. By 1982, the number of beneficiaries had gone up to 28,000. Finally, on 1 October 1983, Yunus launched the country's bank for the poor, Grameen Bank. Business soon caught up and, by July 2007, Grameen

Bank had extended credit worth $6.38 billion to more than 7.4 million borrowers. 'As of October 2011, Grameen Bank has 8.349 million borrowers, 97 per cent of whom are women. With 2,565 branches, Grameen Bank provides services in 81,379 villages, covering more than 97 per cent of the total number of villages in Bangladesh.'[38]

It is to be noted that 97 per cent of these borrowers were women, which is a very purposeful direction of lending credit, as women are deemed more family-oriented in the utilization of their financial resources. Talking to *The Guardian* in March 2017, Yunus lauded the entrepreneurial skills of the poor women, 'There are roughly 160 million people all over the world in microcredit, mostly women. And they have proven one very important thing: that we are all entrepreneurs. Illiterate rural women in the villages, in the mountains, take tiny little loans—$30–$40—and they turn themselves into successful entrepreneurs.'[39]

In the late 1980s, Grameen Bank started to diversify into many other areas of rural economy in Bangladesh, such as agriculture, fishing and telecom. Separate organizations were created and, soon, it became a diversified group of profitable and non-profit ventures. The concept of microcredit soon spread far and wide, establishing a footprint in nearly a hundred countries, including in rich ones such as the US. In India, too, microcredit to self-help groups through microfinance companies is a vibrant mode of financing the poor. Village-level self-help groups come together by forming a pyramid of groups across wider geographies. Going by the sheer number of beneficiaries, they become a force to reckon with for any

---

[38]https://www.grameen-info.org/about-us/

[39]Miriam Cosic, '"We are all entrepreneurs": Muhammad Yunus on changing the world, one microloan at a time', *The Guardian*, 29 March 2017

marketing company selling their wares to them.

Yunus founded the Yunus Social Business in 2011 and started setting up Yunus Social Business centres in universities across the world. Through these centres he expanded his concept to developed countries too. 'Globally, the issues are the same,' he says. 'In terms of poverty of welfare recipients, housing problems, water problems, in terms of healthcare problems. These are common problems, rich country or poor country. Australia has poor people, America has poor people, Europe has poor people.'[40]

Yunus's pioneering work in social engineering is widely recognized across the globe. In 2006, Yunus and Grameen Bank were jointly awarded the Nobel Peace Prize for 'their efforts through microcredit to create economic and social development from below'. As the Nobel Committee observed, 'lasting peace cannot be achieved unless large population groups find ways in which to break out of poverty' and that 'across cultures and civilizations, Yunus and Grameen Bank have shown that even the poorest of the poor can work to bring about their own development'.[41]

Yunus is a leader who had a dream to take the poor out of a life of destitution and impoverishment. And he translated that dream into reality, thereby transforming the lives of millions across the globe. As his Nobel Peace Prize citation reads,

> Muhammad Yunus has shown himself to be a leader who
> has managed to translate visions into practical action for
> the benefit of millions of people, not only in Bangladesh,
> but also in many other countries... Yunus's long-term
> vision is to eliminate poverty in the world. That vision

---

[40]Miriam Cosic, '"We are all entrepreneurs": Muhammad Yunus on changing the world, one microloan at a time', *The Guardian*, 29 March 2017
[41]https://en.wikipedia.org/wiki/Muhammad_Yunus

cannot be realised by means of micro-credit alone. But Muhammad Yunus and Grameen Bank have shown that, in the continuing efforts to achieve it, micro-credit must play a major part.[42]

What Comes First—Vision or Action?

The traditional understanding of leadership is that leaders have a vision of the future, which they articulate passionately to their followers to collectively translate into reality. In a way, castles are built in the air first and foundations are subsequently laid underneath. The American poet and philosopher Henry David Thoreau, in a way, was close to the idea when he said, 'If you have built castles in the air, your work need not be lost; that is where they should be. Now put the foundations under them.'

However, there are situations to the contrary, when some small action or incident leads to the building up of a broader and grander vision, which gets implemented at a mass level later. Nothing explains this better than the story of Make a Wish International, an organization dedicated 'to grant[ing] the wishes of children with life-threatening medical conditions to enrich the human experience with hope, strength and joy'. The seed of the idea was sown in 1980 in Phoenix, Arizona, when a small group of caring individuals went out of their way to ensure that the wishes of a terminally ill boy were fulfilled. Born on 13 August 1972, the seven-year-old, Christopher James Greicius, who was undergoing treatment for leukaemia, had a strong desire to become a police officer. When the US customs officer Tommy Austin heard of this, he decided to help Chris realize his dream and lift his spirits. He got in

---

[42]https://www.nobelprize.org/prizes/peace/2006/press-release/

touch with the Arizona Department of Public Safety and, with their cooperation, planned an experience for the little boy. Chris was flown to the police headquarters, where he underwent a motorcycle proficiency test, which he passed with some assistance. Dressed in a custom-made uniform, he was sworn in as the first honorary public safety patrolman in the history of the state. He spent the day as a police officer and was elated to have this experience of his lifetime.

Chris died soon after, on 3 May 1980, but he left behind the seeds of a great movement. The incident inspired similar instances of people coming forward to fulfil the wishes of children in similar situations. What started with the fulfilment of just one wish led to the creation of the Make a Wish Foundation. In 1993, Make a Wish International was formally launched in five countries outside the US. Today, it has taken root in fifty countries across five continents and over the years has granted more than 415,000 wishes to children across the world.

Creating a Vision in the Modern World

While visions could be lofty and transformative or mundane and ordinary, in the modern world, visioning has acquired certain added dimensions.

For new-age leaders, an exciting vision is the all-important instrument to inspire their teams, sustain leadership of an informed and enlightened workforce, and keep the organization afloat. This is becoming all the more critical for the simple reason that in an environment of constant volatility and upheavals, the very task of keeping an organization on track and carrying out its daily routine can be frustrating and exhausting. The leaders, therefore, have to create a captivating dream, a fascinating vision of the future that can keep the trust, hope and faith of not only the workforce and shareholders but also of other stakeholders. Further, focusing on a transformative agenda could also help a company take advantage of the diverse business opportunities coming up in the marketplace and provide it with a competitive edge over others.

A Transformative and Disruptive Vision

Organizations of today are under constant pressure to create transformative and disruptive visions for themselves to remain competitive. An important driving force behind such disruptive visions is the technology that is developing at a fast pace, enabling them to bring about radical transformations in the way products and services are consumed. Some of them also aim at enabling humanity to scale new horizons.

One of the greatest leaders of our time, Elon Musk, the CEO of Tesla Inc. and SpaceX, provides an excellent example of creating a transformative and disruptive vision, which is closely integrated with a larger social purpose. Under Musk's leadership, Tesla is constantly reimagining, realigning and reinvesting in itself to lead the world's transition from fossil fuels to clean and sustainable energy sources. Musk, an entrepreneur par excellence, has always maintained that Tesla's purpose is not simply to make electric cars but to help humanity transition from fossil fuels to clean and sustainable energy sources for survival. In his original Master Plan, he called Tesla a conduit 'to help expedite the move from a mine-and-burn hydrocarbon economy towards a solar electric economy, which I believe to be the primary, but not exclusive, sustainable solution'.[43] Then, in the 'Master Plan, Part Deux', he reasoned out the need of

---

[43]https://www.tesla.com/blog/secret-tesla-motors-master-plan-just-between-you-and-me

creating 'a sustainable energy economy or we will run out of fossil fuels to burn and civilisation will collapse'.[44]

On the whole, Musk is driving human civilization towards a seemingly Utopian goal of an electrified and low-carbon society through his multipronged product lines. His SolarCity roofs can be seamlessly interconnected with Powerwall battery solutions. His self-driving electric cars can lead to safer roads while addressing the world crisis of high carbon dioxide emissions. His other venture, the Boring Company, is constantly trying to increase the speed and reduce the cost of travel in a way never imagined before. Going further, his SpaceX is envisioning making humanity an interplanetary civilization with a colony planned on Mars.

Leaders in modern times develop their vision keeping in mind critical hypotheses around areas such as managing the planet, innovating for the future, workforce motivation, customer preferences, stakeholder alignment and mutual trust. This calls for a different kind of thinking and appreciation of future demands, latent customer predilections and technological challenges. It goes without saying that it is the transformative power of the modern leaders' visions that stirs stakeholders to support futuristic projects; it is the magnetic pull of their grand ideas that attracts the best talents across the globe. The future of mankind as well as that of our planet is being reshaped by these visionaries.

---

[44]https://www.tesla.com/blog/master-plan-part-deux

6

The Collaborators and Co-Creators

The best executive is one who has sense enough to
pick good men to do what he wants done,
and self-restraint enough to keep from
meddling with them while they do it.

—THEODORE ROOSEVELT, FORMER US PRESIDENT

How does Zubin Mehta, the celebrated music director of the Israel Philharmonic Orchestra and the main conductor of Valencia's Opera House, create the symphonies and the musical masterpieces that the world enjoys? At first glance, his work may not look akin to the performance of a leader in a modern business house, but a deeper insight would reveal a close similarity. In the emerging knowledge economies, where most jobs are done by trained and trusted professionals with knowledge and expertise, the role of the leader at the top is similar to that of the conductor of an orchestra. At a broader level, the core functions of the conductor of an orchestra can be described as managing relationships, deciding on the programme, the selection of musicians, coordinating pieces to be played and, finally, collaborating and co-creating with the musicians the overall symphony for the audience. Much in the same manner, a business leader, too, orchestrates all his people and resources to create a harmony and produce the symphony of a product or service needed by customers.

Drawing an interesting analogy between the work in an orchestra and modern workplaces, the illustrious Israeli music conductor Itay Talgam observes that just like musicians, employees in modern workplaces are demanding greater involvement in the task they are required to perform, seeking meaning in what they do. As he puts it, 'Whatever you do in life, there's content and form; only those two put together create special meaning of a great work of art or great interpretation of music or a great story that you tell.'[45]

Talgam goes on to suggest that leaders have the responsibility of creating an organizational culture wherein everyone in the team is able to find meaning and purpose in whatever he or she is doing, even though it could be an everyday mundane job performed on a routine basis. Emphasizing the point, he cites an interesting example from the world of music and relates the story of the famous Italian conductor Riccardo Muti, who had to resign as the musical director of the Teatro alla Scala Orchestra in Milan in 2003 because of an internal dispute with musicians in his band. Fed up with his authoritative and dominating style, the musicians wrote to him asking him to resign.

'You are using us as instruments, and because you are using us very good, the results are always good. But on the way to getting this wonderful result, we are losing our souls. We don't like the music we play.'[46]

In modern workplaces too, employees' search for meaning and purpose in their work underscores the silent revolution,

---

[45]Vikas Kumar, 'Israeli music conductor Itay Talgam believes leadership is all about those you lead', *The Economic Times*, 23 December 2011
[46]Ibid

both in style and substance, that leadership is undergoing in contemporary times.

The Traditional Top-Down Image of a Leader

What are the lingering images of a successful business leader that have been passed on to us for generations? Most commonly, it is the heroic image of a dynamic chief executive who joins a sick corporation struggling for survival. He generates high hopes by reinventing the organizational vision, mission, goals and structures. He redefines strategies and directs everyone on what to do and how to do them. Down the line, he rewards those who come up to his expectations while disincentivizing underperformers. Finally, with his charismatic personality, he takes the company out of the sticky situation and heralds a new dawn of growth and profitability, generating happiness and satisfaction among all the stakeholders.

This vertical view of the leader at the head of the triangle is essentially an image drawn from the days of Victorian-era factories. Deeply entrenched in the leadership ethos, this top-down approach has always seen leaders at the apex of a triangle wherefrom all knowledge, wisdom and inspiration trickles down to the followers. The prevalent individualism of the West has also added to this notion of top-of-the-hill leadership, where the outcomes of an organizational action are disproportionately attributed to the actions of individual leaders while underplaying the role of other factors. This has been central to the study of most transformational and charismatic leaders. No wonder, then, that leadership scholars from the West have tended to study the leadership phenomenon in terms of leaders, structures, roles and functions, ignoring the other factors relevant to the leadership process.

Leaders as Collaborators and Co-Creators

However, to be effective and deliver results in the changing environment, imperfect leaders of today consciously move away from the romance of leadership and shun the heroic image of a leader nurtured and promoted so far. They no longer project themselves as all-powerful persons who can single-handedly lead the organization to the realization of its cherished goals and objectives. Their focus remains on grooming leaders and placing them at relevant points in the organizational structure so as to speed up problem-solving and decision-making. In this sense, they reflect the spirit of the American industrialist and philanthropist Andrew Carnegie's oft-quoted desire to put on his gravestone, 'Here lies a man who knew how to put into his service more able men than he was himself.'

Thus, new-age leaders see a drastic change in their role profiles. They believe in teamwork, where they see their role as both a player and a coach. Instead of command and control, they strive to collaborate and co-create with their teams to provide collective solutions to common problems, devolving the leadership in a manner where everybody sees themselves as contributing to the common cause. Jack Welch, the former chairman and CEO of General Electric, captures the essence of it when he says, 'Before you are a leader, success is all about growing yourself. When you become a leader, success is all about growing others.'

Challenges: Leadership at the Point of Action

In a world that offers no easy solutions to complex problems, leaders no longer can take critical decisions and manage just sitting at the top, at a distance from the scene of action. They have to lean on the experience and expertise of their team members to respond to the challenges emanating from the operating environment. Consider the following two examples, one from the Indian Army and the other from the Indian paramilitary forces—CRPF—that showcase the changing landscapes in which leaders of today are required to operate.

The Quick-Thinking Army Major

9 April 2017: It was the day of the parliamentary by-elections in the Budgam district of Jammu & Kashmir, the insurgency-affected state of the Indian Union. Major Leetul Gogoi of 53 Rashtriya Rifles, a counter-insurgency unit of the Indian Army, received a distress call from the Indo-Tibetan Border Police (ITBP), intimating that a violent mob of around 1,200 stone pelters had surrounded a small team of ITBP personnel and polling staff in the polling station in Utligam village. The mob, consisting of men, women and children in a frenzy, was threatening to set the polling booth ablaze.

When the Major rushed to the spot with a small team of five personnel, the mob started throwing stones at them. Even boulders were attempted to be dropped on them from rooftops, making it impossible for them to get out of their vehicle. The crowd did not respond to repeated announcements made by the Major.

Struggling to get out of the situation without any violence, the Major saw a short person close to his vehicle, who was acting as the ringleader. With some difficulty, the Army men caught hold of him and entered the polling booth arena in their mine-protected vehicle. They rescued four of the civilian polling booth staff, seven ITBP personnel and one constable from the local police.

But, as luck would have it, while coming out of the polling station, their mine-protected vehicle got stuck in the mud. Seeing this, the mob started to throw stones at them once again. Even a petrol bomb was hurled, which fortunately did not explode. The Army men were somehow able to pull the vehicle out of the mud even while being pelted with stones.

At this point, the Major had a flash idea. He ordered the ringleader captured by them to be tied to the front of their Jeep. As this was happening, a shocked crowd stopped throwing stones for a while. In that small window of time, the Major ordered his men to get into the vehicle immediately, and they drove out of the area safely without any bloodshed.

Once the news of the 'human shield' broke in the media, there was a furore, with human rights activists condemning the step taken by the Major. Even some retired Army generals expressed disapproval at the Major's actions, stating that it was neither prudent nor in line with the Army's standard operating procedures (SOP).

Briefing the media later, Major Gogoi said, 'This thing I have done only to save the local people. Had I fired, there would have been more than 12 casualties… With this idea, I have saved many peoples' lives.'[47]

On 15 April 2017, the Army convened a Court of Enquiry (COI) into the incident. The COI gave a clean chit to the Major, and he was awarded the Chief of Army Staff (COAS) commendation for sustained efforts in counter-insurgency operations.

Restraint Shown by CRPF Personnel

In a similar incident in the Budgam district on the same day, a few belligerent youngsters heckled some CRPF personnel who were walking on foot on election duty for the parliamentary bypolls. The hecklers kept following them, raising slogans and

---

[47]PTI, 'Army Major Gogoi, probed over Kashmir human shield, tells media he saved lives', Livemint, 23 May 2017

often punching and pushing the armed men. However, even though armed with guns, the soldiers remained calm and kept moving unprovoked.

When the video of the incident went viral on social media, there were intense reactions—some condemning the militants, others praising the restraint shown by the CRPF personnel. Commenting on the incident, the director general of police, S.P. Vaid, praised the restraint shown by the CRPF personnel and said, 'Any armed force in the world would have retaliated with force.'

These incidents described above highlight the two emerging dimensions of leadership today. First, we are operating in a landscape where a delay in decision-making or a wrong decision could risk serious damage and even extinction itself. Further, there is no time to seek directions from the higher-ups and, therefore, decision-making has to be taken closer to the scene of action. Secondly, while in normal times, one could follow the SOP, there are times that require leaders to improvise their responses as per the demand of the situation. Here, in the first episode, the Army Major deviated from his SOP and took one of the protesters as a human shield to save the lives of people. In the other case, the CRPF personnel refused to follow the traditional approach of retaliating at their hecklers and showed exemplary restraint.

While these leadership stories from the armed forces are telling enough to bring home the point of improvising local strategies, responding with speed and providing leadership at the point of action, they are equally relevant to leadership in its wider context. The business scene in the modern world in many ways resembles conflict situations with constant upheavals and disruptions.

Here, too, the challenges arising out of local situations need to be responded to with speed and action while considering local culture, circumstances, rules and regulations. For modern corporations, the added dimension is that their skilled and educated workforce aspires to have an enriching and fulfilling job role and content, which goes beyond routine compliance with instructions from above. Employees look forward to using their creativity in facing organizational challenges as partners in realizing their collective vision and mission.

Hence, there is a need for modern organizations to devolve leadership to the different layers within the organization. There is also the need to inculcate the culture of displaying leadership at the grass-root level so as to remain competitive and survive in today's challenging times.

Need for Improvisation

In an article titled 'Leader Challenge: What Would You Do?' in the *Journal of Asynchronous Learning Networks* (Volume 15: Issue 3), the following vignette is quoted from a *New Yorker* article in 2005, which gives an example from the American Army experience to illustrate the critical importance of embedded knowledge in war-like situations: 'A small unit of American soldiers was walking along a street in Najaf, when hundreds of Iraqis poured out of the buildings on either side. Fists waving, throats taut, they pressed in on the Americans, who glanced at one another in terror. The Iraqis were shrieking, frantic with rage. From the way the lens was lurching, the cameraman seemed as frightened as the soldiers... At that moment, an American officer stepped through the crowd holding his rifle high over his head with the barrel pointed to the ground... "Take a knee," the officer said, impassive behind surfer sunglasses. The soldiers looked at him as if he was crazy. Then, one after another, swaying in their bulky body armour and gear, they knelt before the boiling crowd and pointed their guns to the ground. The Iraqis fell silent, and their anger subsided. The officer ordered his men to withdraw.'[48]

Like the leaders in the two episodes in Jammu & Kashmir, the leader of the American troop in Iraq, too, exemplified the importance of the embedded knowledge, personal insight and understanding that one is required to marshal in dealing with sudden, complex and chaotic situations of the modern world. For the US army, which operates in 120 countries today, many of them being extremely hostile terrains, a high degree of insight into the local psyche, culture and understanding of ever-evolving situations is critical to success.

Distributed Leadership Works Better

I start with the premise that the function of leadership is to produce more leaders, not more followers.

–RALPH NADER, AUTHOR, AMERICAN POLITICAL ACTIVIST AND
GANDHI PEACE AWARDEE

Imperfect leaders of today learn a lot from the flight of the geese discussed earlier. To promote collaboration and co-creation within their organizations, leaders create a culture of 'distributed leadership', where leadership does not rest solely with the person at the top—it is distributed across the organization.

The concept of distributed leadership makes a radical departure from the traditional leader-follower dualism, wherein the leader is supposed to be in the driver's seat and the followers are the passive travellers. This new perspective makes an

---

[48]Dan Baum, 'Battle Lessons', *The New Yorker*, 9 January 2009

attempt at understanding the leadership phenomenon with a systemic approach in terms of interactions among people in complex organizations. It refuses to see the act of leadership as the product of one individual's traits, styles or actions and emphasizes that leadership is not something a leader does to his followers or to the organization. Rather, it considers the leadership process as a group activity, where both the leader and his followers play active roles.

Explaining this concept, leadership scholar and author James P. Spillane states in his article titled 'Distributed Leadership':

> Distributed Leadership is first and foremost about leadership practice rather than leaders or their roles, functions, routines, and structures. Though they are important considerations, leadership practice is still the starting point. A distributed perspective frames leadership practice in a particular way; Rather than viewing leadership practice as a product of a leader's knowledge and skill, the distributed perspective defines it as interactions between people and their situations. These interactions, rather than any particular action, are critical in understanding leadership practice.[49]

In fact, looking at leadership activity is akin to looking at an iceberg. What is not visible is much more than what meets the eye. This new approach underscores the fact that with the change of situations, leadership also passes from one individual to the other. Therefore, it can be fair to say that leadership could be convergent and concentrated at some point in an organization, depending upon the leader's expertise or influence. At the same time, it could be dispersed and shared

---

[49]James P. Spillane, 'Distributed Leadership', *The Educational Forum*, Volume 69, Issue 2, 2005

when the job demands multiplicity of experience and expertise. In this sense, the traditional divide between the leaders and their followers gets blurred.

This multidimensional view of leadership has both vertical and horizontal aspects. At the vertical level, this pluralistic approach to leadership aims at developing and nurturing dynamic and capable leaders at different levels within organizational hierarchies, so that decision-making is faster and the response to challenges is more prompt and appropriate. This approach also ensures that organizational think tanks get replenished with new ideas and strategies for meeting current, emerging and potential challenges. As the leadership remains deeply embedded within the organization, yet at the same time spread wide across different cultures, markets and geographies, it is able to provide multifaceted perspectives and grab emerging opportunities crucial in today's competitive marketplace.

At the horizontal level, distributed leadership involves restructuring of the organization, making it less hierarchical and creating empowered units that can move faster while operating within the ambit of organizational goals and philosophies. This involves innovating job designs to ensure proper distribution of power, responsibility and accountability within the organization. This new understanding of leadership does recognize the role and influence of leaders in determining organizational outcomes, but, like an iceberg, there is much more that remains submerged under water.

In order to be effective, leaders also create organizational structures that promote leadership at different levels in the organizational hierarchy. This helps them prepare their organization better to respond to the challenges coming from the external environment with speed and expertise. They are also not afraid of the multiplicity of leaders within the hierarchy, simply because they realize that having more leaders around doesn't diminish their own position, power or influence—it only complements it.

Nurturing Leadership within an Organization

To embed the culture of leadership within themselves, leaders need to nurture it using a systematic approach, whereby employees with leadership potential can be identified, developed and groomed for leadership roles.

The most critical step in this direction is putting the focus on employee empowerment. Here, simply talking about employee empowerment is not enough—organizations have to create an environment in which leadership voices are protected and encouraged. This means new ideas, even if coming from the lowest strata of the organization, are not frowned upon, and there is some tolerance for mistakes within the system. For employee empowerment to be effective, leaders have to create organizational structures, hierarchies and job designs that clearly spell out the roles, responsibilities and points of accountability within the system. The next step is to empower employees with decision-making authority and encourage them to take decisions on issues relevant to their roles. Depending upon the role and responsibilities, empowerment could include decision-making on crucial issues such as SOP, product launches, talent acquisition and employee separation, such as resignations, retirements, terminations, etc. And in the process, if they struggle, leaders can give them the necessary guidance and support. Decision-making is a complex process and, often, people at lower levels in the hierarchy tend to push it up while leaders at the higher levels lap it up, as it adds to the heroic perception of their leadership. Leaders must avoid this temptation and understand that it is not for them to solve problems—they should enable and encourage relevant leadership teams within the system to do the same. Employees will be encouraged to take decisions if they feel that they will be supported and protected, even if decisions taken by them in good faith prove to be wrong or counterproductive. This will help the leadership pipeline in the organization grow and employees can step into leadership roles as and when required.

By embedding and encouraging leadership at different levels in the organizational structure, organizations also enhance the collective self-esteem of their employees. When employees look upon themselves as contributing significantly to their organizations, their level of commitment for and engagement within the organization gets enhanced and they feel good about themselves as well as their organization. It leads to a win-win situation, in which the organization not only experiences higher productivity, but it also remains prepared to respond to potential challenges and opportunities emanating from internal and external environments, something that can keep it ahead of the competition.

Test of Leadership: Dissent, Teamwork, Information and Conflict

It is commonplace for top leaders to say that people must speak their minds on matters of organizational importance. But the test of such assertions comes up when we hear dissenting voices from below, challenging the conventional wisdom in any organization. How do we react to them? How do we respond to a whistle-blower who raises an issue, inconvenient and uncomfortable to the leadership?

It is indeed in these moments that the seriousness and commitment of the organization to promote leadership across the hierarchy gets tested. It is, therefore, for the leaders at the top to create a culture where employees feel free to express even diverse and dissenting opinions with the confidence that they will be heard and examined objectively and dispassionately. It is only in such an environment that creativity can flourish. As we know, creativity needs a host of new and sometimes even weird ideas before we get one good idea worth implementing. In an institution, scoffing at new ideas is a sure way of shutting the doors on creativity and innovation. Therefore, organizations have to ensure that leadership voices from across the hierarchy are heard and protected.

Teamwork is another bugbear. To be effective and to deliver results in a diversified and connected work environment, organizations must encourage employees to look beyond their silos and cooperate and collaborate with relevant groups in the search for effective solutions. Setting up cross-functional teams and encouraging and rewarding employees to exhibit leadership roles, both formal and informal, will go a long way in developing leaders at different levels in the hierarchy. Apart from improving internal communication, this can also help the organization identify market opportunities and capitalize on them.

Happy teams make for a free flow of information. There are two kinds of information available today. One that is publicly available, and thanks to information technology and social media, it is available to everyone. The second is specific to a company or an industry. Access to company or industry information is generally not available to everyone in the company.

No doubt, in today's scenario, information is power, which is one of the reasons why people privy to information tend to withhold it from others. However, it must be realized that a free flow of information on industry, business, markets and customers is critical for decision-making and leadership success. If leadership is to be distributed across the organizational hierarchy, there has to be an unhindered and transparent flow of required information within the system. This not only helps employees in taking more appropriate decisions benefiting their organizations, but it also helps them grow as leaders.

Where there are multiple leaders, conflict is a given. In an environment of distributed leadership, where more than one leader is sharing the decision-making space, conflicts will happen. As perspectives and priorities differ, different people come up with varied solutions to a problem and conflicts take place while selecting the best course of action. The leadership-development programme of an organization, therefore, must focus on honing the soft skills of leaders. They must be encouraged to appreciate and acknowledge the competing perspectives on an issue put forth by different stakeholders. While articulating their own expectations, they must also try to understand the expectations of others. While communicating, they must also listen to others. This will help them explore common grounds and manage the expectations of different competing interests.

Apart from helping potential leaders cultivate their conflict-management skills, on the organization's side, a clear delineation of roles and responsibilities, well-defined job designs and meaningful delegation of authority could help everyone understand their functional boundaries and exercise authority in their own functional areas. In essence, leaders must learn and practise how to share power while maintaining authority. This will go a long way in creating a positive environment and a high morale within the organization, minimizing conflict.

Trust and EI: The Magic Keys to Distributed Leadership

Under the contemporary leadership ethos where vertical power-based commandments are no longer effective, the focus has shifted to certain intrinsic qualities, such as relationships, authenticity and emotional intelligence. Trust is a product of all the three above and hence a major tool in the leadership repertoire today. No wonder that the trust in power is fast giving way to the power of trust as the defining factor for leadership success today.

Trust, however, is not a one-sided phenomenon—it operates on a pluralistic platform. To realize the power of trust, leaders not only have to develop trustworthiness, they also have to learn to trust others. For example, no amount of emphasis on employee empowerment can generate trust in the leader if employees have to run each of their decisions past the leader for confirmation. Therefore, leaders must learn to inculcate both the dimensions of trust—how to trust others and how to develop trustworthiness. Trust does involve risk—the risk of being betrayed or the person trusted with some responsibility not coming up to expectations. However, the upside of trust is much higher than the downside of the risk arising out of it.

An environment of trust can be created only on the bedrock of emotional intelligence (EI). EI is a measure of a person's self-awareness, empathy and sensitivity to other people, relationships and authenticity. In an environment where leadership space is shared and decision-making keeps happening at different points in the organizational structure, it is essential for leaders to demonstrate a higher level of EI so as to understand and appreciate the perspectives of the different stakeholders. In his article 'Getting Along—At the Top',[50] Daniel Goleman, author of the bestseller *Emotional Intelligence*, stresses the point that in collaborative work situations, where leaders have to share power and where different leaders bring their own skills, expertise and

---

[50]Daniel Goleman, 'Getting Along—At the Top', Korn Ferry Institute, 5 September 2017

perspectives to the table, those with higher EQ competencies are more effective and successful.

Goleman identifies six EQ competencies for managing a shared leadership environment: emotional self-awareness, emotional self-control, adaptability, empathy, organizational awareness and conflict management. Emotional self-awareness enables you to understand how your colleague's action impacts you while empathy puts the focus on the other person's perspective. Self-control allows you to think before reacting. Organizational awareness empowers you to see the big picture relating to the organizational context, goals and objectives while adaptability enables you to embrace alternative strategies without changing your goals. Finally, conflict management involves understanding and appreciating differing perspectives and finding a common ground. A higher EQ level on these counts obviously helps you in managing better in an environment of shared leadership.

It goes without saying that leadership-development programmes have the task cut out for themselves. They must equip leaders with the attributes of developing and gaining trust as well as managing the related risks. At the same time, they must devise ways and means whereby potential leaders can learn to enhance their emotional quotient in order to prepare themselves for dealing with the new realities of modern workplaces.

How to Develop New Leaders

Developing new leaders is a constant preoccupation in any organization, whether it is for succession planning, promotions or managing a new unit. Going beyond this, cultivating leadership at different points within the organization can be the need of the hour for adding vitality and dynamism to the institution.

However, before embarking upon a leadership-development plan, an organization must examine the following two aspects. First, it must ask itself what its understanding of leadership is or what kind of leadership it is looking for. This is relevant, since, in practical terms, leadership means different things to different people. At the same time, leadership styles could vary from one organization to the other. Therefore, an organization must determine the leadership type or styles suited to it and then focus on promoting it within the institution. It could be an attempt to promote a uniform style throughout the organization or certain complementary leadership styles, depending upon the specific need or circumstances of the organization.

Secondly, the current literature on leadership assumes that leadership is displayed and demonstrated within an organization in a uniform manner, irrespective of the hierarchy at which the leader is operating. This is one dimension that is most often glossed over in leadership-development programmes, which usually focus on all the attributes of leadership without differentiating between the hierarchical needs.

There is a need to challenge this assumption. Just to illustrate the point, creating a vision and ushering in organizational transformation can be a more pronounced leadership attribute for the leader operating at the top, while people orientation and being an effective role model can be more relevant at a lower level in the hierarchy. Therefore, if leadership is required to be 'distributed' within the expanse of the organization, it is critical to identify the traits and core attributes required to be displayed by leaders in different segments and at different levels in the organization, and chalk out the leadership-development framework accordingly.

Once the leadership styles and attributes required by the organization have been identified, the next question is who the potential leaders could be. This takes us to the classic question about whether leaders are born or made. While scholars have taken positions on the issue at both ends of the spectrum, the reality is not all that black and white. In real life, people are not born with a clean slate—they do possess some innate attributes that determine their natural behaviour and dispensation. It therefore goes without saying that while choosing potential leaders, if we focus on persons who display a natural flair for leadership, we would be trying to maximize the potential that is already there among people.

Further, leadership programmes in organizations must focus on developing leaders rather than training them. In essence, training is centred on the known and the familiar. It focuses on the standard and best practices available in the current state of things. Development, on the other side, is oriented towards the future—it deals with the unknown and aims at developing capabilities that may be needed to meet the emerging unexpected challenges. The leadership-development process involves coaching and mentoring with a view to maximizing the potential within the individual. All these nuances are critical to developing leadership within an organization to serve its needs in these uncertain and volatile times.

7

The Agile Jugglers

The glaring difference between successful people and those whose careers falter...is their ability to wrest meaning from experience, i.e., learning agility.

–MCCALL, LOMBARDO AND MORRISON[51]

Why is it that leaders who happen to be effective in one company start looking inept and ineffective when they move to another? How come successful leaders often fail to deliver when elevated to a higher level, even in their own company? Isn't it surprising that out of the thirty best CEOs in the world, chosen by the American magazine *Barron's* in 2008, only five made the grade in an identical list in 2012? What explains the fact that of the fourteen companies marked for their excellence by Robert H. Waterman Jr and Tom Peters in their epoch-making book *In Search of Excellence,* quite a few couldn't live up to their reputations and dropped out of this exalted list? There could be a long array of companies stumbling and faltering as external environments change and the top leadership proves unequal to the task ahead and gets fired.

If there is one factor common to all these situations, it is the inability to manage the transition; the breakdown in

---

[51]Morgan W. McCall, Michael M. Lombardo and Ann M. Morrison, *Lessons of Experience: How Successful Executives Develop on the Job*, Free Press, 1988

leadership caused by the volatility, uncertainty, complexity and ambiguity of the VUCA world.

As the business environment remains in constant flux, ambiguous, bereft of essential skills and expertise, leaders find it difficult to interpret business situations correctly and make logical and rational choices. But the ambiguity and murkiness of the operating landscape is going to continue into the future, with constant change and transition being the new normal now.

Kevin Cashman, Korn Ferry's global leader in CEO and Executive Development, draws a very apt comparison when he says,

> Living and leading today are much like swimming in the unpredictable, treacherous Lake Superior, the fourth-largest body of fresh water in the world. We dive into the water, and we never really know what is going to happen next. Although we operate under the illusion that life remains constant, clear, and under our control, this is far from reality. Everything is always changing, and often situations and choices are unclear, uncertain, even murky.[52]

A significant consequence of this volatile and ambiguous business environment is that transition confronts leaders with novel situations in unforeseen circumstances. At the same time, it brings to the fore opportunities hitherto unexplored by the organizations. To deal with this situation, new-age leaders are required to keep adapting to the changing environment and renewing the repertoire of their leadership skills on a continuous basis. They must be able to interpret their past experiences properly and apply the learning to their new situations. In addition, they also need to be comfortable with

---

[52]Kevin Cashman, 'The Five Dimensions of Learning-Agile Leaders', *Forbes*, 3 April 2013

ambiguity and uncertainty and make sense of the hazy situation by analysing and assimilating ideas, trends and information available to them. Quite often they are required to take quick decisions to grab the opportunity available in the marketplace, even though they may not have the time and data available to make a compelling case of choosing between the available alternatives. In a nutshell, adaptability, flexibility and the ability to deal with complexity and ambiguity in the new normal business environment are the keys to leadership success today.

Learning Agility in a Globalized Market

The illiterate of the twenty-first century will not be those who cannot read and write, but those who cannot learn, unlearn, and relearn.

–ALVIN TOFFLER, AMERICAN WRITER AND FUTURIST

The ability to learn and adapt, called learning agility, is a major differentiating factor between leaders who will be successful tomorrow and those whose leadership journey is going to get derailed. In an article titled 'High Potentials as High Learners',[53] authors Michael M. Lombardo and Robert W. Eichinger highlighted the relationship between learning agility and leadership potential. They maintained that the leadership potential of a person is determined more by the person's ability to learn novel ways and means to handle complex and unforeseen situations rather than the abilities already demonstrated by them on the job. The need to acquire new skills gets further accentuated when individuals are required to play their roles in different geographies and cultures. Equally

---

[53]Michael M. Lombardo and Robert W. Eichinger, 'High Potentials as High Learners', Wiley Online Library, 8 January 2001

important is that they need to unlearn old skills that have become obsolete with the change in their roles and operating landscapes. This ability of unlearning and learning is something that differs from one individual to the other, and, therefore, is a critical determinant of leadership potential. Highlighting the importance of this competence, Lombardo and Eichinger say,

> To deal with change, organizations need to find and nurture those who are most facile in dealing with it. Identifying those who can learn to behave in new ways requires a different measurement strategy than often employed—one that looks at the characteristics of the learning agile.[54]

The idea has seen considerable acceptance among leadership strategists in the recent past. Learning agility today is being considered one of the most important traits for evaluating leadership potential in a volatile and complex world, more relevant than even many of the celebrated virtues of earlier days, such as academic excellence, IQ or EQ.

What Is Learning Agility?

Learning agility denotes a person's mental ability to learn, unlearn and re-learn continually and rapidly from people, situations and experiences, and devise suitable models, practices and behaviour patterns to respond to complex and unfamiliar situations. It is a complex set of skills that enables a person to draw meaning from their experiences and observations, find patterns in them and apply the learning to a new situation to get the desired results.

---

[54]Michael M. Lombardo and Robert W. Eichinger, 'High Potentials as High Learners', Wiley Online Library, 8 January 2001

In the White Paper 'Learning about Learning Agility' (Centre for Creative Leadership), Adam Mitchinson and Robert Morris put it very succinctly,

> Our research supports the view that learning agility is a mindset and corresponding collection of practices that allow leaders to continually develop, grow, and utilise new strategies that will equip them for the increasingly complex problems they face in their organizations.[55]

Explaining the concept further, leadership experts Kenneth P. De Meuse, Guangrong Dai and George S. Hallenbeck in 'Learning Agility: A Construct Whose Time Has Come', observe:

> ...There appear to be three defining characteristics of learning agility relative to other constructs. First, the construct of learning agility ties closely to the developmental job experiences. Second, it is multidimensional, reflecting the complex requirement of challenging jobs. Third, it is an early indicator of leadership effectiveness. Therefore, learning agility can be most appropriately construed as a 'metacompetency' (i.e., an individual attribute that is prerequisite to the development of other competencies; cf. Briscoe & Hall, 1999).

The concept of 'metacompetency' has been defined as 'a competency that is so powerful that it affects the person's ability to acquire other competencies'.[56] For example, the competency of reading can be cited as an analogy for metacompetency;

---

[55]https://www.ccl.org/wp-content/uploads/2015/04/LearningAgility.pdf

[56]Jon P. Briscoe and Douglas T. Hall, 'Grooming and picking leaders using competency frameworks: Do they work? An alternative approach and new guidelines for practice', *Organizational Dynamics*, January 1999

once a person is able to read, it opens the gates for all other kinds of learning that can be communicated to him through the written word.

In the same manner, learning agility is also described as a metacompetency, which includes learning from past experiences, the ability to comprehend the complexity of hazy and volatile environments and finally the ability to demonstrate the flexibility and adaptability to respond to complex situations. It provides only an indication of the leadership potential of an individual; the end product of learning agility is an agile leader who demonstrates these competencies in real-life situations.

The concept of learning agility has added some crucial dimensions to our understanding of leadership development. In the past, the most important criteria for elevating a person to the next higher role in the leadership hierarchy or selecting someone for a new leadership role had been the past performance of the person. It was assumed that if an individual had performed well in his current role, he would perform well in his next higher position as well.

However, this approach is essentially flawed and loses sight of the fact that every role in an organization demands a new insight and understanding. Also, the behavioural patterns that are effective at one level or in one position may not be useful in another. Added to this is the increasing volatility and complexity of modern organizations.

Therefore, in the context of judging an individual's potential for leadership, his current skill sets are less relevant in comparison to his ability and willingness to learn new skills needed for managing the new role.

This becomes obvious when we observe that the leadership attributes that were someone's proven strengths in one situation turn out to be definite weaknesses in another. There have been instances of leaders who have failed in their roles as they were perceived as being too visionary or too much of a strategist. Yet some others have failed for being too aggressive or too humble. There are instances when the virtues of a participative management were considered crippling weaknesses. For example, the Italian music conductor Talgam recounts one of his own experiences, recalling the time of the collapse of the Soviet Union, which had led to the immigration of a large number of Russian Jews into Israel.

'The orchestra was full of Russian musicians. I had just come back from working with Bernstein, and my whole mindset was about dialogue,' he says. 'At one point I stopped the rehearsal and told the orchestra, "This really doesn't work. What should we do?" There was dead silence, and then one of them rose and said, "Where we come from, the conductor would not ask what to do. He would know what to do." So you see, I failed him. But I thought I was honouring them.'[57]

The Age of Start-Ups

With the advent of nimble-footed business start-ups, the relevance of learning agility becomes all the more critical. Start-ups try to fulfil the varying needs of customers, some of which can be felt and spoken, while others are the latent needs and aspirations of customers. These companies are inventing new products and designing new processes that need a high level of nimbleness in thinking and approach. Companies have to imagine solutions and design products even though there may be considerable uncertainty and ambiguity about

---

[57]Vikas Kumar, 'Israeli music conductor Itay Talgam believes leadership is all about those you lead', *The Economic Times*, 23 December 2011

their effectiveness and acceptability. Leaders have to take quick decisions even in the absence of definitive data analysis. At the same time, if a solution doesn't work, they have to be quick in dropping it and starting afresh with a new approach. In the process, they need to interpret their experiences to derive meaning, which could explain their success or failure. Based on the new learning, they need to reorient their approach and strategy to the task at hand.

Hence, the importance of learning agility to manage today's complex and volatile environment can never be overstated. In the words of Mitchinson and Morris of the Centre for Creative Leadership,

> It is clear that learning agility is part of any successful leader's repertoire. The willingness and ability to learn from experience not only influences the extent to which we grow as individuals but also how we are perceived by others. Ultimately, our ability to continuously learn and adapt will determine the extent to which we thrive in today's turbulent times.[58]

People who are learning-agile are more adaptive and flexible. In the brave new world, success doesn't necessarily go to the person who is bright, brainy and smart—it follows those who are adaptable and keep evolving in a dynamic, fuzzy and uncertain environment.

Measuring Learning Agility for Leadership Agility

Given that learning agility is an important tool for assessing leadership potential and predicting performance, it is critical to

---

[58]Adam Mitchinson and Robert Morris, 'Learning About Learning Agility', Center for Creative Leadership

measure it as well. Organizations, too, find measurement tools relevant as people differ in their capacity to learn. Leadership experts have developed various models for assessment of learning agility. Prominent among them is Korn-Ferry's Lominger Learning Agility model, developed by Lombardo and Eichinger. This model defines four characteristics of learning agility:

People Agility: Persons gifted with this ability have high self-awareness. They are receptive to other people's points of view and have a high degree of interpersonal relationship skills. They promote teamwork and encourage collective performance. These persons have high resilience and respond to change and conflict in a constructive manner.

Results Agility: People high on results agility are result-oriented, with a penchant for completing tasks even in difficult circumstances. They build high-performance teams and drive performance. They exhibit confidence and inspire others to do their best.

Mental Agility: This relates to a person's ability to think through complex problems and get to the root cause of problems. Such people are gifted with a high degree of curiosity. They love to explore alternative solutions to difficult problems and are comfortable with complexity and ambiguity.

Change Agility: People with change agility thrive on challenges. They like experimentation, look out for new ideas and respond to change in a positive and constructive manner.

Each of these four dimensions of learning agility is crucial to determining leadership potential in a new environment. However, these characteristics are not evenly distributed among people—they are gifted with these attributes in varying proportions. Leadership in the new age belongs to those who are able to develop their key strengths across all four dimensions of learning agility and unlock their strategic potential. This is the present, and the future is not going to be any different.

As learning agility has emerged as a critical means of evaluating leadership potential, it is essential that leadership- development programmes factor it as part of their strategy. This, however, needs to be further supplemented by another factor—the willingness to learn new skills and competencies to operate under unusual and tough conditions to get the desired results.

Challenges: Agile Leadership or Cautious Management?

New-age leaders are often faced with a strange challenge—the choice between agile leadership and cautious management. The complexity of the business environment today demands leaders to take critical decisions even when there is insufficient data or evidence to support the decision. This involves increasing risk, and leaders are expected to take risks and be agile enough to respond to challenges before them.

At the other end of the spectrum, there is a tendency towards increasing management caution and control. The intensity of competition and increasing transparency is opening up businesses to scrutiny by analysts, media, regulators and the public at large. Further, there is an ever-increasing demand from organizations to adhere to compliance and accountability not only to laws, regulations and accounting norms, but also to emerging factors like local culture or public sensitivity. We have recently seen a host of organizations, such as JP Morgan Chase, Barclays and others paying billions of dollars in penalty towards regulatory violations and market manipulations, while other mighty organizations, such as the Lehman Brothers, the Enron Corporation and Arthur Andersen, have gone out of business. Such instances have only added to the management exercising control, along with regulators and governments.

On a theoretical plane, this would appear to be a classic conflict between leadership and management, with each pursuing differing perspectives. As popular perception goes, leaders do the right things while managers do things right. The incongruity of such an assumption is that it considers leadership and management at opposite ends of the organizational spectrum. However, nothing can be farther from the truth. Both leadership and management are meant to complement each other for an organization to grow and excel. For example, an organization with a strong leadership but a weak management would inspire people with its great vision and dynamism, but remain critically short on implementation skills such as planning, budgeting and execution. On the other hand, organizations with a strong management but weak leadership are bound to end up staid, static and pedestrian.

The current impasse facing businesses today is a result of the swing in favour of leadership earlier at the cost of management control. In the 1990s, the business world saw the emergence of a number of narcissistic leaders, who, with their electrifying vision, daring and dynamism, promised to lead the world into a different future. These skilled orators and passionate dreamers, with their larger-than-life personalities, were able to inspire people and attract followers to their strategies of shaping the future. However, as Freud had rightly analysed, narcissists have their own limitations and weaknesses, and it was not surprising that the leadership idiosyncrasies of some of these leaders resulted in the downfall and collapse of their organizations.

A natural consequence of this development has been the shifting of organizational focus from leadership to management. Not only have organizations started to focus more on compliance, even regulators are coming out with fresh sets of regulations, preferring to err on the side of caution. Increasing globalization has only added to this trend. As organizations get more integrated, with many of them having transnational holdings, a regulatory violation by a company in one geography impacts its parents and subsidiaries in other geographies as well. Likewise, the increasing tendency to be in line with public sensitivities and adhere to moral and ethical codes is bringing back greater focus on compliance. Thus, a German company won't buy carpets from India based on the perception that the Indian manufacturers employ child labour for the job. Investors, too, may shy away from investing in a product or sector that might offend shareholder sensitivities. For example, shareholders of Reliance Industries Ltd persuaded the management to ensure that its subsidiary Reliance Retail didn't sell non-vegetarian products.

An unwelcome consequence of this trend is that inspired leaders in modern corporations turn into staid administrators, harping all the time on planning, review and compliance. Most are apprehensive that in an age of quarterly reviews and shareholder activism, any breach of norm might lead to decline in valuation and market share, inviting the ire of their shareholders, analysts and the public at large.

Managed Too Much, Inspired Too Little?

The leadership crisis facing the world today is partly a reflection of this phenomenon. Never before in history has leadership been in such short supply. In a turbulent and traumatic world, organizations need agile leadership to steer them on the path of success and keep them relevant in the constantly changing environment. Going beyond, in an age of increasing trust deficit in corporations, it takes exceptional leadership to inspire people and make them believe in a cause worth pursuing with passion and perseverance.

It needs to be realized that stakeholders in any organization are not looking forward to compliance as their primary objective. They look for growth and development, innovating new products and charting newer territories. Therefore, leaders of today cannot stop dreaming. They cannot close their eyes to emerging business trends and customer needs; they cannot stop innovating the future to satisfy these compelling needs. A relentless passion to interpret the chaos, an unbounded daring to face the turbulence and an inspired vision to reshape the future remain the demand on the leaders of today.

Contemporary leaders need to strike the right balance between management control and leadership vision. They must define boundaries that are sacrosanct for the organization but facilitate and nurture creativity and innovation to flourish within the same. They must adopt a 'glocal' approach—thinking global, acting local—and ensure that they are on the right side of social and cultural sensitivities, and if at all some sensitivities are offended and transgressed, they don't hesitate in mending their ways and retracing their steps. However, the relentless pursuit of their vision has to remain their passion, which they can't compromise on. As they say, 'Leadership is striking the right balance between vision and execution, continuity and change, poetry and prose.'

Organizational Agility Versus Organizational Stability

Leadership agility and organizational agility have a reciprocal relationship—one thrives when the other does. Although it might sound contradictory, organizational agility is not conflicting with stability—it is, rather, complementary to it. Organizational agility denotes an organization's capability to move fast, be responsive to its environment and take decisions with speed and nimbleness.

Agile organizations have two things in common—they show speed and dynamism in responding to the challenges before them, and they have a very solid and stable foundation that remains resilient to change. It is anchored in some deeply embedded values and beliefs within the organization that continue to remain its driving force even in the face of frequent storms in the environment. It is like the operating system of a computer, which provides a platform anchored on which various other software applications provide nimble solutions to our problems. Let's take Amazon, for example. It may add to its product line, change its structure, enter new markets, but all across its different products and markets, it retains its customer-centricity. It is a cultural mooring that doesn't change with the change in market, product or processes.

A nimble-footed start-up, operating from a garage, may not bother about stability in the beginning. But as it moves out of the garage and starts expanding to new geographies, it designs and develops SOPs and cultivates an organizational culture to provide stability. On the other side, large and established organizations strive to become nimble and agile, although they struggle in the process. The key challenges in their journey to agility emerge from their legacy systems, hierarchical structures and, above all, the mindsets of their leaders who have tasted success coming their way through their tried-and-tested methods. In a networked structure, when they are asked to share power with others and take decisions through cross-functional teams, they become uncomfortable, uncertain and apprehensive. As a reaction, they exert more control, devise new rules and impose greater authority, thereby frustrating the organizational drive towards greater agility.

In view of this, new-age leaders have to strive hard to

infuse agility into their organizations. They have to reinvent their systems and processes and re-imagine their organizations as closely networked entities, as against existing hierarchical models with large spans of control. A networked organization will not only bring its leaders closer to their people and their customers, it will also break the silos in which organizations work today. The integrated and networked teams, therefore, will be able to understand the complexities of the challenges at hand and respond to them with agility and learn as they keep going.

In the process of infusing agility, leaders have to walk a tightrope balance and simultaneously work on infusing stability into their organizations. They have to ensure that the organizational backbone, be it its culture, its common purpose, a commitment to quality or anything that binds the organization together, remains robust and resilient and doesn't change too soon, too frequently.

Lack of Organizational Agility: A Sure Recipe for Failure

In the relatively stable economies of earlier days, organizations could manage their businesses with single-minded focus. The complexity of business was less; their supply lines and customer segments were also stable. Thus, companies like Tata Steel could focus on making steel, Reliance Industries Ltd could concentrate on refining crude and producing petrochemicals, while commercial banks could busy themselves primarily with collecting deposits and financing projects. Competition being low, the threat perception to businesses was also low. Moreover, the slow speed of business coupled with the relative opacity in the business environment provided leaders some comfort that they could make mistakes and learn from them without much damage.

Way back in the early 1980s, when Britain's Caparo Group chairman Lord Swraj Paul had launched a well-publicized takeover bid for two Indian business houses—Escorts and DCM—the total holdings of the promoters in their companies were only 5 per cent and 10 per cent, respectively. Lord Paul was able to buy 7.7 per cent of Escorts and 13 per cent of DCM stocks. However, for years, both these companies refused to register the purchase of these shares, and the Indian judicial system also took ages to decide in favour of Lord Paul. Having got enough breathing space and with the support of local industrialists who felt equally threatened, promoters were able to ramp up their own shareholding in their companies. Finally, with the support of public sector undertakings, which had considerable stakes in these companies, they were able to frustrate the corporate raid on them.

The business environment of the 1980s helped these companies realize their mistakes and rectify the same. However, a similar takeover bid in the current scenario and the blocking of transactions would have raised a global hue and cry about shareholders' rights and the need for fairness and justice in the system. And yes, possibly, the results would have been different.

In modern business landscapes, however, organizations have threats coming from many other sources. Today, competition—and that, too, from unusual quarters—is always knocking on the doors of companies. Technology is opening up new frontiers, and if organizations don't respond to them, there are others who are going to avail of the opportunity and threaten the incumbents.

Quite clearly, the future will belong only to those organizations that are agile and nimble enough to grab the opportunities appearing on their horizon and are able to reimagine and restructure themselves in keeping with the requirements of time and place.

Leaders as Agile Jugglers

The organizational agility exhibited by corporations today adds certain new dimensions to leadership. It is not enough for leaders to be just agile—they are required to be agile jugglers. The complexity and versatility of modern corporations demands that leaders keep juggling their different priorities with ease, grace and agility. All of these priorities may carry their own urgency, and may need different sets of skills and expertise as well. Further, they need to be handled with the ease and grace of an expert juggler so as not to break the rhythm.

These priorities emanate from various sources. First, as organizations keep expanding their geographical footprints, crossing national boundaries and going global, they become susceptible to the business ecosystems of global markets. Second, today's businesses are becoming more and more complex as business houses pursue varying lines of businesses, each having its own specific challenges. Thus, along with their traditional businesses, entities such as the Tata Group, Reliance Industries, Godrej or Bajaj have also stepped into new-economy businesses such as insurance, telecom, organized retail and commercial finance. Each of these business lines has its own ecosystem, and demand and supply dimensions, besides threats and opportunities. This demands an understanding of the challenges specific to the sector and suitable responses. Leaders, therefore, not only need to be multiskilled, they also have to be agile and capable of juggling different priorities, using different skill sets and understanding.

In her book *The Leadership Spectrum: 6 Business Priorities That Get Results*, author Mary Burner Lippitt advocates a priority-based leadership framework that responds to the priorities of different life-cycle stages of an organization. She identifies six life-cycle stages of an organization—inception or rebirth, growth, stature, prime, maturity and renewal. According to her, each of these six stages requires a distinct business priority and leadership framework.

> The business priorities are: developing new products or services, gaining and satisfying customers, building an effective infrastructure, increasing efficiencies, developing a high performance culture, and positioning for the future. The correlating leadership framework— the Inventor, Catalyst, Developer, Performer, Protector, and Challenger priorities, respectively—shifts with the organization's life cycle.[59]

The idea is equally relevant to group corporations. As modern business houses pursue multiple business lines, it is only natural that different companies in the group are at different life-cycle stages. For example, within the Reliance Group of Industries, while their refinery at Jamnagar in Gujarat is at the maturity level, the PX Phase 2, commissioned in April 2017, is only at the start-up phase. At the same time, its telecom company, launched in 2016, is at the growth phase, while Reliance Retail is trying to get into the stature stage. Likewise, many other companies in the group are operating at different stages in their life cycle. It is only natural that the group's leader, Mukesh Ambani, keeps juggling his business priorities as he deals with the different businesses in his group. The situation is no different for other leaders in different business houses.

The need for juggling priorities also emanates from the volatility and ambiguity of the business environment, where each day brings with it fresh challenges.

Modern leaders, therefore, cannot find any comfort in

---

[59]Mary Burner Lippitt, *The Leadership Spectrum: 6 Business Priorities That Get Results*, Nicholas Brealey Publishing, 2002, p.xviii

the traditional leadership stereotypes; they have to be agile learners and, in turn, understand their business priorities, their co-workers and their business environment. They are required to make quality decisions using diverse skills while juggling multiple priorities on the ground. However, while juggling their priorities, they must never lose sight of the larger picture and the long-term priorities of the organizations.

8

The Champions of Diversity and Inclusion

Diversity is not about how we differ. Diversity is about embracing one another's uniqueness.

–OLA JOSEPH, AUTHOR AND MOTIVATIONAL SPEAKER

Cisco Systems, a leading provider of Internet protocol-based networking systems and equipment, faced a business challenge.[60] As a global business leader providing networking solutions, the company felt an urgent need to understand the demands of its diverse customer groups, including persons with disabilities (PwDs), with respect to using various communication networks. The company's response was to reflect the diversity of its customer groups in its workforce to understand and appreciate customer perspectives, and design and develop products that could help their diverse sets of customers connect, communicate and collaborate with one another.

The company partnered with NGOs such as Enable India and the Association of People with Disability to understand in depth the problems faced by PwDs, and diversify its workforce accordingly. Consequent to this, Cisco India recruited a number

---

[60]Pooja Shahani and Kate Vernon, 'Diversity & Inclusion: Building the Business Case-Stories From India', Communitybusiness.org, April 2014

of persons with disabilities in its various functions. They were hired as product inspectors and engineers, and entrusted with the task of testing and validating a range of assistive technology offered by Cisco. What the company experienced was something novel and invaluable. Not only did these persons offer the company real and first-hand insight into the design and development of products and technology, they were also helpful during product development. Among the many notable examples was one visually impaired employee who conducted tests on Cisco's WebEx platform and provided deep insights that were critical in improving its accessibility for visually impaired persons. Yet another example is of Cisco's IP phones, which have built-in computers and operate through a network. The team was facing serious challenges in making it PwD-friendly. Finally, with the help of its disabilities team, it was able to integrate new features, such as a hearing-aid compatibility, within the device.

This initiative of Cisco has helped it achieve many goals. First, the enhanced perspective of specific needs of the PwD segment, as well as first-hand feedback from its differently abled employees, helped the company renovate its products and bring it closer to the aspirations of its customers. Second, it helped the corporation reach out to new market segments with a competitive advantage and as a differentiated brand. Finally, the success of this initiative hugely served the cause of workforce diversity, changing employees' perception about the capabilities of PwDs and increasing the acceptance of PwDs in the mainstream.

Diversity and Inclusion: New Mantras for Success

The Cisco story reconfirms the established notion that whenever we see a great business story, we can see an equally great people story behind it. Under contemporary leaders, diversity and inclusion (D&I) is fast becoming the cornerstone of business strategy, with multiple objectives. It is not driven by a sense of social justice alone, as organizations are fast realizing that focus on minority groups such as women, PwDs, the LGBT community and people from diverse ethnicities broadens the talent pool. Within the workforce, diversity fosters creativity and innovation, while inclusion improves collaboration and reduces conflict. To top it all, it improves the brand image of an organization, making its products more acceptable to the wider customer segment.

What Constitutes Diversity?

A lot of different flowers make a bouquet.

–UNKNOWN

Workforce diversity is an idea that suggests that modern workplaces should have fair and equitable representation from different sections of society. The thought processes of modern civilization have evolved to a level today where stakeholders in a business organization are not limited to its promoters, employees and customers. As businesses have a give-and-take relationship within the society in which they operate, society itself is considered an important stakeholder. This realization gives rise to the moral justification of workplace diversity and fair and equitable opportunity for the different constituents of society.

In most studies, workforce diversity has been studied and analysed from the perspective of representation of women in the workforce. It is understandable as women constitute about 50 per cent of the population. However, going beyond the gender divide, diversity is a more inclusive concept that embraces other sub-sets of the population as well, e.g. nationality, ethnicity, colour, beliefs and religion. It broadly arises from the following two sources: Inherent diversity, which refers to demographic characteristics emanating from sex, race, colour and age, and acquired diversity, which arises from education, skills, culture, knowledge and experience.

Interestingly, there is a generational divide in the understanding of diversity. While earlier generations related to diversity only in terms of gender, colour and religion, those belonging to the millennial and Gen-Z generations include softer aspects such as values and beliefs too. Also, the practical implementation of the concept has varying implications depending upon the geography, culture and circumstances. For example, in the US, diversity includes women, the LGBT population, people of colour and different ethnicities in the workforce. In India, it relates, apart from including women and religion, to state social groups such as Scheduled Castes and Scheduled Tribes.

Drivers of Workforce Diversity

There are three important drivers for workforce diversity. First, leaders are driven by their own sense of fairness and justice arising out of their human and social consciousness as well as personal experiences. In an article titled 'Great Leaders Who Make the Mix Work', the authors cite the personal experience of Carlos Ghosn, CEO of Nissan Motor Company. Ghosn tells the story of his mother, which helped shaped his attitude and approach to diversity. She was a brilliant student and wanted to become a doctor. However, she had to give up her ambition because, with limited resources, boys in the family were prioritized for education while girls were expected to marry and settle down. Ghosn is quoted as saying, 'After hearing that story, I said I would never do anything to hurt someone based on segregation.' For Ghosn, gender parity is a personal cause.

'When I see that women do not have the same opportunities as men, it touches me in a personal way. I think it's some kind of refusal related to my sisters or to my daughters,' Ghosn states.[61]

Second, for the baby boomers and Gen-X, ideas such as diversity, inclusion and equal opportunities were acquired as desirable virtues, whereas for millennials and Gen-Z these values are part of their natural self, integrated into their personalities, an outcome of the social environment in which they were born and brought up. As the majority of employees and customers today consists of younger groups such as millennials and Gen-Z, they not only expect their institutions to support these causes, they also drive the attainment of these organizational goals. No wonder we find modern companies flaunting the tag 'We are an equal opportunity organization'.

Third, and most important, going beyond the horizons of righteousness and moral force, contemporary leaders realize that diversity opens up new opportunities for growth and expansion for their organizations. As Josh Bersin, the principal and founder of the HR research and consulting firm Bersin by Deloitte, says, 'Companies that embrace diversity and inclusion in all aspects of their business statistically outperform their peers.'[62]

In a study, published by *Harvard Business Review*, the author, David A. Thomas, showcases IBM's initiative towards achieving gender diversity and the diversity task-force initiative launched by its CEO, Louis V. Gerstner, in 1995.[63] The strategy saw the creation of eight task forces, with each focusing on a specific segment—such as women, Asians or LGBT—that became a

---

[61]Boris Groysberg and Katherine Connolly, 'Great Leaders Who Make the Mix Work', *Harvard Business Review*, September 2013

[62]Josh Bersin, 'Why Diversity And Inclusion Will Be A Top Priority For 2016', *Forbes*, 6 December 2015

[63]David A. Thomas, 'Diversity as Strategy', *Harvard Business Review*, September 2004

critical component of the company's HR strategy. Apart from broad-basing IBM's talent pool, this strategy brought about significant business results for the company. For example, the women's task force helped the company reach out to women-owned businesses and business partners in the US. According to this report, this initiative boosted IBM's revenue from this segment from $10 million in 1998 to $300 million in 2001.

Globalization has come up as one of the other drivers of diversity today. As organizations cross their national boundaries, they come face-to-face with varied sets of market dynamics, customer attributes, languages and cultures. They are also required to comply with a diverse set of local laws and regulations. It is, therefore, only natural that the workforce of a multinational organization should reflect the diversity needed to understand and cater to these multicultural markets.

A Social Cause That Makes Business Sense

Workplace diversity reflecting equal opportunity has become a social cause today, and organizations that reflect the diversity of their target markets and are attuned to the sensitivities of their customers are also loved by their customers. The long history of cause marketing is testimony to the fact that customers love and respond to a brand that is seen to be promoting a social cause. In India, Hindustan Unilever's campaign to link its detergent brand Surf Excel with the 'save water' cause earlier and more recently with the Swachh Bharat Abhiyan (Clean India Movement) is just one example of how customers respond favourably when a brand integrates the promotion of a social cause with the sale of its product. IBM offers another example of an organization that has extended the concept of diversity beyond its workforce and achieved a fair degree of supplier diversity. Today, its suppliers in the

US include minority-owned businesses, as well as businesses owned by the disabled. While supplies are still based on merit, the organization creates a level playing field for its suppliers.

Challenges: Diversity without Inclusion Is Ineffective

Diversity is being invited to the party.
Inclusion is being asked to dance.

—VERNA MYERS, DIVERSITY EXPERT

Often, diversity and inclusion are considered synonymous and used without distinction. However, they are not the same, as they represent different facets of workforce dynamics. Conceptually, diversity is about identifying, respecting, valuing and embracing the difference among humans and recognizing their identities and individualities. It is expressible in quantitative numbers by showing a numeric representation of different demographic groups within the workforce. Inclusion, on the other hand, is a qualitative issue and signifies how integrated the diverse groups are within the organizational system. It may be used to define the corporation's purpose or to collaborate and co-create to achieve the same. It is a step that follows diversity and aims to empower diverse groups within the workforce to harness the uniqueness of their skills, expertise and experiences to achieve organizational goals.

Diversity on its own doesn't lead to inclusion; inclusion has to be driven with a distinct and specific strategy. While organizations find it difficult to achieve workforce diversity, ensuring inclusion is often a challenge. It involves reaching out to the hearts of employees and instilling in them a sense of belonging. Therefore, leaders must not stop at ensuring diversity—they must undertake effective steps to make sure that the people who have been brought on board participate in the organization's actions wholeheartedly. The lack of a sense of belonging can happen to any employee irrespective of his or her gender, skin colour, background or position in the organizational hierarchy, and it could be counterproductive, rendering the entire D&I exercise futile.

Inclusion generates a sense of belonging, which is important for the well-being of the organizational entity. Research says that a sense of belonging is a basic human need; we are all hard-wired to desire belonging to someone, to our families, to our teams. An increased sense of belonging promotes emotional and psychological well-being and encourages performance. Therefore, D&I can become a productive exercise and provide competitive advantage to an organization only when different sub-sets of the workforce feel that they are loved, cared for and that their opinions count.

In spite of the fact that human societies today realize the importance of D&I, our progress in achieving these objectives has been facing roadblocks. Let's look at one of the major factors that impede the progress of D&I today—cognitive biases and prejudices.

Recent studies in cognitive psychology and behavioural economics tell us that our behaviour patterns are most often guided by our subconscious minds rather than our overt, conscious and rational choices. Our subconscious mind is the place where all our values, emotions, beliefs, preferences and prejudices are stored, and it is from here that our instant, instinctive and emotional responses are triggered in response to external stimulation. As a result, our thoughts and actions are often guided by our intuitive biases that impact our decision-making at the workplace as well.

Most of our biases and prejudices emanate from the following sources:

Assumed Stereotypes: As a result of our personal experience and emotions, quite often we develop implicit stereotypes, imparting specific characteristics to different demographic groups, even though they may not have any rational basis. For example, women could be perceived to be emotional and men to be better at networking. Likewise, PwDs could be seen as non-productive and taller persons taken to be more confident.

Partiality and Favouritism: People generally develop a sense of affiliation to their own groups, which could be based on class, religion or nationality. Their inclination to promote and prolong the interests of their own group could impact their decisions at the workplace. Sometimes, a person may favour his or her group also in expectation of a reciprocatory favour at a later time.

Comfort of Homogeneity: People draw a lot of comfort from the homogeneity of their respective groups arising out of similar thought processes, norms, customs and cultures. Familiarity with norms also leads to predictability of behaviour patterns within a group, which is comforting. Diversity, on the other hand, requires people to learn new behaviour patterns and accommodate unfamiliar points of view.

The prejudices that people develop as a result of these biases often impact decision-making within an organization. They form roadblocks to diversity, often coming in the way of recruiting or promoting people from minority groups representing a different ethnicity, gender, culture, religion, sexual orientation or language.

Minority Group Stereotypes: Who to Blame?

Women and other minority groups often contribute to the perpetuation of the prevalent stereotypes around them, and for understandable reasons. Given the chance, women are often not as forthcoming as men in their acceptance of a leadership opportunity or a new opportunity needing relocation. In such situations, while men are usually ready to grab the opportunity and even do the required networking to ensure that it happens, a woman might be hesitant, thinking, 'Can I handle this?' or 'Let me check with my family'. The reasons are not far to seek. While men look at their jobs as their primary responsibility, a woman's priorities, apart from her job, include issues such as family, children and social causes. These factors demand their time and impact their mobility too.

Why do women not assert themselves and demand their rightful positions in organizations? Sheryl Sandberg, the chief operating officer of Facebook and founder of Lean In, a global community dedicated to helping women, says it is because women get mixed messages about their careers.

> Think of a career like a marathon: long, gruelling, ultimately rewarding. What voices do the men hear from the beginning? 'You've got this. Keep going. Great race ahead of you.' What do the women hear from day one out of college? 'You sure you want to run? Marathon's really long. You're probably not going to want to finish. Don't you want kids one day?' The voices for men get stronger, 'Yes, go. You've got this.' The voices for women can get openly hostile. 'Are you sure you should be running when your kids need you at home?'[64]

The issue doesn't stop here—it is something deep and intrinsic as well. Though not scientifically proven, leadership experts could vouch for some essential differences between the

---

[64]Joanna Barsh, 'Facebook's Sheryl Sandberg: "No one can have it all"', *McKinsey Quarterly*, April 2013

leadership styles of men and women. While men tend to be aggressive and focus on networking and career advancement, women prefer to be more collaborative, open to listening and relationship-oriented. Given a task, women usually focus on completing the job at hand rather than vie for being in the spotlight like men.

Women are not alone in their lack of aggression and reticence about their accomplishments or career advancement goals. There are other minority groups, too, that are not so vocal about their ambitions and aspirations, and hence not perceived to be leadership material. In reality, their reticence might arise out of certain other reasons and circumstances. Minority professionals in the US, for example, don't like to talk about the excellent leadership work being done by them within their communities, because religion and ethnicity are big taboos in corporate circles. Their reluctance to network might also arise from their instinct to hide their minority identity so as to avoid creating an impression that they got the job not on merit but on account of affirmative action.

New-Age Champions of D&I

In these times of uncertainty and ambiguity, organizations that do well are the ones that think differently, learn differently and act differently. Driven by this realization, contemporary leaders have lifted D&I from the HR manager's desk and made it part of their own agenda. With renewed focus from the top, D&I has thus acquired some new dimensions as well. The idea has moved beyond the realm of gender and other demographic diversities and now includes issues such as diversity of thought and removal of corporate biases. The approach towards inclusion is not just to tinker with stray ideas such as giving maternity benefits to female employees but to provide a pleasant employee experience by aiming at individual wellness and work-life balance. In terms of implementation strategy, it has moved from training, education and sensitization to the executive key result areas (KRAs) and accountability for results. The approach is to counter prevalent biases and create an environment through managerial and technological interventions, where the cognitive biases of managers do not adversely impact the hiring processes.

In its fifth annual Global Human Capital Trends report,[65] Deloitte beautifully summed up this new perspective on D&I, highlighting the differences between the old and the new approaches.

D&I: Old Rules Vs New Rules

Old rules	New rules
Diversity is considered a reporting goal driven by compliance and brand priorities.	Diversity & inclusion is a CEO-level priority and considered important throughout all levels of management.
Work-life balance is considered a challenge for employees to manage, with some support from the organization.	Work-life balance, family and individual wellness are all considered part of the total employee experience.
Companies measure diversity through the demographic profile of designated groups defined by attributes such as gender, race, nationality and age.	Companies measure inclusion, diversity and lack of bias in all recruitment, promotion, pay and other talent practices.

---

[65]'Rewriting the rules for the digital age', 2017 Deloitte Global Human Capital Trends, Deloitte University Press

Diversity is defined by gender, race and demographic differences.	Diversity is defined in a broader context, including concepts of 'diversity of thought', also addressing people with autism and other cognitive differences.
Leaders are promoted on 'merit' and experience.	'Merit' is unpacked to identify built-in biases; leaders are promoted on their ability to lead inclusively.
Diversity & inclusion is a programme of education, training and discussion.	Diversity & inclusion goes beyond education to focus on debiasing business processes and holding leaders accountable for inclusive behaviour.
Companies regularly report progress on diversity measures.	Companies hold managers accountable for creating an inclusive culture, using metrics to compare them against each other.

Source: Deloitte University Press

Being an Inclusive Leader

The process of ensuring D&I in the workforce calls for a new set of skills—experiential learning, continual improvements, transparency, accountability and a data-driven approach. It requires organizations to undertake some decisive strategies and exhibit some definitive attributes, as discussed below.

Commitment and Courage: Quite often, D&I initiatives face rough weather owing to resistance from the larger group of employees, who draw psychological comfort from the homogeneity of their teams. Added to this are the widespread biases prevailing about minority groups with respect to their performance, knowledge and skills. Inclusion of women, for example, could be resisted not only by the peer groups but by managers as well, owing to the prevailing perception about women employees' mobility, readiness to work long hours or prolonged absence during maternity. Similar perceptions may prevail in larger groups about other minority groups in different geographies, based on religion, sexual orientation and skin colour.

Even in the face of resistance to change, organizations that are committed to the cause show the determination to carry forward their agenda.

Let us take, for example, the case of women in the workforce. In a country like India, not even half its population of women join the organized workforce after finishing their formal education. Further, even those who take up jobs are often discriminated against and lose out on their career prospects because of issues like maternity, childcare, parental care, long travel times, etc. In such a situation, the ICICI Group in India has shown how certain unconventional decisions to encourage and support women to overcome their personal challenges in pursuing their career prospects can lead to greater participation of women in the workforce and benefit the organization. For example, their initiative iWork@home, launched in 2016, enables and facilitates female employees across hierarchies to work from home for up to one year. Another initiative aimed at female managers with children of up to three years of age, provides for the travel and stay of the child and a caretaker or family member.

The result of such initiatives towards empowerment of women employees, taken by the group over a period of time, has been quite impressive. According to a *Forbes India* report,[66] women employees account for 30 per cent of the

---

[66]Shruti Venkatesh, 'ICICI Bank takes two steps to foster women's career goals', *Forbes*, 7 March 2016

ICICI bank's total workforce of 73,000. Going further, the larger participation of women in the workforce has seen women getting into leadership positions at the bank, which has become a leadership factory not only for its group companies but for the Indian financial service sector as well.

Breaking Barriers: The leadership of Goldman Sachs offers an example of how a difficult D&I agenda can be carried forward successfully through proper commitment, communication and sensitization of the workforce. Pursuing its commitment to promoting equal opportunities for the LGBT community, Goldman Sachs has worked for years with organizations such as Community Business, Stonewall and others supporting the LGBT cause. Further, it has systematically thought through the business case, taken inputs from other successful organizations, sensitized its employees and involved its senior leadership to champion the cause. In Europe, the Middle East and Africa (EMEA), its senior diversity council works in close coordination with the global talent development team to maintain the diversity in the leadership pipeline. The MD Ally programme provides the needed support and guidance to the community in various ways.

The company's LGBT network in India, too, promotes an environment that facilitates, welcomes and supports LGBT professionals, and encourages them to contribute their best to the organization. With a dedicated website, periodic newsletters and regular hosting of LGBT-related events, the network has not only attracted over 300 LGBT professionals, it has also generated a lot of awareness and sensitization within the workforce about this minority group. In 2013 the company launched another initiative, Beyond Barriers: Out and Proud. This new platform provided that any employee could join a one-hour anonymous call, chaired by the heads of the LGBT network and representatives of the Office of Global Leadership and Diversity. Based on the feedback from the call sessions, the company started the practice of making short presentations on the need to eliminate biases about the LGBT community and how to support these professionals in contributing to the organizational mission.

The business case of this initiative has been quite obvious. While Indian society is yet to accept the LGBT community within its fold, through its initiative, Goldman Sachs has a wider access to the talent pool and facilitates a higher level of employee engagement and performance. The icing on the cake is the differentiated brand image that it has been able to develop in the financial services industry, where it is considered to be an employer of choice.

Minimizing Biases

Modern organizations set up an institutional mechanism to minimize biases. Some of the strategies that can be adopted towards this end are discussed below.

Training and Sensitization: Education, training and sensitization are the age-old methods of influencing human behaviour. Although D&I didn't figure on the training agenda earlier, considering its critical importance in today's scenario, it now forms the core of employee-training programmes. By quoting trustworthy voices from within and without the organization, sharing success stories of diversity and busting popular stereotypes about minority groups, employees are led to question their own notions and develop a new perspective on the issue. Fostering empathy among employees and making them role-play representing minority groups also goes a long way in sensitizing employees and making them feel where the shoe pinches.

Technological Interventions: Technological interventions come in handy when preventing human biases in critical processes such as recruitment, promotions, succession planning or positioning people for leadership roles. Analytics and data tools today can decipher patterns and indicate possible biases in recruitment and promotions effected by the organization. Successful companies today have been able to reduce managerial biases using tools such as Entelo, Hire View and Success Factors, which can identify and dissect managerial patterns in recruitment.

Process Interventions: Changing operational processes and monitoring them closely is yet another method adopted by companies to check bias in decision-making. For example, there are companies that mask names and other personal details in candidates' resumes while carrying out the recruitment process. There are yet others that have made the selection and recruitment processes data-based and automated to reduce the role of human biases.

Accountability for Results: One of the key drivers of diversity in modern organizations is different functions across the organization having diversity targets on their agenda, which are specific and measurable. For example, in 2017, when the Tata Group decided to chalk out its diversity roadmap up to 2020, it decided to have 25 per cent representation from minority groups. Out of this, while women would account for 20 per cent, the rest would come from the LGBT community.

While executives are empowered to carry forward the D&I mission, accountability for performance on this score is also fixed by integrating the D&I targets with the performance review and compensation packages of executives.

Appointing D&I Champions: Organizations promoting D&I have found it useful to position D&I champions in different functions within the organization. They become the role models and conscience keepers of the organization in matters of diversity. These diversity champions could head committees comprising of employees belonging to specific minority groups. The role of these committees could be to identify specific challenges faced by these groups and highlight them before the larger group in an effort to generate awareness and sensitivity, and also to suggest solutions to these.

Building a Strong Business Case for Diversity: There is a strong business case for organizations to reap good dividends by encouraging diversity at the workplace and ensuring that employees develop a sense of belonging to the institution. Rather than telling this to employees at a theoretical level, they can make it a demonstrated case of organizational effectiveness. This makes it easier for the mainstream workforce to accept diversity and embrace inclusion.

Standard Chartered India did exactly this by showcasing examples of how diversity could be utilized to solve the pressing business problems of an organization. The bank had been experiencing a high attrition rate of 25 per cent among its frontline employees dealing with telesales. In 2009, conscious of the fact that PwDs were loyal and engaged employees, it decided to diversify its talent pool to include the recruitment of persons with disabilities. In consultation with a charitable trust, EnAble India and the National Association for the Blind (NAB), the bank tried to figure out the types of jobs visually impaired persons could perform. Starting with a pilot of three employees entrusted with making 'welcome calls' to new customers, in 2010 the bank went on to recruit ten visually impaired persons as full-time employees and placed them as telecallers for selling its financial services products. It further raised the number of hires for this segment to twenty-seven employees working in different functions.

To support this initiative, the bank also took a few other steps. With the help of NAB, it organized programmes and prepared training modules to train and sensitize its other employees on working and collaborating with visually impaired persons. To support its visually impaired employees, it provided them software applications such as JAWS—Job Access with Speech. The bank went on to make the workplace environment friendly for them by installing talking ATMs, providing special chairs with instructions in Braille at workstations and accessible transport facilities.

This diversity initiative of the bank paid rich dividends. While the attrition rate in frontline sales was extraordinarily high, the group of visually impaired persons had a 90 per cent retention over a three-year period. The productivity of this team has been on a rise. What is a bonus for the bank is that it also received awards, honours and recognition as a brand with a difference, committed to hiring persons with disabilities.[67]

Facilitating Collaboration: Employees feel included in the team if their voices are heard, their insights are respected and their expertise valued. When their self-respect is protected by the organization, they contribute to the organizational mission wholeheartedly. Translating this strategy into action at the workplace may mean creating mixed teams with representation of minority professionals based on their experience, skill and expertise. The team leaders have to ensure that the participation of minority professionals is encouraged and recognized. This may involve deep listening to the opinions coming from minority professionals, asking follow-up questions and allocating them responsibilities, besides recognizing and rewarding

---

[67]Pooja Shahani and Kate Vernon, 'Diversity & Inclusion: Building the Business Case - Stories From India', Communitybusiness.org, April 2014

their performance. The entire idea is to make the minority professionals feel that they and their opinions are as welcome and valued as those of the dominant groups within the system.

Promoting the Four R's of Inclusion: The critical tools in the hands of leaders for creating an environment of collaboration are the four R's of Inclusion: respect, recognition, responsiveness and responsibility. These attributes are not unidirectional— they need to flow in all directions, from leaders to followers, from followers to leaders, and among followers themselves. As leaders have a critical role in driving organizational strategies and culture, they are also required to ensure that these four R's of inclusion are followed by everyone in the institution.

The inclusion-strategy of IBM launched in the late 1990s offers a unique example of such an initiative. Under its CEO Louis V. Gerstner, IBM created eight task forces, each focused on a minority group, such as women, LGBT, blacks, Asians etc. Each group was assigned the task of unearthing and recognizing the uniqueness of the group as well as to uncover its perceived threats, challenges and aspirations. This was a deliberate attempt to highlight the issues facing the group and bring it to the notice of the larger group of employees for their understanding and appreciation.

In this exercise, each group was assigned a senior executive as its sponsor, whose role was to understand the concerns, challenges and aspirations of the group and give it a voice before the senior management. The sponsors were assigned in a manner that could lead to synergy in operations as well as support to the groups in their function. For example, the senior VP of research and development was assigned the PwD task force, in the hope that he would get first-hand knowledge of the issues facing this segment of the population—an insight that could help IBM's product innovations for its target groups.

In the same manner, the global VP of sales and marketing was made the sponsor of the women's group in the expectation that it would help women develop new markets for women-owned businesses.

Collaborations of this kind not only brought about greater understanding among different employee groups, it also helped IBM employees accept and appreciate the differences among them. The business outcome of this initiative was encouraging. The professional successes achieved by these groups as a result of the enterprise-wide collaboration further enhanced the image and reputation of different groups, bringing all of them closer to one another and developing a sense of belonging to the institution.[68]

In pursuing their D&I agenda, leaders who act out of courage and conviction make a real difference to society. When ABB India, an engineering company, decided to recruit female engineers, it opened up new frontiers for women in an industry that had so far been considered an exclusively male domain. Likewise, the decision of Thomson Reuters India to recruit persons with disabilities into their knowledge-intensive domain gave renewed confidence to the PwD segment about their own worth and importance. These employees with disabilities include those who are visually, speech- and hearing-impaired, and yet are able to work in functions such as market analysis, accounting, data entry and recruitment. Initiatives such as these have obviously sent strong messages to the society at large to shun its apprehensions about the capabilities of women and PwDs in performing difficult and complex tasks, inculcate diversity and create inclusive workplaces for the greater good of its members.

---

[68]David A. Thomas, 'Diversity as Strategy', *Harvard Business Review*, September 2004

9

The Inventors of the Future

When Alexander the Great visited Diogenes and asked
whether he could do anything for the famed teacher,
Diogenes replied: 'Only stand out of my light.' Perhaps
someday we shall know how to heighten creativity. Until
then, one of the best things we can do for creative men and
women is to stand out of their light.

—JOHN W. GARDNER, FOUNDER OF COMMON CAUSE
AND INDEPENDENT SECTOR

'We didn't do anything wrong, but somehow, we lost,' said Stephen Elop, Nokia CEO, while announcing its takeover by Microsoft.

Indeed, Nokia didn't seem to have done anything wrong. It was a great company, a leader in the global market of smartphones. Even though it didn't do anything wrong, the world around it changed, and changed too fast. As the smartphone market was growing rapidly, the game was changing from a simple battle of handsets to a full-fledged war between mobile ecosystems, involving hardware, software, mobile applications and customer service. Nokia couldn't anticipate the change—it missed out on the learning, and lost the battle. As a consequence, it not only lost the opportunity to make it big in the smartphone market, it lost the battle for survival as well.

The story of another smartphone giant, BlackBerry, is no different. Who could have anticipated that this iconic brand, which was selling over 50 million phones per year until 2011, would have to bow out of the market and be sold out to another company? BlackBerry, too, failed to see the future. It had simply fallen in love with its QWERTY keyboard, which was once the favourite of the corporate world for the convenience it offered in sending mails and messages. But due to lack of foresight and vision, it failed to see that the future of smartphones was going to be determined not by corporate clients but by the huge mass of consumers across the globe. It did try to stage a comeback with touchscreens in its BlackBerry 10 model, but it was too late. By the time its romance with QWERTY keyboards ended, the world had already been taken over by Apple and Android devices.

The Nokia and BlackBerry stories provide an important message for leaders today: Just because you created the empire, don't think you'll remain the emperor forever. You can't rest on your laurels of yesterday and hope to survive in the market; you need to continue anticipating the market trends and keep inventing the future.

As the old saying goes:

Businesses which change after the change will **Survive.**
Businesses which change with the change will **Succeed.**
Businesses which cause the change will **Lead.**

The doyen of innovations Steve Jobs hit the nail on the head when he said, 'Innovation distinguishes between a leader and a follower.'

On the Crossroads of Change

Modern corporations are at a crossroads today. In the industrial economy of earlier times, organizations could pursue the goal of zero defects by building strong hierarchies, achieving process standardization and eliminating risks. A well-conceived strategy with efficient implementation would not only ensure that the uncertainties in the ecosystem were eliminated to a great extent, it would also keep the company ahead of its competitors.

However, that was possible only so long as the business environment was relatively stable and predictable. In today's turbulent times, business landscapes are continuously getting reshaped by an accelerating pace of technological advancements, demographic shifts, environmental changes, economic developments and geopolitical adjustments. Factors such as social media, big data, advanced analytics and artificial intelligence are continuously redefining the way organizations communicate with their customers, analyse and understand their markets, transact their businesses and respond to competition. It is therefore only natural that existing business models, product lines and operational processes are facing serious challenges, both internally and externally. Not only is technology proving to be a constant disrupter, workforce disposition and workplace dynamics, too, are undergoing drastic transformations.

Are twenty-first-century leaders equipped to face the continuous ongoing disruptions? We find a lot of them on the crossroads, unsure of the road to take. Not surprisingly, there are a lot of companies gasping for breath and quite a few losing the battle for survival altogether. To retain the competitive advantage of their organization, leaders of today have to be more creative in their approach, keep an eye on the future, anticipate market trends and customer aspirations, and introduce products and services to serve customer needs and create value for all stakeholders. To lead and excel in the face of constant disruptions, they need to come up with a compelling and transformative vision to keep their teams inspired and customers hooked.

There is no dearth of visionary leaders today who have looked at the past, analysed the present and invented the future. They have ushered in some of the finest innovations around existing products and services by reimagining the established operating models and resculpting customer offerings in a manner inconceivable and unthinkable a decade earlier. We have Uber, the largest provider of passenger taxi services in the world, with no fleet of its own. We have Airbnb, the world's largest accommodation provider owning no real estate. Then we have Alibaba, the world's most valuable retailer, with no inventory at all. Facebook, too, stands out in the list as the most popular media company which doesn't create any content of its own. These are examples of products and services created by some of today's highly innovative business leaders, who have mesmerized the world. But there are millions of others around the world whose innovations may not be as life-changing as those of Travis Kalanick (Uber), Mark Zuckerberg (Facebook) or Jack Ma (Alibaba), but their creativity and innovation are making a difference to their businesses and society at large.

Pursuing Excellence Instead of Perfection

Serial innovation is the key to staying competitive and retaining market leadership today, as the rules of the game have changed. We are living in an age of constant innovations and disruptions. Hence, even though a company might come up with a ground-breaking innovative product or service, this may not be enough to keep its market leadership for long. Being in competition today is like riding a tiger—you may get down at the cost of your own peril. The reasons are obvious. In our days of competitive technologies, it doesn't take much time for a product to be copied and replicated in the market. Hence, even after introducing ground-breaking innovations, organizations need to follow them up with constant renovations—incremental innovations that add value to the products and services. For the simple reason that they never know where their next competitor is going to come from. In the more stable economies of earlier days, you could keep your competition always in focus, understand what new things they were working on and prepare yourself accordingly. But in our knowledge-driven economy today, we may suddenly have a start-up coming from nowhere and springing a nasty surprise on us, disrupting our business. The impact of this new reality of business is here for all of us to see. Businesses no longer aim for perfection today while carrying out innovations—they aim for excellence. Perfection obviously takes more time, and you can be sure that by the time you introduce a perfect product in the market, from somewhere around the world someone else will bring in a not-so-perfect product which could rob your product of its novelty and appeal. The Apple-Samsung battles are a case in point.

The strategy, therefore, has to be to bring in excellence through innovation—something better than what is currently on offer to the customers. So, gone are the days when a Sony Corporation would introduce a unique product to the market and reap the benefits for years before coming up with another distinctive product. Product life cycles have become shorter and companies indulge in self-cannibalization of their own products by introducing their enhanced versions to stay ahead in the competitive race. This approach is well reflected in the Apple strategy of launching one unique product and following it up with incremental innovations and improvements. The great saga of Apple iPad tablets and iPhones and their multiple versions is nothing but an original innovation being followed up with incremental renovation, making the latest one better than the previous ones.

Quite clearly, creativity and innovation provide the competitive advantage to organizations in today's turbulent times. In earlier days, organizations were able to achieve success and fulfilment by focusing on management tools such as structure, strategy, technology and organizational culture. The Japanese auto manufacturers such as Toyota and Honda are classic examples of how companies could become global leaders by focusing on these management tools. However, in our brave new world today, these conventional tools alone prove to be inadequate for organizational success. Creativity and innovation are the additional critical tools for staying ahead of competition and delivering stakeholder values. Therefore, new-age leaders are required to have high innovation quotients. Companies ignoring this will be doing so at the cost of their own success and survival.

Creating Value through Leadership

Across all ages in the evolution cycle of human civilization, leadership has remained a source of competitive advantage to the organization. It has always stood out as the invaluable string that passes through all the organizational nuggets, such as strategy, culture and technology.

Hence, it is not surprising to observe that organizations that remain vibrant and perform well under a dynamic leader become sluggish and slip into a zone of non-performance when a weak leader takes over. The story of the Indo-Japanese joint venture Maruti Suzuki India Ltd is a case in point. It was under its iconic leader, R.C. Bhargava, that, braving challenging circumstances, this small-car manufacturer started fulfilling the dreams of an average Indian to own a car. Its first indigenous production, Maruti 800, in 1983 caught the attention of the common man, who till then was forced to choose between the tank-like Ambassador and the unappealing Premier Padmini. Soon, Maruti became the dream car of Indians, and the company became the leading auto manufacturer in India, with 81.25 per cent market share in 1997. But as Bhargava retired in 1997, his successor found it difficult to maintain the tempo. Even in the face of increasing competition from the entry of Korean cars in the market, the company didn't come up with new models to beat the competition. Consequently, it rapidly lost market share. The leader at the helm was often charged with incompetence, and the Japanese partner found it difficult to work with him. However, with Bhargava back at the helm in his second stint, the institutional dynamism was back in motion. Today the company is competing in the Indian market with global brands from Japan, South Korea and the US, and still commands 51 per cent of the passenger car market. What is more, the Indian subsidiary has become the hub of production, sales and product development in the emerging markets for its Japanese partner.

The way leadership impacts organizational dynamism, it impacts creativity and innovation too. No innovation can succeed unless the leader is fully committed to it. It is primarily the leadership team that sets the direction and drives the culture within the organization.

In this background, it is good to see contemporary leaders as innovators of the future. They define and articulate their innovation strategies to facilitate their teams to buy into the same. They also emphasize how strategy could boost and support the organization's overall vision. They develop their innovation priorities and do not hesitate in making trade-offs that could support their overall business strategies.

As innovators, modern leaders essentially keep moving between order and chaos. While they usher in chaos within an established order, with their disruptive innovations, they also develop a new order out of the chaos by deciphering a meaning and pattern from the complexities and ambiguities prevailing in the environment and innovating products and solutions on the back of it.

Innovations for Social Good

Driving innovations cannot be an end in itself for organizations; innovations must add value to society and stakeholders at large. We are in an age wherein corporations are judged not only on the basis of their revenues and profits, but also in the context of whether they are adding value to the larger objectives of society. Even an excellent innovation that in any way adversely impacts dominant social values, such as environmental protection and conservation, equality, inclusion or fairness, is going to face backlash from customers. In India, the global brand Uber, which revolutionized private transport services, initially faced a lot of customer ire as the drivers registered with the company were often seen involved in crimes against women. Likewise, its Indian counterpart, Ola, is facing resentment for its practice of introducing what is perceived to be inordinately high surge pricing during peak hours.

In an interview, David J. Haines, CEO of Grohe, the market leader in sanitaryware, says that while enhancing customer experience, they do realize that they have a responsibility—in fact, an obligation—to conserve water, which has become the world's most scarce resource now. According to him,

> We invest an awful lot of money, time, and effort into finding innovative showering solutions where the consumer gets the same shower experience using 20, 30, 40 percent less water. Nothing is more environmentally unfriendly than a leaking tap: we invest in our cartridges

to make sure that even 20 to 30 years after you've put in the tap, it doesn't leak.[69]

Innovative Leaders Create the Future

Innovative leaders don't just see the future, they summon it, braving all the challenges—law, regulations, constraints and incumbents. In the 1990s, when Sunil Mittal pioneered the mobile telephony revolution in India, the import of mobile phones was not permitted. But his company Bharati Airtel overcame the problem by importing the parts and assembling them in India. Over the years, Bharti Airtel emerged as the biggest mobile-phone service provider in India. There are numerous similar tales of ardent entrepreneurs who have defied the norms and brought about change and transformation in society.

With their penchant for creativity, new-age leaders make innovation part of their organization's DNA. They transform the culture of the organization and make it innovative as well. The example of Jack Welch is a case in point. He was the leader who instilled the culture of innovation in General Electric and transformed it into a successful and innovative organization. The story of K.V. Kamath, the MD and CEO of ICICI Bank Ltd, is yet another example that shows how a leader with a high-innovation quotient can not only catapult his company into the leadership position but also transform the entire industry itself.

---

[69]'How Grohe finds growth through innovation', McKinsey & Company, August 2015

The Visionary Banker Who Summoned the Future

There are leaders who shine when they are at the helm and fade away as they step out. But there are a few who dream big and think of changing the world. They dream with their eyes open, nurture their dreams, give them wings and make them fly. They are the ones who bring about transformation in society.

K.V. Kamath, the visionary banker and the former MD of India's leading private-sector bank, ICICI Bank Ltd, is one such person who made a tremendous difference not only to his company, but to the banking industry and society as well. In the late 1990s, when the Indian economy was still in the process of opening up post the economic liberalization of 1991, he saw opportunities in India's banking space that none of his contemporaries could. He reimagined the banking business and revolutionized retail banking and consumer finance. Recognizing the growing income and the rising aspirations of the Indian middle class, under his leadership, the bank reshaped its product portfolio and initiated different lines of businesses, like home finance, car finance and securities trading.

As the entire consumer finance business was at a nascent stage in the country, there were uncertainties and ambiguities in the environment. There was no previous experience, there were no past guidelines. People had to grope in the dark to find their way, stumble and learn from experience. Under such circumstances, Kamath developed a vision as to what the consumer finance business was going to look like in the near future. In line with his vision, he brought about structural changes and leadership alignments within the organization to ensure that his vision was practically implemented on the ground. The result is for all of us to see—the consumer finance business in India stands completely revolutionized.

Kamath was simultaneously fighting on another frontier: He had a vision to transform retail banking in India as well. In order to get an edge in this segment, he had to compete with the expansive branch network of public-sector banks and foreign banks operating in India. As building up a countrywide branch network was not a viable option, he took recourse to technology and set up a pan-India network of ATMs, which could facilitate basic day-to-day banking transactions. This was one experiment that changed the face of retail banking in India, facilitating ease of banking as well as giving customers an experience hitherto unknown to them.

Kamath had been quick to recognize the business opportunities in the environment and ready to seize them as well. Anticipating the upsurge in Internet usage, ICICI went online in 1997, thereby becoming the first financial institution in India to offer online services. Later, it also launched its online platform for equity trading as well as dealing in mutual funds and other financial securities.

History will undoubtedly remember Kamath as an iconic leader who transformed a nondescript ICICI into a dynamic and innovative business house, changing the face of banking in India. His stint in the ICICI Group reveals some of his dominant characteristics. He was an institution builder. He has not only been an agile leader ready to spot business opportunities and seize them in time, he has also been the one who has been able to inject the spirit of creativity and innovation into the DNA of all his group companies. It is a compliment to him that ICICI Bank and all its subsidiaries have been at the forefront of innovation and command leadership positions in their respective business domains, be it in banking or insurance or home finance or asset management.

Fostering an Organizational Culture for Innovation

Innovations do not happen by accident. Nor do creative organizations come up by chance. They are nurtured and developed by creating a culture of innovation within the organization. The critical role of leadership in this is to ensure that the innovation hubs within the organization get the freedom to be creative; that they are not chained by bureaucratic structures and processes; and that they are encouraged to take risks in an environment of uncertainties and ambiguities, rather than looking to the hierarchies for direction. Successful leaders create the necessary environment to ensure that from concept to creation, there is a collective ownership of the initiative. They recognize that their challenge is to gather a diverse set of people with varied skills and experiences, who should be able to develop and nurture the creative ideas into actual deliverables for the customers and be able to say to themselves, 'Wow, we brought this innovation!' To put it in Scottish novelist John Buchan's words, 'The task of leadership is not to put greatness into people, but to elicit it, for the greatness is there already.'

For sustaining a culture of innovation, leaders have to ensure that no one blocks the light for their creative geniuses. A new idea is required to be protected like a sapling, because it is common for people to write it off in the first instance simply because they find it difficult to divorce their existing beliefs and accept new ones. If something has worked for them in the past, they continue to believe that it will work even when the circumstances have changed. As Roger von Oech, American author, speaker and toymaker, puts it, 'It's easy to come up with new ideas; the hard part is letting go of what worked for you two years ago, but will soon be out of date.'

The history of human civilization shows that it has not been possible for even some of the greatest men to embrace new ideas and smell the success around the corner. Just consider the following examples:

New Ideas Take Time to Sink in[70]

- *The horse is here to stay, the automobile is only a novelty, a fad.*
  −President of Michigan Savings Bank, 1903, advising Henry Ford's attorney to not invest in Ford Motor Company. He did anyway and parlayed $5,000 into $12,500,000.
- *I think there is a world market for about five computers.*
  −Thomas J. Watson, Chairman, IBM, 1943
- *That's an amazing invention, but who would ever want to use one of them?*
  -US President Rutherford B. Hayes, participating in a trial telephone conversation between Washington and Philadelphia, 1876
- *Television won't be able to hold on to any market it captures after the first six months. People will soon get tired of staring at a box every night.*
  -Darryl F. Zanuck, Head of 20th Century Fox, 1946

To take the culture of innovation to the next level, new-age leaders go beyond the baseline and pursue a set of clear-cut strategies to foster an environment where diverse ideas bloom, and creativity and innovations flourish.

Diversity in Human Capital: Recruitment in organizations generally follow the pattern of merit, whereby higher the merit, greater the chances of selection. This practice could be good for administrative and managerial functions, but may not be

---

[70]The Office of Formation and Discipleship, The Roman Catholic Archdiocese of Atlanta

ideal for encouraging creativity. Merit-based selections can't necessarily ensure that the selected personnel will bring in any diversity in thinking and approach, so critical for creativity. Innovation requires new ways of looking at a problem and finding novel solutions for the same. But in an organization, if everyone keeps thinking alike, the stream of new ideas will get choked. As Walter Lippman, the American writer, reporter and political commentator, puts it, 'When all think alike, then no one is thinking.' Einstein, too, echoes the same when he says, 'If you always do what you always did, you will always get what you always got.'

For promoting creativity and innovation, organizations need a constant flow of new ideas and unconventional thinking. Hence innovation-oriented leaders always make conscious efforts to introduce diversity within the organization in terms of age, sex and ethnicity, as well as psychological types. They go beyond their wish list and devise clear-cut strategies with defined targets to create a think tank where new ideas flow and the organization is benefited by its diverse-thinking, preferences, expertise and experiences coming from people with different backgrounds. For example, a few years ago, when Severin Schwan, CEO of the Roche Group, a highly innovative company in the domain of pharmaceuticals, looked at diversity within his organization, he found a very low representation of women in the leadership of the group. The group set up a goal of increasing the representation of women in the top 400 leadership positions from 13 per cent to 20 per cent. Within five years, they were able to take it to 23 per cent. Likewise, while expanding into emerging markets, the company decided to increase the number of leaders from these markets by 30 per cent. This inclusion of leaders from emerging markets helped the company understand local markets, communities and cultures in a much better way.

Challenging the Status Quo: Any advancement in human history was done by challenging the status quo. History tells us how Chrysler Corporation, once known for its engineering innovations, had to bow out of the market; or Polaroid, once a market leader in instant film and cameras, now looks like a shadow of its former self because it refused to embrace change. The story of The Eastman Kodak Company is yet another example showing how suicidal it can be to not open the door when opportunity comes knocking. The company that had maintained a dominant position in photographic films during most of the twentieth century had seen the emerging trend of photo films giving way to digital photography. But it was slow to embrace the new technology, as it required moving the focus away from photographic films, which was its main revenue grosser. Its sluggishness in adapting to the emerging technology, saw this highly profitable company struggle financially in the late 1990s. Finally, in January 2012, the unfortunate Kodak Moment came, when it had to file for Chapter 11 bankruptcy protection in the United States District Court for the Southern District of New York. It was only in September 2013 that the company came out of bankruptcy after exiting several businesses and selling most of its patents to other companies to settle its liabilities.

Confronting the status quo is, however, not an easy task. First, it involves courage to leave the known and embrace the unknown; to discard something that was working and paying dividends, and instead, exploring something that is neither tested nor tried. Secondly, confronting the status quo does involve risk—of antagonizing stakeholders and inviting the risk of failure.

However, leaders look at change as an opportunity and not as a threat. In spite of all the odds, they confront the status quo in a bid to create a new market offering, enhance customer experience and edge past competition. They nurture creativity, promote innovation and strive to ensure that this softer side of corporate culture is hard-coded into the organizational DNA through diversity, teamwork and a spirit of risk-taking.

Leveraging Shared Vision: According to common perception, vision is developed by a leader who shares it with his team. Effectively, it denotes that in an organization, ideas percolate from the top to the bottom. This was more or less true in the command-and-control style of leadership of the industrial economy, where leaders were expected to do the thinking and employees were required to simply follow the command and deliver. Ford reflects this perspective when he says, 'If I had asked people what they wanted, they would have said faster horses.'

However, in complex and connected organizations, success and failure are never individual attributes—they are always a team performance. Before an idea becomes an innovation, it has to be hatched and nurtured by a host of individuals managing diverse functions and holding relevant expertise. Keeping this in mind, leaders need to create a shared ownership of ideas as well as shared responsibility for its success or failure. This not only promotes the willing participation of teams in the innovation process, it also enhances employee engagement, as they feel empowered. It further adds to the employees' self-esteem, as they perceive themselves contributing significantly to the organizational purpose. Thus, an environment of distributed leadership with enthused and empowered employees is the ideal situation where innovation and creativity can flourish.

Removing Fear of Failure: In normal life we are taught to see success and failure as opposite ends of the spectrum. But in the journey to any successful innovation, the two always travel together as companions. There has hardly been any innovation that has not been preceded by failures. Most of the times, ideas that lead to great innovations are so crazy and absurd that they are bound to be rejected. Before Edison finally invented the electric bulb, he had failed about a thousand times in his earlier attempts. In fact, when one is not failing intelligently or learning from the failures, one is not doing anything creative at all. As Hollywood movie mogul Woody Allen says, 'If you're not failing every now and again, it's a sign you're not doing anything very innovative.'

Why, then, are people afraid of failure? It's because failures are usually perceived negatively and often followed by punishment. It is this fear of failure that prompts employees to play safe, avoid trying anything new and maintain the status quo. Therefore, for building a culture of innovation within the organization, leaders go the extra mile to eliminate the fear of failure from the minds of people and instil the trust and confidence in them that failures are an essential part of creativity. They love doing what Charles Kettering, the American inventor and holder of 186 patents, describes as the basic responsibility of leadership, 'We often say that the biggest job we have is to teach a newly hired employee how to fail intelligently. We have to train him to experiment over and over and to keep on trying and failing until he learns what will work.' This is the mindset of a true leader.

Leveraging Experience and Expertise: With their learning agility, leaders are quick to draw meaning from their past experiences and apply the insight so gained to the jobs at hand. Likewise, they are also able to replicate the knowledge and experience gained in one industry or business into another set of businesses. In the McKinsey interview cited earlier, Haines explains how his company was able to apply the features of digital technology to its bathroom showers in its pursuit towards enhancing customer experience through innovation.

'...[We] copy many of the things done in other industries using icons. For example, we have a shower now that you can pause while you wash your hair. So rather than just leave the tap running you press the pause button. Then they press the pause button again to go back to showering at the pre-set temperature. That's a little example of digital technology in the water space providing superior customer experience.'[71]

Doing More with Less: Today, innovations are acquiring a new meaning and a larger purpose. New-age leaders are aware that the global economy has been facing serious challenges. The available resources are proving drastically inadequate to fulfil the needs of seven billion people on our planet. Added to the problem is the temperamental shift in the new generations, which are used to instant gratification and the fulfilment of their needs and desires. No wonder that the unmet demands and unfulfilled aspirations are resulting in conflict and strife, often leading to even war and terrorism.

The problem with Western innovations is that they guzzle money and natural resources. Consequently, the resultant products become costly and available only to the select few in the upper crust of society. In their effort to distinguish their products from competition, companies add new features and price them increasingly higher. It is basically a more-for-more model—the more the features, the more the price. Apple's iPhones and iPads are typical examples of this game. The same is applicable to innovations in certain critical sectors like pharmaceuticals, healthcare or even financial services. A large section of the population, even in developed countries

---

[71]'How Grohe finds growth through innovation', McKinsey & Company, August 2015

such as the US and France, cannot afford to avail of formal banking services due to the high cost. Thus, there is a widening gap between the needs and aspirations of the masses and the affordability of products and services available to them.

Frugal Innovation: Advancements in technology, however, are enabling leaders to bridge this gap by resorting to frugal innovation, a way of doing more with less. These creative entrepreneurs are coming up with amazing solutions to the problems facing humanity today. As they have limited access to external resources, they tend to utilize what is available to them in abundance—human ingenuity. Thus by utilizing minimum resources, they are able to create more social and economic value, and make their products and services available to a large mass of humanity.

There are three basic reasons why these entrepreneurs are able to make their products affordable for the masses. First, they keep it simple—they try to solve a problem rather than impress their customers by embedding exotic features in their products. Second, they do not try to reinvent the wheel—they prefer to use existing technology commonly available to people. Third, instead of scaling up the value chain, they try to scale it horizontally to benefit the masses.

Some business start-ups have indeed done a remarkable job in this direction. For example, to address the problem of preventable blindness among poor people in remote areas, the Indian healthcare start-up Forus Health has brought out an innovative device, 3nethra. It is a technological innovation which is able to screen common eye problems that can lead to blindness. It is a simple, rugged and portable device that can be operated even by a minimally trained technician. Further, with cloud-based technology, its retinal imaging digital camera can capture, store and transmit images. Thus, people even in far-off areas without medical facilities can afford to have diagnosis and treatment from competent ophthalmologists based out of cities and even different countries.

Another such example is Vodafone's M-Pesa, which is being used by a large population in Kenya, as the poor there do not have access to formal banking services. It is a fine example of frugal innovation, which combines economic efficiency with social purpose. Access to this mobile payment solution is driving some of the disruptive business models in sectors such as energy. Kenyans who cannot buy the solar power solution, M-KOPA, are able to make an initial payment and bring home the solar solution box consisting of a solar rooftop, three LED lights, a solar radio and a cell phone charger. The rest of the payment is made in micro-payments every month using M-Pesa. Once the threshold is crossed, the solar solution gets unlocked and the customer can have free and clean energy at his disposal.

Shaping the Future of Humanity

In a way, these leaders are bringing in social and economic transformations in communities where people have low income but high aspirations. They use their human ingenuity to solve bigger problems by turning adversity into opportunity.

During the Bangladesh war of 1971, when Dr Dilip Mahalanabis showed the efficacy of the oral rehydration salt (ORS) solution, it was nothing short of a revolution. Prior to the war, millions of refugees had crossed over to India, resulting in the outbreak of a cholera epidemic. At this point, patients had to depend on intravenous fluid therapy for diarrhoeal dehydration treatment, clinical infrastructure for which was simply not available. This solution, which can be taken with just a glass of water, was immensely useful not only during that period but over the years, as it has saved the lives of millions of children suffering from cholera and diarrhoea across the world.

Though it is early days, contemporary leaders are using innovations not only to further the business interests of their own organizations, but also to lead the society at large to a better future. When Elon Musk declared that he would be open-sourcing the intellectual property of Tesla, the world took note that he was doing something extraordinary, going beyond the conventional approach of commercial organizations towards driving profits. Musk was clearly thinking of a larger purpose in his business and trying to appeal to the large group of millennials, Gen-Z and Gen-Now customers and employees who care for the planet and its limited resources.

Innovative leaders of today inspire trust and confidence in our shared future and make us believe that there is hope for humanity.

PART III

Building Resilience for Success and Survival

The problem with modern organizations is that they have third-generation strategies, supported by second-generation organizational structures, and implemented by first-generation managers.

–UNKNOWN

Eagles live for around forty years. By the time they are around thirty years old, their beaks become dull and bent, their talons lose their flexibility and they are unable to have a grip on their prey. Their feathers, too, grow thick, inhibiting flight.

Around this period in their lives, eagles go through a process of renewal and rejuvenation. They retreat to an isolated place high in the mountains, and over a five-month period, systematically pluck out their feathers and talons, and knock off their beaks by hitting them against the hard rock. It is a painful process wherein they bleed extensively. Then follows a period of regrowth and renewal, whereby they are able to grow a new set of beak, talons and feathers, and renew and revitalize their *energy and strength. Without this, they won't be able to live their normal life.*

The success of any organization is essentially the success of its leadership. In these times of trial and tribulation, just like eagles, contemporary leaders need to undergo a continuous process of unlearning and relearning: unlearning some of the old values and skills, and relearning the new ones needed for survival and success in the neo-normal. They need the resilience of an eagle to lead their people in these tumultuous times to realize their cherished vision and mission.

CR

10

Secrets of Leaders Who Deliver

Leadership is the capacity to translate vision into reality.

—WARREN BENNIS, AUTHOR AND PIONEER OF THE
CONTEMPORARY FIELD OF LEADERSHIP STUDIES

The study of leaders and their leadership stories clearly tell us that leaders across ages and from different walks of life have been imperfect; their leadership doesn't necessarily flow from their high moral virtues or a rich repertoire of essential traits. Gandhi could provide transformational leadership to a nation and inspire generations of people across the globe, even though quite often he was self-opinionated, undemocratic and dictatorial. Likewise, few leaders in modern times have shaped the way we look at the world as significantly as Steve Jobs has. But he was a maverick and didn't display the classical traits of a leader. We have seen people scaling the heights of leadership by overcoming their known weaknesses—be it personal morality, communication limitations or individual idiosyncrasies—in a transparent and networked society, where there are no hiding places for leaders.

This implies that analysing leaders in terms of their conformity to personal morality, adherence to principles and consistency in approach or possession of a set of mandated positive human traits is simplistic. At the beginning of the twenty-first century, former US President George W. Bush exercised a top-down assertive leadership approach, reminiscent of the nineteenth-century style of leadership. It goes against the conventional wisdom of leadership today, and yet, as pointed out by David Gergen, the American political commentator and former presidential advisor, he got some of the highest approval ratings in contemporary presidential history. Contrast this with the highly democratic, participative and value-based leadership of former US president Barack Obama, who, too, scored an exceedingly high approval rating. The fallacy of studying leadership success with reference to traits or styles is quite obvious from this contrast.

The question arises, however, that if it is not merely traits or personality types, what is the secret of leadership success in the twenty-first century? What are the leadership models that organizations should build on and budding leaders should follow? These are questions that demand answers.

Effective Leadership

While there is a lot of difference in views on what leadership is or what makes a good leader, there are no two opinions on what effective leaders do: they get results. As management guru Peter Drucker puts it, 'Effective leadership is not about making speeches or being liked; leadership is defined by results, not attributes.'

Leadership, in fact, is determined more by the results that leaders deliver than by their personality types or inherent traits. History counts only those as successful leaders who are able to make a difference to society for good or bad. No one remembers a general who was ethical and humane but never won a battle. The much-celebrated counter-terrorist hostage-rescue mission carried out by Israeli commandos in July 1976 at the Entebbe airport in Uganda is remembered as an act of heroic leadership. But the same operation would have been termed a failure of leadership if hostages held by the terrorists had been killed. Taking the point further, the botched-up attempt of Americans to rescue their hostages in Iran shook the faith of people in the leadership of President Jimmy Carter.

Hence, in addition to the skills and attributes required for leading in the VUCA world, leadership also needs to be studied in the context of what leaders do to get results and enhance their effectiveness. The focus, therefore, is also on leadership behaviour and the underlying principles and practices that determine success in increasingly complex, integrated and interdependent societies, where members pursue multiple and often-conflicting priorities. It is only when we start focusing on behaviour patterns of effective and successful leaders, along with their skills and attributes, that we provide a model for aspiring leaders to build themselves upon or for the institutions to put in place a meaningful leadership-development programme.

This is not to say that the debate over what constitutes good leadership is over or that leadership can be taken out of its context. Also, this is not to prove a point that there can't be a well-accomplished leader who could measure up to Daniel Goleman's idea of a leader who could keep alternating between the six distinct leadership styles—coercive, authoritative, affiliative, democratic, pacesetting and coaching—'each in the right measure and at just the right time'. The world will not be bereft of charismatic leaders who transcend all barriers of leadership definitions and mesmerize audiences with their charm and appeal.

However, modelling leadership development on the lines of such leaders is a sure recipe for failure as everyone cannot be a charismatic leader; people have limitations and quite often life doesn't give them enough time and opportunity to acquire and hone skills and styles that they don't possess in good measure.

The advantage of focusing on leadership behaviour is that, unlike traits and styles, it is easier for people to acquire and adapt the behaviour patterns which lead to effectiveness and desired results. These behavioural skills can be acquired, taught, emulated and practised. Secondly, this approach can also help in leadership assessment as the effectiveness of leaders' behaviour can be judged with relative ease on the touchstone of the results they achieve. And finally, this gets rid of the moral and ethical conflict, the typical Hitler dilemma, which attempts to see leadership in the context of ethics and morality. It also refuses to see leadership in the context of winners versus losers in a conflict, where the winners are invariably painted as leaders, and losers dumped as villains, irrespective of the individual merits of their leadership.

Focus on Results

To say that leaders need to get results is like saying that we need to breathe for living. As leaders, getting results in line with their vision and mission has to be their primary focus.

In the article 'What Makes an Effective Executive',[72] management guru Peter F. Drucker lists the eight practices that successful leaders across geographies, industries and personality types followed to get results. He writes:

> What made them all effective is that they followed the same eight practices:
>
> - They asked, 'What needs to be done?'

---

[72]Peter F. Drucker, 'What Makes an Effective Executive', *Harvard Business Review*, June 2004

- They asked, 'What's right for the enterprise?'
- They developed action plans.
- They took responsibility for decisions.
- They took responsibility for communicating.
- They were focused on opportunities rather than problems.
- They ran productive meetings.
- They thought and said 'we' rather than 'I'.

According to Drucker, the first two gave them knowledge and insight that they needed to steer the organization in a particular direction. The next four prepared the ground for effective action. Finally, the last two were tools to instil responsibility and accountability in the people and the system.

A focus on delivering results implies that there cannot be any laid-down approach or strategy that can lead to leadership success. If there were one, leaders could decode the same and bask in the glory of achievements. The ground realities are, however, different and the solutions that worked for a company or in one context may not work at all for another company, or even for the same company in another context. Therefore, an organization's strategies and plans of action have to be contextualized to its circumstances and environment, which may include its legacies, competitive challenges and its own health.

Leaders, therefore, are known by the results they deliver and not by the strategies they adopt. Nothing explains this better than the difference in the leadership strategies of Jim Parker, former CEO of Southwest Airlines, and Anne Mulcahy, former CEO of Xerox, both of whom adopted diametrically opposite strategies to take their companies out of crises. Both of them were successful in their goals and were thus hailed as celebrated leaders.

Jim Parker: Resilience through Employee-Centricity

At 8.45 a.m. on 11 September 2001, when the unthinkable happened, the airlines industry was shattered. Following the terrorist attacks on the twin towers of the US World Trade Center, airlines were forced to shut down for days while the country struggled to recover from the crisis. This effectively meant that all airline passengers, pilots and crew members were stranded, with their planes all across the country. There was despair, dejection and despondency all around.

While other airlines' stranded employees were sitting idle, waiting for the next set of instructions, Southwest Airlines encouraged its employees to take care of their customers, taking them to movies and places of interest. This was a master stroke in building customer relationship and enhancing customer loyalty.

Southwest Airlines made a difference in another area as well. In the aftermath of 9/11, most of the airlines started downsizing their workforce by around 20 per cent to protect their bottom lines. However, Jim Parker, then the Southwest CEO, decided against downsizing. On 8 October 2001, he declared, 'We are willing to suffer some damage, even to our stock price, to protect the jobs of our people.'

Going a step further, he also declared a $179.8 million profit-sharing plan for its employees.

How did Southwest Airlines stand the test?

The airline has a long-standing history of being an employee-focused company where layoffs are the last resort for survival. Its earlier CEO, Herbert Kelleher, once made the classic observation, 'Who comes first, the employee, customers, or shareholders? That's never been an issue to me. The employees come first. If they're happy, satisfied, dedicated, and energetic, they'll take real good care of the customers. When the customers are happy, they come back. And that makes the shareholders happy.[73]

This strategy proved to be excellent in good times and Southwest's bottom lines swelled in earlier decades. But Parker's strategy of employee-centricity proved to be equally effective in the time of distress, as commitment to employees created a strong organizational resilience to fight back the crisis. As a consequence, Southwest Airlines was the first to recover from the crisis. While other airlines lost billions of dollars, Southwest's balance sheet remained in the black all through the succeeding quarters. Its stock prices also showed the quickest recovery among all US airlines.

Contrast Parker's strategy with that of Mulcahy, who followed an altogether different strategy at a time of crisis. Faced with the prospect of Xerox going for Chapter 11 bankruptcy, she showed no hesitation in downsizing and sending home more than 25,000 employees to take the company out of the woods.

Anne M. Mulcahy: The Accidental CEO

When Anne Mulcahy was named CEO of Xerox Corporation in 2001, the person most startled at the decision was Mulcahy herself. Having spent the larger part of her career in Xerox in sales and HR, and without a strong background in finance, she felt she was not CEO material at all. To make matters

---

[73]Charles A. O'Reilly and Jeffrey Pfeffer, *Hidden Value: How Great Companies Achieve Extraordinary Results with Ordinary People*, Harvard Business School Press, 2000

worse, as the announcement hit the market, Xerox stocks dropped 15 per cent.

'I took on this position feeling equal parts excitement and dread,' she told a packed auditorium while delivering her address as part of the 2004-05 'View from the Top' talk series.

An accidental CEO though she was, she was the best thing to have happened to Xerox in one of its worst times of crisis. When she took over the helm of affairs at Xerox, the company was going through a deep financial crisis. It was practically on the verge of Chapter 11 bankruptcy. It had accumulated over $17 billion in debt and had recorded losses for the preceding six years continuously. To make things worse, its recent sales force reorganization plan had gone bad and there was severe disenchantment among customers. As if this was not enough, the US Securities and Exchange Commission had found it guilty of accounting malpractices in its Mexico unit.

Mulcahy started with a no-holds-barred approach and devised an aggressive turnaround plan aimed at debt reduction, operational efficiency, clear communication and focus on research. She confronted her employees with a no-nonsense approach. As she put it, 'I gave people a choice to make: either roll up your sleeves and go to work or leave Xerox.'[74]

Faced with the task of downsizing the company's workforce by 30 per cent, she took a bold decision and slashed over 25,000 jobs. She also sold off $2.3 billion worth of non-core assets to reduce debts and, in the process, got rid of the entire desktop portfolio of Xerox.

Xerox finally returned to profitability in 2004, and that was followed by a period of spectacular growth. Its return to

---

[74]Lisa Vollmer, 'Anne Mulcahy: The Keys to Turnaround at Xerox', Graduate School of Stanford Business, 1 December 2004

> profitability was declared by *Money* magazine as 'the great turnaround story of the post-crash era'.
>
> Mulcahy's courageous leadership in the face of extreme adversity was recognized across industries. In 2008 she was named CEO of the Year by the *Chief Executive* magazine. She was hailed as one of the world's most influential women in 2005 and then again in 2009. The US News & World Report celebrated her as one of America's best leaders.

The message from these two stories is crystal clear. Leadership strategies are contextual to the organization and, therefore, the approach of successful leaders to the challenges facing them is determined not by their traits but by the context in which they are operating. Hence, it is more relevant to study leadership with reference to the behaviour patterns that lead to success rather than to study it in the context of traits and personality types, which essentially limits our understanding of the leadership phenomenon.

What They Don't Teach You in Leadership Programmes

What contributes to leadership-effectiveness? If leadership is so contextual, which are the behavioural models that organizations should promote for success rather than merely trying to clone leaders based on traits and personality types?

A study of leadership across ages would reveal that a small sub-set of behavioural characteristics are common to many successful leaders who have faced difficult challenges and overcome the same. Some of these behavioural approaches would make idealists uncomfortable, as they are not in conformity with established norms and values. It is understandable why these are never taught as part of leadership- development programmes. But that also explains why the much-acclaimed leadership models are so much at variance with the ground realities.

It would be relevant to study some of these critical behavioural attributes for grooming our future leaders.

Be a Principled Pragmatist: Conventional wisdom would like us to believe that leaders are men of principle who would rather give up their position than compromise on their principle. They are said to live by their convictions and are believed to be focused on and committed to their vision. A case in point is Gandhi, who lived by the principles of truth and non-violence and didn't give them up even in cases of extreme provocation. In recent times, Obama has been a shining example of principled leadership, standing up for all the positive values in our personal, social and political life. His call for 'equal justice for all' received universal acclaim and reinforced global initiatives towards this objective. No wonder that he has been rated as the twelfth best president in the history of the US as per the C-SPAN 2017 Survey of Presidential Leadership.

While these are some of the finest examples of principled leadership, there is no dearth of evidence to show that when there is a conflict between priorities and principles, successful leaders try to strike a balance between the two, compromising on their own principles in the interest of the larger cause they are espousing. It would, in fact, be naïve to assume that a leader could work in isolation and lead others by their own beliefs, principles and priorities. Leadership is essentially a multidimensional phenomenon involving both leaders and their followers, who impact and influence one another. While it is obvious that leaders influence followers, what does not get highlighted often is that followers, too, influence their leaders. We are living in a multidimensional world, where all of us have multiple alignments, affiliations and commitments, depending upon a host of factors such as race, class, religion, language, ethnicity and gender. As a result, a follower's commitment to their leader's vision is neither total nor unquestioned—it is always conditioned by their own commitments, orientations and affiliations.

The leader-follower dualism is essentially an exercise in influencing each other, whereby both sides move some distance from their original positions. In addition to this, a leader's principles and commitments are also influenced by the circumstances in which the leader or their organization is placed. We have seen this clearly in the leadership examples of Parker and Mulcahy.

To realize their stated objectives, leaders quite often have to resort to pragmatism by making some small or temporary deviations from their beliefs and principles. In his blog post titled 'The Leader as Principled Pragmatist', the eminent US presidential historian Richard Norton Smith emphasizes the point that successful leaders combine principles with pragmatism. He goes on to say,

> …[It] goes without saying that we want our presidents to be men and women of principles. What happens, however, when principles come into conflict with one another? Thomas Jefferson worshipped before the altar of strict constructionism, if no other. Yet history applauds him for putting aside his deepest convictions about limited government when Louisiana came on the market. More precisely, Jefferson's constitutional principles took a back seat to his continental vision of the United States.[75]

Smith goes on to describe a number of American presidents such as Lyndon Johnson, Herbert Hoover and Harry Truman,

[75]Richard Norton Smith, 'The Leader as Principled Pragmatist', *Harvard Business Review*, 6 October 2008

who had taken a pragmatic approach even in the face of principles to the contrary, originally espoused by them. In recent history, Richard Nixon was a hardcore anti-communist but when he realized that it was in the interest of the US to cultivate a positive relationship with China, he did not hesitate to take the initiative, giving up his personal convictions. Smith lays down the marker for the success of the presidents, and says, 'Great presidents spend themselves in causes greater than themselves, for purposes nobler than re-election.'[76]

The political journey of Abraham Lincoln, one of the most celebrated presidents of the US, is yet another magnificent example of a principled pragmatist. In the group biography, *Team of Rivals: The Political Genius of Abraham Lincoln*, the acclaimed presidential historian Doris Kearns Goodwin portrays how the little-known lawyer and a one-term congressman rises from obscurity and takes on his more accomplished and privileged rivals to become the most transformative president of the US. On 18 May 1860, when the Republican National Convention in Chicago voted in favour of Lincoln over his more gifted and reputed rivals William H. Seward, Salmon P. Chase and Edward Bates, it was an acknowledgement of Lincoln's extraordinary potential as a leader of the American people.

What emerges from Goodwin's masterpiece is that when Lincoln started his public life, he didn't have any chance of becoming a heroic figure. However, he kept evolving as a leader, learning and building on his experiences. He was always looking to gauge what others were feeling and what their motives and aspirations could be. While pursuing his long-term goals, he didn't hesitate when the exigencies of circumstances demanded him to take painful decisions and make uncomfortable

---

[76]Richard Norton Smith, 'The Leader as Principled Pragmatist', *Harvard Business Review*, 6 October 2008

adjustments. For example, the constitutional amendment outlawing slavery saw Lincoln make quite a few unpleasant deals to gain the support of legislators.

The vision and pragmatism of American presidents was also reflected in the way former Prime Minister of India P.V. Narasimha Rao steered the economic liberalization of the country in 1991.

The Quintessential Pragmatist: P.V. Narasimha Rao

The visionary Indian leader and scholar P.V. Narasimha Rao, who served as the country's prime minister from 1991 to 1996, is credited with transforming the Indian economy. The Statement of Industrial Policy announced by his government and the reformist budget presented by the then Finance Minister Manmohan Singh on 24 July 1991 set the process for liberalization of the Indian economy from decades of bureaucratic socialism, and its consequent integration with the liberal global economy. It was a mammoth task taken up in the face of the deeply entrenched socialistic convictions within his own political party, the Congress. He faced stiff opposition from his party men, who, all their life, had lived and sworn by socialism. What was worse, his party didn't enjoy a majority in Parliament and he had to depend on the support of regional parties.

It is now widely known that being a pragmatist, Rao made many compromises within his own party to soften the Opposition to his economic programmes, playing a cat-and-mouse game. He also compromised on his principles to get support from a regional political party which was out to claim its pound of flesh. While making these short-term compromises, Rao always kept his vision focused on the larger cause of transforming the Indian economy—and succeeded in his mission.

The life of many successful leaders would show that they are often confronted with intricate and complex dilemmas with no easy choices. They are required to exercise prudence and opt for the least harmful option. And yet, if luck is not with them and the choice boomerangs, they are doomed. Often, going against the teachings of the moral brigade, they show traces of inconsistency, changing their proclaimed stand on issues dear to them. They are also known for indulging in strategic misrepresentation, not opening up their entire agenda to the Opposition so as to keep them guessing. Some of our most admired leaders, such as Winston Churchill, Nelson Mandela, Abraham Lincoln, Jeff Bezos and Narendra Modi, have shown that they didn't hesitate in making compromises on the way to achieving their ultimate objectives.

It is obvious that leadership is an intricate issue and that it can't be explained in straight terms like good or bad, consistent or inconsistent. Quite often, you have bad people doing some good and some good people compelled by circumstances to do something not-so-good. Sometimes leaders veer away from their declared path, showing inconsistency in their declared positions on issues, which could just be a trade-off with their opponents for a larger purpose. Of course, it opens up the eternal debate about whether the end justifies the means or whether for the end to be acceptable, the means, too, must be pure. But it makes sense to keep leadership out of this debate and dilemma.

Expand Your Power Base

Nowhere in the world has any leader got unfettered power or authority to lead absolutely in the manner he or she wants. When the much-celebrated leadership expert and author John Maxwell says that a leader is one who knows the way, shows the way and goes the way, he is obviously presenting an idealistic and oversimplified understanding of leadership. There are always counter-balancing forces in the environment, sometimes in multiples, representing different interest groups, pulling the leader in different directions. Particularly when a leader joins a new organization, he has to understand the milieu and the different power centres operating within the environment. To be effective, he has to negotiate with different stakeholders in the system and strike a balance among the different centres of power.

However, in the process of balancing the various interest groups, leaders also gradually keep building their own power base within the system. They do it by first aligning the neutral bystanders in the system to their side. Also, instead of taking their critics and opponents head-on, they explain their vision and strategies to them over a period of time and win them over to their side. As they keep aligning more centres of power with them and increase their power base, it becomes easier for them to carry their agenda forward smoothly.

Initially, in the process of negotiating with competing narratives, leaders have to give up some of their priorities or dilute some of their original messages. For example, when Prime Minister Narendra Modi's government decided to introduce the path-breaking Goods & Services Tax (GST) in India, it had to dilute the overall architecture in multiple ways to make it acceptable to the various interest groups, including manufacturing and consuming states. Of course, the attempt was to get it started first and make improvements on the course.

While this kind of balancing between priorities is common in politics, where stakes are higher and multifarious vested interests keep pulling in different directions, it is not uncommon even in professionally managed business organizations. In public-sector companies, labour unions often act as power centres and leaders have to keep a balance between their demands and organizational needs. In the private sector, the clash of interest could arise out of differing business or cultural priorities, and the leader has to keep balancing his goals to take all the stakeholders along.

When I worked for an Indo-Japanese company, the cultural differences were obvious. During meetings, while it was difficult to make a Japanese executive speak, it was equally difficult to stop an Indian from speaking. But, lighter side apart, with their long-term perspective, the Japanese were content with moderate business-growth targets, but, at the same time, they were highly committed to ensuring zero-defect processes and business outcomes. On the other hand, the Indian side was highly aggressive about business targets, which were practically never achieved. On the issue of process accuracy and business outcomes, their approach was to keep improving the customer experience as the business built up momentum and maturity.

In your leadership journey, as you go along balancing these priorities, you gain new supporters and partners, who add to your power base. It is only after you are able to align the power centres to your side that you are in a position to carry out your agenda in an unhindered manner.

Accomplish the Art of Influencing People

Closely connected to the aspect of building one's power base is the need to practise the art and science of persuasion and influence. Influencing people and aligning them to their mission are two of the basic responsibilities of leaders. Therefore, leaders must be adept at the art of influencing people. However, in the interconnected environment in which organizations operate today, people are open to multiple influences. The complexities of jobs create multiple dependencies, while the cultural, demographic and geographical diversities within the organization lead people to pursue diverse priorities. In such a situation, leaders have to master the art of influencing people to follow the agenda set by them.

While influencing people is ultimately an art, there is a lot of science behind it too. In his book *Influence: Science and Practice*, Professor Robert Cialdini explores the various ways in which people can be influenced. Backed with numerical empirical studies, Cialdini makes the point that in an environment where people are overloaded with information, they can be influenced to act on the basis of certain generalizations and unconscious thought patterns. He has identified six key weapons of influence: reciprocation, commitment and consistency, social proof, liking, authority and scarcity. Cialdini drives home the point that human beings are susceptible to these tools even if they are aware of it.

As influencing people is critical to leadership-effectiveness, it is critical for leaders to learn this science of influence and hone the art of persuading and influencing people. In fact, the art and science of influencing people must form a critical component of all leadership-development programmes.

Balance the Ethics-Effectiveness Trade-Off

Leadership literatures are replete with words of wisdom impressing upon us the importance of ethics and morality for leadership. There are numerous leadership tales advocating fair play, honesty, justice, authenticity, truthfulness, employee-centricity and benevolence. On the other hand, there are a few empirical researchers who are able to find positive outcomes out of supposedly negative attributes, such as manipulating people and situations, self-promotion, narcissism, power play and a top-down approach. Going further, when we take a close look at the lives of some of the most admired leaders, we find them willing to make deviations from the accepted path of morality and fairness and making compromises to achieve their long-term goals and objectives.

Why, then, is it that leadership tales are still wrapped around ethics and morality? Why is it that the only picture of leadership that we see is that of a caring, empowering, responsive and benevolent leader whose primary concern is the greatest good of everyone around? The answer is clear—leadership studies confuse the two questions 'What is leadership?' and 'What is good leadership?'. The difference between the two needs to be appreciated. The first demands a description of facts and realities, while the second expects a value-based normative answer. The other reason for this misplaced perception is the psychological phenomenon that impels people to believe what should be rather than what actually is.

As leaders we need to separate wheat from chaff and look at the comprehensive picture. There is always a thin line between ethics and effectiveness. Sometimes, being ethical leads to effectiveness. A religious leader, for example, has to be ethical for being effective. It holds true in the case of commercial corporations too. James Burke, former CEO of Johnson & Johnson, was considered an ethical leader, when, in 1982, the company recalled 31 million bottles of Tylenol capsules from store shelves after a few bottles were found to be poisoned. The company provided free replacement to customers in the form of safer tablets. This unusual act of product recall, probably a first in history, was considered highly ethical and added to the company's effectiveness. Within a period of two months, the market share of the product, which had fallen from 37 per cent to a mere 7 per cent after the crisis, recovered to 30 per cent after the company launched tamper-proof packaging.

On the other hand, there are situations when ethics and

effectiveness do not go hand in hand; in business and in the political space, it is rare to find leaders displaying both these attributes simultaneously. There are leaders who are ethical but not very effective and then there are leaders who are highly effective but whose ethical standards are questionable. Some of the most successful leaders, such as Abraham Lincoln, John F. Kennedy and Martin Luther King Jr, would not pass if their lives and careers were put to ethics and morality tests.

Leaders have to have a holistic perspective in balancing ethics and morality with result-orientation. While one must aspire to be a moral and ethical leader, one also has to be conscious of the fact that people do not operate in a perfect world. They keep balancing between their self-interests on the one hand and the larger interests of society and the organization on the other. It is only natural for leaders, therefore, to keep moderating their responses to situations to get the desired results. Effective leaders do make a trade-off between ethics and effectiveness in practical work situations while being conscious that they are expected to act in conformity with ethics and morals.

Address the Organizational Context

We know of great and successful leaders who took their organizations to great heights or transformed the world they lived in. Yet, if we want to draw some common threads of leadership behaviour for success, the effort would be more confusing than rewarding. We would find that each leader had his unique circumstances and exceptional challenges. Hence the learning gleaned from each success story is unique in itself and cannot be replicated in other situations.

The reason is simple. As we have seen it, leadership is highly contextual. To deliver results, leaders have to understand the organizational context—the background and the environment in which they operate. They are required to relate their strategies to the nature of the industry, its legacies, the competitive environment, laws, regulations, the financial health of the company and a lot of other factors. Therefore, for people leading their organizations or for leadership-development programmes grooming people for leadership positions, it is critical to understand and appreciate the importance of applying appropriate behaviour patterns suited to the organizational context. For example, concern for people may take precedence over process discipline in a business organization under certain circumstances, but in a nuclear power plant, process discipline would be non-negotiable under any circumstances.

The importance of organizational context is so critical that, as the context changes, the behaviour of the leader also has to change for delivering results. There are, of course, certain baseline behaviours that have universal relevance, but beyond the baseline, leadership behaviour has to be modulated under varying circumstances, depending upon the priorities of the situation. The leadership approach in a sick company needing revival would be different from that in a thriving company on top of its competitors.

Seen on a wider spectrum, the political leadership of Myanmarese political leader Aung San Suu Kyi provides some insight into shifting leadership priorities arising from changing circumstances. Kept in captivity by Myanmar's military regime, this pro-democracy icon of freedom, held in as high esteem as Nelson Mandela, was the world's most famous political prisoner for nearly two decades. Writing the foreword for the first edition of her book, *Freedom from Fear: And Other Writings*, the famous Czech playwright Václav Havel said, 'She speaks for all of us who search for justice.'[77] Acclaimed for her fight for human rights and non-violence, she was awarded the Nobel Peace Prize in 1991. However, after she assumed de facto leadership of the country in 2016, post the 2015 general election, her approach to human rights violations arising out of ethnic clashes in the country was different.

Entrusted with the responsibility of managing peace and integrity in the country, she has remained reticent on the plight of the Rohingya insurgents, whom she has described as 'terrorists'. Even in the face of global condemnation, she has held fast to her position, stating that the global powers have created a 'huge iceberg of misinformation'.[78]

Focus on Your Behavioural Skills

There are a few important messages that we get from the above narrative. First, behaviour and traits are not exclusive of one another—they, rather, complement each other. To a participative leader, the behaviour of seeking diverse opinions to resolve a problem would come naturally, almost as a reflex. To a servant leader, caring for people would be next to his nature. Traits do reinforce behaviour but traits alone cannot lead to leadership success. We have seen leaders with differing personality types and traits leading their respective organizations effectively at the same point in history. It is, therefore, advisable to focus on improving your behavioural skills, which could make your leadership more effective. These skills could relate to communication, conflict management, time management

---

[77]Aung San Suu Kyi, *Freedom from Fear: And Other Writings*, Penguin Books, reprint edition 2010

[78]Michael Safi, 'Aung San Suu Kyi says "terrorists" are misinforming world about Myanmar violence", *The Guardian*, 6 September 2017

or resilience development. As part of your learning, you need to identify the behavioural skill most relevant to your given situation and focus on improving it.

The interesting part is that the behavioural skills that lead to success can be learnt and improved like any other skill, such as cycling or learning a foreign language. Like ordinary persons, leaders, too, have a learning curve. The life history of great leaders such as Lincoln and Gandhi shows that they were not as heroic as they turned out to be. They learnt their leadership skills and climbed the leadership ladder step by step. Hence, everybody can be a leader by learning the appropriate behaviour skills and using them suitably.

Last, the path of leadership is straight and narrow, fenced on both sides by virtues such as ethics, morality, benevolence, and acts of caring, nurturing and listening. But successful leaders have shown how to stray momentarily into narrow bylanes to quell some temporary fire, only to return to the original path to accomplish their cherished vision and mission. By doing so, they have shown that it is important for leaders to take responsibility for the task they have undertaken. If there are obstacles on the way, leaders have to weigh the trade-offs and step into the arena to tackle them. Alternating their behaviour patterns suitably is a critical factor that differentiates between leaders who make a difference to society and those who end up blaming their circumstances and fade into oblivion.

11

Discovering Your
Leadership-Effectiveness

It doesn't matter who you are, where you come from.
The ability to triumph begins with you. Always.

–OPRAH WINFREY, AMERICAN TELEVISION PERSONALITY

It was a Monday morning and as I was glancing at my schedule, looking forward to an eventful week, my chain of thought was broken as my secretary announced an unscheduled visitor. As he came in, I was unable to place the tall and handsome young man immediately.

After pleasantries, he said, 'I came to show you something.' He smiled at me and took out a trophy from his bag, 'I owe this to you.'

I looked at it closely and said, 'Young Leadership Award! Oh, congratulations!'

'I owe this to you. I could get it because of you,' he said again. And looking at my puzzled face, he quickly introduced himself and went on to add, 'You see, I'm heading an important regional sales team of this fairly big organization. We have a very structured and mandated sales process—fixed reporting times, defined scripts, cold calling, lead generation and field visits. But that's not my forte—sales is more relationship-oriented and I've groomed my team too on the same lines.'

'And your team is doing well?' I asked.

'Oh, yes! In fact, we have always been among the good performers in the country.'

'What's the problem then?'

'Not much, except that every year during the annual review I was advised to change my leadership style and abide by the organizational mandate. I used to feel disheartened—neither here nor there—I was full of self-doubt and distrust, even though I kept getting my bonus and incentives.'

'But this trophy...?'

'Oh, that's where you come in. Last year I heard you at a leadership seminar, and your message to leaders was to work from their strengths. I knew then what I needed to do. I followed my approach sincerely. And you see this trophy? My team topped the chart this year.'

'Interesting!'

'And, you know, this year during the annual review, when my CEO raised the issue once again, I simply said, "Is there a business case for this?" He looked at me and smiled.'

'You're absolutely right! Delivering results is the primary responsibility of leadership. As for the mandated sales models and leadership stereotypes, your company would do well to develop and nurture alternative models rather than stick to just one.'

He left after that. I couldn't have asked for a better start to the week.

◆

Amid all the clutter of leadership theories and larger-than-life images of charismatic leaders, it is natural for someone to get lost in the cross-currents of competing theories, each demanding a budding leader to cultivate an array of traits or model on the lines of some personality or the other. In the process, leaders tend to forget what they are and keep struggling to become what they are not. The result is that either we produce leaders who remain unsure of who they are and what they are doing, or they become unnatural clones of great personalities. It is only natural, then, that the imported traits and values in the leaders do not ignite the kind of passion and perseverance that are the hallmarks of good leadership. People are able to see through the imposter in the leader when they find that the leader is not able to practise the professed values consistently or that his heart is not where his mouth is. This adds to the lack of authenticity and trust deficit that leaders around the world are facing today.

Clearly, the existing leadership models have failed to respond to the demands of the new environment and the complexities of the operating landscape. There is, therefore, an urgent need to define a leadership framework that could be common to all, but which, at the same time, retains the individuality of everyone. Here are a few insights into some psychological orientations and behaviour patterns that can help you improve your leadership-effectiveness and authenticity.

Be Yourself and Believe in Yourself

Always be a first-rate version of yourself, instead of a second-rate version of somebody else.

–JUDY GARLAND, ACCLAIMED AMERICAN
ACTOR, SINGER AND DANCER

Leadership speaks in many voices and you need to find your own. Your journey of finding your own voice begins with you being yourself and believing in yourself. The beauty of everyone in this world lies in their own individuality, originality and uniqueness. Therefore, we must visit our life stories and find our individuality and distinctiveness; we must understand what inspires us and what troubles us. Understanding ourselves is critical to determining the message we want to give to the world. Unfortunately, very often we lose the precious gift of our uniqueness by constantly trying to fit into someone else's shoes. In the process we sabotage our own tryst with destiny by speaking in someone else's voice and telling someone else's story. Steve Jobs had good advice for all of us when he said, 'Your time is limited, so don't waste it living someone else's life.'

The point to remember here is that the world has never seen a great leader who was not being his honest self. Hence, you must assure yourself that it is safe to be you, and that is the only way you can ever become a leader. This awareness and self-acceptance can be the stepping stone to developing a credible leadership.

Believing in yourself is the next essential attribute for credible leadership. The history of leadership tells us that every human being has the potential to become a great leader. What is required, however, is that we believe in the sincerity of our dreams and work on them to make them come true. As Eleanor Roosevelt put it, 'The future belongs to those who believe in the beauty of their dreams.'

As the central message in some of the previous chapters says, for becoming an authentic leader, you must recognize your core strengths and embrace your imperfections. Your core competence could be in any area—communication, conceptualization, strategy formulation or technology. You must identify it, invest in it and build your leadership around it, since working on your strengths is going to be more rewarding than anything else. Further, it is always good to be conscious of your blind spots as well. But in this age of collaborative leadership, it is better to have someone else in your team who can supplement your weak areas with his core strength. Thus, with everyone in the team working on their core competencies, the organizational outcomes are certainly going to be exemplary.

Nurture the Tiny Buddha Within

The leader is not a different kind of person. Every person is a different kind of leader.

−UNKNOWN

Hidden within everyone's life story is a tiny Buddha waiting to enlighten the world. To be an authentic leader, you need to wake up the Buddha within you and develop a purpose in life that goes beyond your personal interests. Purpose is something that is an intrinsic part of you; something that drives your leadership, guides all your actions and helps you stay on course during adversity. It gives meaning to your leadership and doesn't allow you to rest or sleep until it is achieved. It ultimately becomes the most precious possession in your leadership journey.

For the purpose to sound authentic, it is important that it emanate from the story of your life and personality. Also, you must tell it to the world in your own voice, with our own passion and emotions. In an impressive article titled 'Discovering Your Authentic Leadership', the authors make an insightful observation, 'The journey to authentic leadership begins with understanding the story of your life. Your life story provides the context for your experiences, and through it, you can find the inspiration to make an impact in the world.'[79]

While people generally draw their messages from the entire canvas of their lives, there are quite a few who find purpose in their lives out of a difficult or traumatic experience, leading to enhanced self-confidence, inner strength and heightened creativity. Bill Wilson founded Alcoholics Anonymous after undergoing prolonged illness and life-threatening conditions. Frida Kahlo became one of the greatest painters of her time after surviving polio and multiple other physical challenges. In her book *When Walls Become Doorways: Creativity and the Transforming Illness,* author Tobi Zausner talks about ways to turn a traumatic life experience into a new and better life. She shows how 'an illness that feels like an impassable barrier can become a doorway to a new and more creative existence'.

When you draw your inspiration from your own life, your commitment to your message to the world is more heightened and passionate, which in turn makes your leadership more authentic. Arianna Huffington, co-founder of *Huffington Post,* entrepreneur and author, is an example of this. Describing the passion behind launching her start-up Thrive India, a unit of Thrive Global, she recounted her nightmarish experience of exhaustion and sleep deprivation that led her to explore methods to bring about behavioural changes in the lives of people to help create a healthy relationship between people and technology. Emphasizing the need for a digital detox in modern times, she says,

> I thought I was a superwoman who didn't need to sleep. When I collapsed, I hit my head on my desk, broke my cheekbones. That was my wake-up call. I looked

---

[79]Bill George, Peter Sims, Andrew N. McLean and Diana Mayer, 'Discovering Your Authentic Leadership', *Harvard Business Review*, February 2007

around and realized there were millions like me and many had had worse breakdowns than me. It occurred to me that there is something very wrong in the way we are living our lives.[80]

Arianna Huffington is just one example from a host of leaders who inspire confidence and authenticity in their leadership with a larger-than-life purpose drawn from their own life stories.

Building Leadership Grit

Success and failures are not opposing ends of the spectrum. They are interdependent. In your journey to success, failures are your faithful companions.

–UNKNOWN

We often have an inclination to simplify leadership and look at it as success stories of great men and women: Gandhi liberated India from British rule, Marie Curie propounded the theory of radioactivity, Steve Jobs invented the iPad, and so on and so forth. These myths about leadership make us believe that what defines leadership is success, whereas the truth is just the opposite: leadership is defined by failures and how we respond to them.

Leaders who sound authentic and ultimately make a difference to society are the ones who believe in their vision, are passionate about their dreams and who do not give up even after repeated failures. A classic example of this is the story of Steve Jobs. He persevered even after a series of failures and believed in his mission in a way that kept igniting his

---

[80]'Our relationship with technology is very flawed', *Mumbai Mirror*, 28 June 2019

dreams. He had co-founded Apple Computer at the age of twenty-one and by the time he was twenty-three, he was a tech celebrity, having earned name, fame and enormous wealth. At thirty, he was driven out of the very company that he had co-founded. He was out in the wilderness, shattered, flirting with different possibilities for his life. But he never gave up on what he loved to do. After a few years in the wilderness, he was back to Apple with a tenacity that saw him marching from one triumph to another.

The life and works of Walt Disney also tell us a similar story. He is remembered as an entrepreneur, animator, film producer and, above all, the pioneer of the American animation industry. But behind his successes there were a lot of failures, leading to bankruptcy, mental breakdown and the loss of the ownership of his first commercially successful character, Oswald, the Lucky Rabbit. After his failures, he could have wandered into Hollywood and made a good living for himself and his family members. But he persevered with his dreams and continued to learn from his mistakes and ultimately became a phenomenon whose creations such as Mickey Mouse, Donald Duck and Disneyland continue to inspire and entertain generations of human beings.

What we learn from the stories of Steve Jobs and Walt Disney is that we should not fear failure but embrace it and learn from it to bounce back. People who are successful in life are not always the smartest or the most intelligent. They are people who display what Angela Duckworth calls 'grit'. In her book *Grit: The Power of Passion and Perseverance*, this professor of Psychology at the University of Pennsylvania defines grit as 'passion and perseverance for long-term goals' and argues that grit matters as much as talent and luck for outstanding success. She further explains that grit combined with a larger purpose in life keeps leaders aligned to their mission and enables them to stay the course even in the face of failure. They don't quit; they don't give up. The determination to achieve their goal makes them more adaptable in approach so that when faced with obstacles, they take a detour to overcome them and come back on course to pursue their mission.

Building Trust and Personal Credibility

People buy into the leader before they buy into the vision.

–JOHN C. MAXWELL, AUTHOR, SPEAKER AND PASTOR

Trust is the essential bedrock on which the edifice of leadership is built. It is, in fact, one of the most precious gifts that leaders can get from their followers, which arises out of one's faith in the honesty, integrity and sincerity of the other person. However, trust is always a multidimensional process. It is not enough that you as a leader inspire trust; you must extend it to your peers and followers as well. In fact, as a leader you must be the first to extend trust, ensuring, however, that it is never blind trust. It must remain a process-based trust, with full responsibility and accountability.

It is only natural that inspiring trust should be among the most important functions in your journey to developing an authentic and effective leadership. Going beyond inspiring trust as a personal attribute, it must be cultivated as an institutional objective too. At an institutional level, trust becomes an economic activity, whereby inspiring trust among customers, investors and other stakeholders adds to the bottom line of the company. The attainment of a high level of trust could be set as an explicit goal and taken up as a focused activity, which is measured, audited and improved.

Experience shows that leaders who inspire trust act like magnets, attracting the best of ideas, talent and capital. Elon

Musk is a living example of a leader who has inspired trust in his transformational vision, thereby creating a band of committed followers across the globe. What is more, even though his ventures haven't been giving returns on expected lines, investors are pouring in money because they believe in the power of his dreams.

To build trust among people, leaders start with building their personal credibility. The three vital factors that build credibility and generate trust in a leader are the leader's character, competence and performance. Character is displayed by one's honesty and integrity, intent and motive under different circumstances. Competence includes factors such as conceptualization, communication, skills and capabilities. Performance, of course, is denoted by one's previous track record and results achieved in pursuance of one's stated vision.

Successful leaders know that trust is an effective instrument for getting their vision translated into reality. There are two basic reasons for this. First, once a leader has been able to establish trust among people, the tribe of his followers keeps increasing, thereby adding strength to his mission and vision, and reducing opposition to it. In a corporate setup, it could mean more employees buying into the leader's vision and getting aligned with their plan and strategy. It could also mean more and more customers trusting the company's products. We have seen a visionary leader like Steve Jobs building a connect with his customers based on the quality and innovativeness of his products. Ever since the first generation of the iPhone was launched in June 2007 and the iPad in April 2010, their users' lives have not been the same.

The second big advantage of building trust is that leaders can ask and inspire their followers to walk the extra mile and make sacrifices on the route to realizing their promised dreams.

The followers then take up the cause and become champions of it themselves.

As a child, I was witness to a classic example of trust-based leadership, when one of India's most loved prime ministers, Lal Bahadur Shastri, had sounded the call to Indians to skip dinner once a week. The background was the India-Pakistan war of 1965, during which the US, siding with Pakistan, had threatened that it would cut off wheat supply to India. The situation was grave, as India was largely dependent on the US for wheat supplies to feed its population and there was an acute shortage of food in the country.

A demure, low-profile and soft-spoken Shastri refused to buckle under the US threat. Rather, he adopted a novel method. One evening, along with his family members, he skipped dinner to understand how his countrymen would feel if he appealed to them to do the same. Next day, he addressed the nation via the All India Radio and appealed to his countrymen to skip dinner once a week. Without any exception, all families in our village followed suit. Even in towns, eateries remained closed on the evening of fasting. As a child, even though I didn't understand much of what was going on, I found it exhilarating to join the weekly fast with an uplifting feeling that I was contributing to a higher cause.

Shastri followed up this move by sounding another call, 'Jai Jawan, Jai Kisan', signifying a resolute focus to boost defence and agriculture. The call to promote agriculture and rural economy led to the promotion of two critically important movements—the Green Revolution and the White Revolution, which, in turn, led to India's self-sufficiency in food and milk production. Building such levels of trust in the age of post-truth is also possible.

Our age of post-truth is uniquely characterized by constant doubting and questioning, as truth is not always black and white—there are ample shades of grey. To sway popular emotions and beliefs, leaders often make statements and assertions that are not necessarily truths but too benign to be called lies either. This not only makes it difficult to cultivate trust, but it also often leads to the erosion of trust already reposed in a leader.

However, as trust happens to be a universal human attribute, even in these trying times, it is possible to build trust among one's followers and utilize it to further a team's collective vision. In recent times, we have seen Obama create a bonding with his audience that has often transcended the boundaries of the US. PM Narendra Modi is yet another shining example of a statesman who has been able to establish his personal credibility and build trust among his countrymen based on the three factors of character, competence and performance. He has established his reputation as a selfless leader with a grand vision to transform India into a developed nation and who has been working tirelessly to achieve this goal. His simplicity and integrity, espousal of social and national causes, and involvement in planning and monitoring of various projects have established his credibility as one of the most transformational leaders India has seen in recent times.

The box below describes the state of affairs post the demonetization of high-value currency notes in India in November 2016, which amply illustrates the power of trust.

The Power of Trust

At 8 p.m. on the evening of 8 November 2016, when Prime Minister Narendra Modi announced demonetization of high-value currency notes with effect from midnight, the entire nation was stunned at the seriousness and enormity of its consequences. The larger purpose behind the move was

---

explained as fighting black money, weeding out fake currency notes and drying up terrorism-funding–issues with which Indians have grappled for ages. The PM implored citizens to bear with the inconvenience for fifty days, during which time the new currency notes would be printed and circulated, and normalcy could be restored in the system.

While the Indian masses appreciated the purpose, the challenges at hand were far more daunting. This, in effect, meant flushing out 86 per cent of the currency from the system and declaring it non-legal tender overnight. In a largely cash-driven economy, the announcement amounted to a near-complete collapse of commercial transactions. The consequences appeared to be catastrophic as the vast majority of the population in rural areas, who dealt primarily in cash, were expected to be the worst victims of the move.

The fifty-day period was indeed a period of trial and tribulation for the Indian masses. The availability of new currency notes was limited as their printing and supply was unable to cope up with the demand. To add to the problem, even where currency notes could be made available, the ATMs could not dispense them as they needed to be recalibrated to be able to do so.

The period saw citizens waiting in long queues before bank ATMs, often returning without getting cash even after hours of wait. The belligerent political Opposition, renowned economists and an unfriendly media kept criticizing the move as naïve and thoughtless, with the potential to ruin the economy. It was even hinted that there could be a mass upsurge against the move.

But the PM had established a connect with the masses, who trusted him as a leader who was working for them honestly, sincerely and tirelessly. Thus, in a cash-dominated economy, people underwent all inconveniences without any complaint. Even when provoked by the media, they simply said that their leader had asked for fifty days and they could bear some inconvenience for a larger cause.

This daring move by PM Modi tasted success simply because he had built up a high level of trust with the masses, who had bought into his dream of transforming India into a corruption-free modern society with equal opportunities for all. It was the trust of the people in their leader that led them to go through serious inconveniences, with the belief that they were partners in nation-building.

It will not be out of place to mention here that demonetization has been attempted the world over by many nations at different points in time, but wherever the leaders did not enjoy public trust, the outcomes were counterproductive. In 1991, when the Mikhail Gorbachev government of the erstwhile Soviet Union banned the currency notes of 50 and 100 rubles to check black money, it led to a coup d'état to overthrow the government. In Myanmar, a similar attempt in 1987 led to bloodshed, with mass protests against the military government, resulting in the death of thousands of citizens.

It was indeed the leadership and the public trust in leadership that made all the difference in such a vast and diversified country as India.

Get on the Helicopter

Most of us get bogged down by our daily routine, so much so that we are hardly able to lift our heads to see the big picture, something beyond the immediate task at hand. This is akin to surveying the area around us while standing on the ground, where our vision is blocked by obstructions around. In corporate life, similar obstructions are created by the limitations of individual roles and responsibilities, departmental functions and pressure to deliver results. Over the years, we get so accustomed to our limited arena of operations that it breeds familiarity and we start drawing a sense of comfort from it.

Effective leaders, on the other hand, tend to leave their comfort zones and take a helicopter view of their operating arenas and environments. What does the analogy of the helicopter view have in common with the leadership view? Let us consider that, as against standing on the ground, when we go up in a helicopter, we get a bigger and clearer picture of the arena being surveyed. The higher we go, the wider the view. You can take the helicopter up to get a panoramic view of the landscape and bring it down to focus on a specific zone.

Leadership, too, involves looking at the bigger picture, seeing not only the trees but the forest as well, seeing not only a part but the whole picture. Thus, leaders go beyond the specifics of a particular situation or problem and take a look at their business and industry in their entirety and their key players, employees, customers, vendors, suppliers, competitors and other stakeholders. They study the interrelations among the stakeholders and try to make sense of their actions and reactions. They develop a historical perspective that captures the flow from the past to the present, leading to the future. Based on a bird's-eye view of the state of the company and the industry, its competitors, its strengths and weaknesses, threats and opportunities, they attempt to build a model for the future. This obviously provides the platform that enables leaders to create their vision for the company or the industry and develop strategies.

Once you take the helicopter view, you as a leader should start asking questions. What is the current state of the industry or the company? What are its strengths and weaknesses? How is competition shaping up? What are the emerging trends and customer preferences? How are the changes in the political and economic climate, demography and technology going to impact the business? What sort of legal or regulatory interventions can be anticipated? How is the scenario going to build up and how is the industry going to look in the next five to ten years?

Once you are able to see the big picture, you should start seeking answers—from yourself as well as from the world around. What will be the impact, if any, of these possible changes? What action should the industry or the company be taking to anticipate and respond to the changes? How is competition going to react to it?

Answers to these will help you draw alternative scenarios of the future, which will need to be articulated and validated. It is a process that leads to a considerable amount of thinking and rethinking, challenging one's previously held notions and assumptions, and reorganizing one's mental map and worldview. It accelerates the process of unlearning and re-learning as well.

A perspective of the present and the future so developed leads to vision and strategy formulation for the future. In doing so, leaders repeatedly bring the helicopter down to focus on specific areas of concern to understand and absorb the details.

Thinking Big and Changing the Rules of Business

Mukesh Ambani, the chairman and managing director of Reliance Industries Ltd, a global Fortune 500 company, could have sat comfortably on his chair and seen his company create new benchmarks in oil exploration and refining. But no! The serial entrepreneur that he is, he explored the global business environment and scanned the Indian business scenario to cater to the emerging needs and demands of the vast Indian population.

A visionary who could rise above the mundane and the ordinary and look at the big picture, he saw the information and communication revolution sweeping the world. He took a helicopter view and looked at the factors driving this revolution—the evolving demographics and the rise of the younger generation, the growing aspirations of people, advancements in communication technologies and the way they were being deployed for transforming the lives of people and societies. A closer look at the Indian scenario revealed that there was a yawning gap between people's needs and their fulfilment. The incumbent service provider in mobile communications had priced both the handsets and the calls at unaffordable rates. As a result, mobile phones had just remained a status symbol in the hands of the rich and the mighty.

Ambani saw the revolutionary potential of the convergence of information and communication, and, in 2002, launched India's largest and strongest communication network then, known as Reliance Infocomm. The company laid out an extensive optic fibre network covering 673 cities. It declared its plans to expand the network and provide connectivity to nearly all the villages and towns in India over the next two years. The services on offer covered voice, video, data and other value-added services.

Ambani realized that data had a greater transformational potential than voice. Data-based solutions could energize business enterprises and open up new avenues of growth and profitability for them. It could encourage outsourcing of business processes and lead to faster and more efficient transactions. He also realized that the availability and accessibility of data could usher India into an era of e-governance, thereby making the lives of common men and women much more comfortable. Visualizing all this in a voice-dominated market, he went for a technology platform, CDMA, which was strong on driving data-based solutions, even though it was used in very few markets. To support his venture, he also created a band of knowledge entrepreneurs who could develop data-based solutions on a revenue-sharing basis for the overarching digital infrastructure supported by state-of-the-art technology.

While Reliance Infocomm continued transforming the Indian economy and the way people interacted with each other, following the demerger of the Reliance Group, Ambani gave up the company.

Later, in 2016, he went on to launch another mega venture, Reliance Jio, which aimed to enable every citizen to live a digital life. In a world that was going digital at an exponential rate, everyone needed the power of data connectivity, advance computing and big data analytics to compete for success. As Ambani said, 'Data is the oxygen of digital life, and oxygen must never be in short supply.'

It is this act of rising above the immediate, taking a helicopter view and seeing the big picture that has made Ambani the great business leader he is. The Indian telecom sector has never been the same again after his intervention.

It needs to be emphasized that as leadership operates at different layers within an organization, leaders operating at the lower levels in an organization are also capable of taking a helicopter view. It is not always essential for a leader to be at the top of the corporate ladder to develop a helicopter view, even though being at the top may be helpful for the process.

Further, taking a helicopter view is a skill that you can acquire. The more you develop this practice, the more accomplished you get at it. This demands a degree of detachment from the immediate surroundings and developing a third-party view of what is happening within the company or the industry. It's only then that we as leaders develop an unbiased view of the operating environment and develop solutions needed for the future.

Discover the Icebergs

Icebergs are deceptive: what is visible above the surface is just a fraction of what is hidden below. In a way, they are symbolic of the state of the human psyche and its behaviour: our behaviours become visible to the external world, but our inner self, which triggers these behaviours, remains hidden. As we know, our subconscious mind is the repository of our memories, beliefs, experiences and thoughts, which are not part of the conscious mind at any given point of time. While remaining submerged within us, our subconscious mind influences our natural behaviour all the time in both positive and negative ways, depending upon the beliefs cultivated by us. Even seemingly routine activities like driving, singing or swimming require a number of skills that are not part of our conscious self, and we keep using them even without being aware of them. Obviously, these skills, honed by training, experiences, reflex responses, intelligence and decision-making, remain part of our subconscious minds, guiding our actions and behaviours.

These icebergs can easily lead us to certain thinking traps and influence our behaviour patterns in ways not logically explainable or desirable. For example, if a person grew up being bullied by his friends during childhood, he may develop an inferiority complex, leading to low self-esteem and the resultant belief that he is inferior to others. He may not be consciously aware of this, but even later in life, it may reflect in external manifestations, such as being oversensitive to criticism or developing anxiety in the presence of strangers.

Therefore, a certain degree of self-awareness is required to understand what our acquired beliefs are and why they are so. In case we find our beliefs or values to be without reason or substance, or out of sync with realities, we can make a conscious effort to change them. It helps us grow as leaders when we discover the icebergs within us and check our actions and emotions on the touchstone of external realities.

A person's subconscious mind is also a repository of various common subscripts—for example, cultural, racial, ethnic and religious—acquired in the process of growing up. Thus, they, too, influence our thoughts and behaviours. Therefore, an insight into these subscripts can help a leader understand their behaviour and influence the same as well. This insight can be utilized to motivate followers, in line with the vision and mission of the organization.

The need for leaders to discover the icebergs has never been felt as highly as in today's environment, where businesses are acquiring global footprints and people are working in cross-cultural environments. To be successful, business leaders do try to discover and understand the submerged icebergs of cultural sensitivities, emotional and psychological orientations, preferences of the markets they cater to and the groups they lead. The better the understanding, the greater their effectiveness in realizing their goals!

In line with this, contemporary leaders think global but act local. They ensure that the products they launch are in conformity with the cultural sensitivities of the targeted markets and their marketing communication takes care of the local cultural sensitivities. It is not without reason that McDonald's is not selling Big Mac in India, as eating beef is taboo for most Indians. Instead, the company has Maharaja Mac in the country, with chicken and lamb as substitutes for beef. While retaining standardization, it introduced a vegetarian burger, McAloo Tikki, too. Likewise, its menu for different countries is different. On the contrary, when Kellogg's initially tried to market a Western product—corn flakes—in India, without understanding local tastes, habits and preferences, they were rejected by the market.

It goes without saying, therefore, that for individuals to lead effectively in today's environment, it is critical to understand and interpret the subscripts that run through the subconscious minds of the persons they are interacting with or the groups they are leading. For modern corporations too, it is crucial to understand the collective consciousness of the community in which they work.

◆

'Do you want to spend the rest of your life selling sugared water, or do you want a chance to change the world?'

This is what Jobs had famously said to John Sculley, head of Pepsi–Cola, before recruiting him as the CEO of Apple. But, in essence, this question is before all of us. All of us have a chance to transform the world bit by bit. Leadership not only provides us an occasion for self-discovery, it is also our opportunity to make the society a better place to live in compared to we have inherited.

The people who change the world are not the only ones with vision and passion. What sets them apart is that they learn from their failures and persevere in their dreams. Human history is replete with stories of great people, for whom the stumble is part of the dance. As they say, the greatest inspiration you can ever have is to know that you are an inspiration to others. Wake up and start living an inspirational life today.

Epilogue

Dealers in Hope

Never before in the history of leadership has a leader's role and responsibility been as daunting and challenging as today. In an increasingly complex world, with constant volatility and ongoing uncertainties, new challenges keep unfolding before leaders with routine regularity. Contemporary leaders have to find their way in a hazy environment where established models and systems are crumbling, failing the test of current realities. Business models are facing deep challenges as organizations are getting reconstructed both from within and without. On the one hand, newer technologies are causing constant disruptions, leaving organizations struggling for survival, while on the other hand, work-related values and prevalent organizational cultures are being questioned by an informed and skilled workforce. To top it all, amid all this chaos and confusion, businesses are embracing new values and adopting novel practices related to emerging issues such as clean energy, climate change, sustainable development, diversity and inclusion. Their range of stakeholders are not limited to just promoters, employees and customers—they include the large spectrum of humanity too.

The lasting legacy of great leaders is that they leave behind inspired men and women who take their vision forward. The most important legacy of the imperfect leaders of the contemporary era is that they give an entirely new dimension to the understanding and function of leadership. With their learning agility, they try to make sense of the fuzzy environment in which they are required to perform and deliver. While on the one hand, they try to bring order to the prevailing chaos, on the other, with their penchant for creativity and innovation, they induce further disruption in the environment. They collaborate with their teams to convert threats from the environment into new opportunities for garnering a competitive advantage for their organization.

Contemporary leaders are shaping the leadership environment in many ways. With them, modern workplaces are witnessing a transition from a macho, omnipotent and infallible alpha-male leadership style towards a softer and more feminized leadership that thrives on collaboration, co-creation and honest communication. They are courageous without being audacious, confident without being conceited, contemplative without being lethargic, and kind and caring without looking feeble and helpless. They are leading the transition from a disconnected world to a networked society, from closed silos to open platforms, from hierarchical ladders to flat structures. They are the ones who lead their teams in navigating from the fixed to the fluid; and the ones who keep converting uncertainties into opportunities by doing more with less. They provide the hope and optimism to take the world out of the crisis facing it today. They are essentially what Napoleon Bonaparte called 'dealers in hope'.

Acknowledgements

Writing a book on leadership had never been on my horizon until the commissioning editor of a publishing house challenged me to do so over a casual conversation about another project. I am thankful to him for putting the seed of the idea into my head.

This book is a modest attempt to put forth my understanding of the subject. However, the credit must go to my numerous colleagues, seniors and entrepreneurs in various organizations—some of whom are iconic figures—whose leadership styles I had the occasion to observe from close quarters and who have enriched my perspective on the subject with their knowledge, experience and insight. I am grateful to them for giving me this opportunity.

Leadership has been extensively studied and researched over the ages. A lot has been written and spoken about it as well. I have had the privilege of benefiting from many of these studies and analyses, and I acknowledge their contribution in developing my perspective on the subject.

Neelima, my wife and soulmate, has been a constant source of inspiration to me in writing this book, and in countless other ways. She has been a partner in this journey and has toiled for days and nights along with me. Her emotional and intellectual companionship has given me great support in accomplishing this task.

This book would not have been possible without the steady and valuable encouragement from my children,

Shweta and Harsh, my son-in-law Subhayu and daughter-in-law Shruti. These new-gen leaders have kept enriching my understanding of new-age challenges—business landscapes, work environments and expectations of leaders. They have been the sounding boards for what the gen-next thinks and how it operates. Their optimism fills me with the faith that all is well with the next generation and also the hope that the future is bright.

I am grateful to Rupa Publications India for having taken up this project and ensured the publication of this book. I have enjoyed working with their enthusiastic, talented and supportive team. I also thank my literary agent, Ms Dipti Patel of WordFamous, who has systematically persuaded me to focus on my writing. Thanks, Dipti, for all your support!